THE
PASSIONATE PAPERS
OF
FIONA PILGRIM

12641-RUBA

THE
PASSIONATE PAPERS
OF
FIONA PILGRIM

*An Epistolary Novel
of
Love and Lust*

John Rubadeau

For

M. H. Kruchten
A dear friend who, with such good-humored grace and such lively wit,
played June Featherstone to my Fiona Pilgrim

and
N. S. Milam

But especially for

L. I. Leon
and
R. D. Pace
and
P. M. Prahin

ACKNOWLEDGMENTS

I should like to thank the following people for their generous comments and helpful suggestions: Timothy D. Ahlgren, Jonathan Barkey, David Barringer, Zachary Bernstein, Braxton Blake, Rebecca Cammack, Karl-Georg Federhofer, Clare Lauwerys, Benjamin Reynolds (author photo), Nick Rubadeau, Pat Rubadeau, Fritz Schafer (cover photos), Daniel Stein.

English Department
Barker Center, Harvard College
12 Quincy Street
Cambridge, MA 02138
December 01, 2001

To the reader:

I was asked, several years ago, to contribute an article to a festschrift celebrating a colleague's fiftieth year of teaching at this institution. In search of a fitting topic for such a tribute, I began by consulting that corpus of scholarship which had—over the passing years—particularly attracted my attention. While rummaging through several boxes containing essays that I had read and had valued for their literary merit, copies of dissertations that I had directed, and various sorts of scholarly articles that had piqued my research interests, I stumbled upon the most interesting find.

Amongst the boxes of literary memorabilia was one containing a sheaf of letters written (and received) almost two decades ago by my old college roommate and lifelong friend, Joseph E. Leonard. Joe had, for reasons known only to him, sent these letters to me for safekeeping; his ultimate design in placing them in my care went to the grave with him.

I have contacted Joe Leonard's heirs, and they have willingly given me permission to publish their late father's correspondence. The letters appear in their unedited form, and I have ordered them chronologically. My only original contribution to the text is the epigraph from Boccaccio, a passage which, in view of the subject matter treated in this epistolary exchange, I consider to be particularly felicitous.

No further commentary seems necessary save to observe that I took much greater pleasure in compiling this collection of my old friend's letters than I did in researching and writing the essay I eventually contributed to the festschrift.

Sincerely yours,

J. K. Douglas

Gordon K. Douglas
Professor Emeritus

Therefore I mean to atone for the wrong done by Fortune, who is ever most miserly of comfort where there is least strength, as we may see in the case of delicate women. As an aid and comfort to women in love (for the needle, the distaff and the winder should suffice the others), I intend to relate one hundred tales . . . . In these tales will be seen the gay and sad adventures of lovers . . . . The ladies who read them may find delight in the pleasant things therein displayed; and they may also obtain useful advice, since they may learn what things to avoid and what to seek. Nor can all this happen without some soothing of the melancholy.

from the foreword to
The Decameron
of Giovanni Boccaccio

May 1, 1982
2801 Hoosier Rd.
Centreville, IN 45480
U. S. A.

Ms. June Featherstone
Harlequin House
Silhouette Lane
Fensucked-on-Strand
Ely, Cambridgeshire
England

Dear Ms. Featherstone:

Honestly, I just don't know how to begin this letter. I feel like a nervous young coed about to discuss a poorly written essay with her English professor. I feel like an aspiring pianist rehearsing for a recital she is about to give for the legendary Horowitz himself. I feel like a puny sapling struggling to grow in the shade of a giant tree: I am the tiny acorn; you, the great oak. I consider you to be the greatest living author of romance fiction, my absolutely favorite genre. From the onset, I want you to know that I have read—many times over—every novel you have published. I think you are a marvelous writer!

I'm sure you must get thousands of adulatory letters similar to mine each year from your admirers all around the globe. Yet I'm crossing my fingers and hoping against hope that, by some quirk of fate, you'll somehow read my letter to its conclusion and be moved enough by its contents to come to my aid. (Before continuing, let me interject that, in addition to having read with so much pleasure every word you've ever penned, your writings have continually been a major source of inspiration to me.) You see, Ms. Featherstone, I am much like that young pianist, nervously fingering the keyboard while making ready to audition for Horowitz. I am an aspiring writer who seeks the tutorial help and expert advice

13

which can only be had by studying under a giant oak such as yourself.

It is for this very reason—to place myself under your nurturing tutelage; to grow, as it were, under the spreading boughs of your authorial foliage—that I write this letter. Of course, I'm not so naive as to expect you to read, or much less respond to, my letter. I suspect that, due to the heavy volume of correspondence you must daily receive from your legions of readers around the globe, my request will fall on deaf ears. Nonetheless, if by some miracle you've read my letter to this point, let me get to the heart of the matter which has prompted me to write to you today.

Ms. Featherstone, I shan't mince my words. Allow me to speak frankly. You are no stranger to me. Having read all of your books— beginning with *Sultry Heart* (1958), your highly acclaimed first novel, and ending with *Quickening Pulse* (1982), your most recent and, in my opinion, your finest work to date—I feel as though we've become old friends through the succeeding years; I actually feel as though I know you personally. I do not wish to impose on our friendship, but might you, as a favor from one friend to another, allow me to send you some selected passages from a work-in-progress? Would you agree to look them over and make any comments or suggestions that you deem might be helpful? Failing that, could you at least take time out from your busy schedule to tell me how one "breaks" into the field which you—unopposed and unchallenged— so masterfully command? What *is* the best method to use when approaching an editor or a publisher with my manuscript? Oh, if you would ever respond positively, I should be forever grateful and eternally in your debt.

Well there! I've done it! I never thought I could summon up enough courage to approach someone of your stature and beg for this sort of help. I apologize for the impudent (Should I have perhaps written "imprudent" here?) nature of my request. But, Ms. Featherstone, I am so desperate!

I want you to understand that I am a serious writer, interested in her craft. Although I've never yet submitted anything for publication, I have allowed my husband to read my manuscript, and he has judged it to be ". . . gripping and moving." And he's very well read.

I shared several selected passages of the novel I'm presently writing (tentatively titled *Tempestuous Summer—The Hottest Season*) with Mildred Milloy, my bridge partner and the moderator of our branch library's weekly book-discussion club. Millie critiqued the segments I had given her and commented that they struck her as being, ". . . divine and heart-rending."

Furthermore, my high-school English teacher once told my mother at a PTA meeting that I had "a gift" for writing. So I'm pretty sure I can write pretty well, and I consider my literary efforts—although assuredly crude in comparison with your refined prose—evidence of my earnest commitment to strive to attain the same niche in the world of books that you have chiseled out for yourself.

A word or two about my novel, just in case you are willing to take on an apprentice and permit her to learn her trade by working under the guidance of a master craftswoman such as yourself. My novel, *Tempestuous Summer—The Hottest Season*, is about a desperate search for true and abiding love in an exotic setting and about how a young woman finally finds the happiness she is seeking when she becomes meaningfully involved with an extraordinarily wealthy man. He may be an OPEC oil sheik, but I haven't yet decided on that. However, I have resolved to make him enormously rich and swarthy, but certainly nothing more than Mediterranean swarthy, if you know what I mean. They meet during the summer—hence, the title. And their relationship up until the dénouement is quite stormy—hence, another part of the title. It is quite a sad story. I myself cried buckets when I reread the rough draft, and that should mean it's good, don't you think?

Well, I've certainly overstayed my welcome at Harlequin House and taken much too much of your time. I apologize. Forgive me, but, at the same time, don't forget me. I must run now, for Peter Paul, my hubby, will shortly finish work and return home, famished and complaining of hunger pains. The boys, Paul and Peter—twins, age eight and mirror images of their father—will soon burst into the kitchen, home from their Cub Scout meeting and ravenous and ready to eat. I'm a den mother, but we have, thank God, rotating meetings. This week, the little rascals are meeting at another den mother's home.

Thus, I can steal a few moments to drop you these many lines. However, I'll soon have to bring this letter to a close, for Priscilla, age twelve, our pudgy princess and a darling (mother's little helper!) will pop her head in the door any minute, pouting because dinner is not yet on the table and over a half an hour has passed since she engorged her after-school snack. Having always been petite and having never been more than a size six, I can't imagine how a daughter of mine could eat so much. I swear the child has an insatiable tapeworm.

I simply must bring this letter to a conclusion and get dinner made and the table set. (A woman's work is never done!) I must lay down my pen, pick up my spatula in its stead, and prepare something to eat. Please—from the bottom of my heart, Ms. Featherstone—oh, please answer my query. I shall be eternally grateful to you.

Can you—will you—oh, do give me some direct aid. Or, at least, steer me in the proper direction and recommend an editor, a publisher, or an agent for me to contact. I await your reply. And even, Ms. Featherstone, if I never hear one single word from you, I want you to know that I've already dedicated *Tempestuous Summer—The Hottest Season* to you.

Humbly and very sincerely yours and forever in your debt if you will but grant me my dearest wish,

Fiona Pilgrim

Fiona Pilgrim

P.S. I shall think of you reading my letter in your garden. I, myself, am a great fan of the English garden. Indeed, I have several books by Gertrude Jekyll, and I suspect her writings have influenced the design of the gardens at Harlequin House. Despite all my efforts at gardening, however, all I seem to be able to cultivate in my tiny plot are weeds, dandelions, and an occasional Queen Anne's lace. By late summer and early fall, a dense growth of ragweed and golden-rod—a hay-fever sufferer's nightmarish garden—prospers where I had once envisioned a lush grouping of black-eyed Susans, sun-flowers, and asters.

I can easily picture the setting: you have just laid aside the pruning shears after having cut the peonies for your lounge. The heady, redolent scent of the white rosebushes, wallflowers, and multicolored lilies perfumes the air while the only sound that dis-turbs the silence is the soft sibilant buzzing of the bees as they fructify the flowers. I can see the shapes and patterns of the espaliered pears growing, vinelike, against the garden walls—the walls are red-brick, are they not? And this picturesque setting is framed against a background of English-green grass, robin's-egg blue sky, and—at the very center of the scene—the imposing Norman façade and great, gray turreted towers of the Ely Cathe-dral. How romantic and inspiring it must all be!

I myself have never been to England, but, two years ago, my cousin, who was "into" cathedrals at the time, toured Great Britain, made a pilgrimage to Ely, and sent me a postcard of your famous monument. Yours, F.P.

P.P.S. I just reread my letter, Ms. Featherstone, and a disquieting thought occurred to me: In the second paragraph, I employed the phrase "hoping against hope." I trust you are familiar with this idi-omatic American expression; otherwise, my words will surely strike your eye and ear as being nothing but sheer gibberish. It means to hope for something with great fervor but with little realistic expec-tation that one's wishes will be fulfilled.

May 29, 1982
2801 Hoosier Rd.
Centreville, IN 45480

Professor Gordon K. Douglas
Department of English Language and Literature
Warren House
Harvard University
Cambridge, MA 02138

Gordy!

Long time no see, no hear, no write—no news whatsoever for the longest period of time. And then yesterday, from out of nowhere (I exaggerate; the postmark clearly indicated Cambridge, Mass., as its point of origin.) comes your note asking if I'm yet to be numbered among the living. Put your mind at ease, old friend. I continue to respire—but only barely. Just how close to terminal am I?

Allow me an analogy.

You remember Mr. Al E. Cat, that flea-bitten old tom you had when we were inebriated undergrads at Wisconsin? You saved him from the hangman's noose at the Humane Society Shelter. He cost two bucks—and that was two bucks too many!—and caused nothing but trouble.

Poor Al was cursed with some horrible malfunctioning of bowel and bladder, an affliction which made him frequent his litter box no less than seven- or eight-hundred times a day. He practically lived there. His damnable toilet reeked like a rendering plant running three shifts a day. As I recall, though, you never seemed the least bit bothered by its effluvium. Never once—in all those years we roomed together—did you volunteer to empty that damned box or add a fresh supply of KITTY LITTER.

But in addition to his incontinence which, in itself, was cause enough to harden the heart of even the most fanatical cat lover, the

19

cursed creature was also plagued by a terminal case of mange. I can still see him—tufts of fur, like batting oozing from an overstuffed mattress, fell out in clumps, and, choking on hairballs, he'd gasp asthmatically, every breath a death rattle. He was always on the brink, but, with nine proverbial lives, the bastard never did kick off. What a piece-of-shit animal! A sure candidate for vivisection if I ever met one. Certainly you remember him?

Well, Gordo, that feline son of a bitch—now there's an oxymoronic juxtaposition, is it not?—was in the pink of health vis-à-vis the blue mood and the black humor in which I now find myself.

End of colorful analogy.

Now that I've set a happy tone for this letter, let me assure you that I'm alive and living in Centreville, Indiana. To be sure—given the incessant progression of the aging process—the more I live, the more I die. Actually, I am alive and dying in Centreville, Indiana. I am not, however, by any means, well.

Let me put some questions to you, the answers to which will clarify instantly why my mood is so morose. Have you ever driven through Centreville, Indiana? Worse, have you ever spent a weekend in Centreville? Worse yet, have you ever thought of wasting the rest of your life in Centreville, a godforsaken little burg a million metaphorical miles from no place and hundreds of cartographical miles from civilization as we know it? Can you possibly imagine what it would be like to be stuck here forever?

Well, maybe it's not forever. Who knows? But one thing's for certain: I'm mired in this cultural backwater until the twins reach their majority; and they won't be eighteen until 1992. That's ten years. Ten years? Shit, Gordy, ten years is a lifetime! In fact, it is forever. Ask any fifth or sixth grader.

Were I a betting man, I'd flip a coin and wager that you haven't been able to make heads or tails out of what I've been babbling about. Let me back up and bring you forward and up-to-date in the troubled life and exasperating times of that struggling, starving, failed, and frustrated author, yours truly, Joseph E. Leonard.

I'm quite sure the last time I wrote you was just after you had left on your Fulbright to Romania. (Incidentally, I was delighted to read in your letter that your research on Publius Ovidius Naso went so well. Congratulations, *tovarish*. As to your request of me, was there ever any doubt in your mind what the answer would be? Of course, I should be honored and hereby agree—indeed, with lascivious glee—to edit your book on Ovid, the Hugh Hefner of the Augustan age.) So while you, lucky devil, were gallivanting about the Balkans and bathing in the Black Sea, I, hapless soul, was stuck in the States.

Towards the end of last September, because I had nothing better to do than fantasize what it might be like to devote myself entirely to my creative writing, free of committee meetings to attend, lectures to prepare, classes to teach, students to advise, papers to grade, research proposals to write, etceteras to be etcetered, I got out paper, pencil, checkbook, savings-account passbook, and abacus. With the figures at my fingertips, I hastily calculated—Quite erroneously! My calculator must have malfunctioned—that I had stashed away enough money to support Betty, the kids, and the Great Scribbler for several years or until one of my novels sold.

Delusional hope and artistic intemperance momentarily replaced good sense, and I admit I did a damned stupid thing. Already counting the prospective royalties from my first novel, I bolted into the Department Chairman's office, resigned my tenured position, called a realtor, put the house on the market, and rented a U-Haul. To make a long and bitter story short and even more bitter, we moved to Centreville because—among many other inducements to living in a small town—I thought such a move would be conducive to my writing.

I imagine you're shaking your head from side to side, tut-tutting your tongue—as if chirruping to some lackadaisical steed—and saying to yourself, "Why did that horse's ass ever settle down in Centreville, Indiana, of all places? Why didn't that fool stay put and let well enough alone?"

Fortunately as I write this, I'm in a mellow mood, although

somewhat depressed, and I can answer your questions civilly by telling you that we came to Centreville—the end of the world; the very anus of Western Civilization—because Betty was raised here. And, despite its many shortcomings (far too numerous to mention even in a lengthy letter), it's a nice-place-to-raise-kids type of town.

Anyway, we moved to Ultima Thule, Indiana. I began to write the Great American Novel, Betty began to remodel the old house we'd bought, the kids began to adjust to their new schools and neighborhood, and my bank account began to dwindle. Before I knew it, I was broke. Shortly before my money ran out, Betty, blaming me for bringing the family to financial ruin, left me.

Her mom and dad, with all their old community ties, pulled some strings for her, and she landed a lucrative position with the county government doing nothing but drawing pay. You know the type of job; there are only two qualifications: You've got to be a card-carrying member of the party holding office at that time, and you have to be alive—not necessarily during the work week, but you must be resurrected by payday in order to draw your check. The old story: it's not what you know, but who you know.

And what about poor (I mean, truly poor) me? To avoid the distractions of social intercourse that come with being neighborly and to allot myself uninterrupted time to write, I had been hermetically bottled up in my tiny atelier and madly scribbling away from dawn to dusk seven days a week for five months. Consequently, as a result of this self-imposed exile from society, I had no connections in town. And there weren't any universities—shit, not even an unaccredited community college—within commuting distance of Centreville, so I couldn't go back into academia unless I moved away.

I thought about it, but I just couldn't bring myself to leave. I felt the kids were at crucial stages in their lives. They needed me as a role model; you've read all that developmental-psychology and/or child-psychology bullshit. Erica, twelve at the time of the divorce, was about to enter puberty. Her menarcheal hormones must have gone haywire and stimulated her appetite. My darling little butterball began to eat enough at one sitting to sustain a Bangladeshi family of five for a full week. Jason and Justin were eight and about to enter Cub Scouts. With Betty's death as housewife and homebody and subsequent rebirth as civil servant and working mother, the twins were suddenly left den-motherless. And the loss of a primary caregiver at age eight (that is, the boys, not Betty, the recently displaced caregiver, were eight) can be a source of much stress and trauma. If you don't believe me, consult the chapters contributed by Freud and Piaget to the *Cub Scout Handbook*.

Actually, I love them—the children, not Freud and Piaget—very much and didn't, and don't, want to be away from them. It was as simple as that. A bad husband I might have been (a matter of opinion: Betty's versus mine); a good father I ever strive to be (a matter of will and effort). I guess I needed them as much as I perceived they needed me.

In order to stay in Centreville, but stay out of jail for nonsupport, I took the only job available. What sort of work can you think of, Gordy, that requires absolutely no background, no training, no intellect, no aptitude, and no morals and whose only prerequisites—both of which I satisfactorily faked during my initial interview, thus making that all-important excellent first impression—are a vigorous commitment to middle-class values and an unquestioning acceptance of the avariciousness that fuels our economy? I confess, hesitantly and disconsolately, that I now earn my daily bread by protecting the accumulation of wealth and its retention in the family after the death of the paterfamilias. I shudder with revulsion to admit it, but the awful truth is—is—is—I am an insurance agent. My confessing this to you is an experience which I can only liken to a wino standing up at an AA meeting and admitting to his fellow lushes that he's fallen off the wagon and that he's back on the sauce. I sell insurance: auto, homeowners', health, business owners' and commercial, and life. *Mea culpa!*

Now a Pied Piper of consumerism and avarice, I play a tune—a funeral dirge, as it were—for all those casualties who have fallen in the service of conspicuous consumption, who have offered their

23

lives to the greedy god Mammon, and who have died in the Great Rat Race. Instead of living for today (*Carpe diem*! *Carpe rosam*!), I convince poor, witless souls that they must purchase life insurance so that, when they eventually kick the bucket and buy the farm, their survivors can live sumptuously from the earnings their deaths have wrought. What a morbid business this is. Is it any wonder I am so morose?

But my depression really hasn't got all that much to do with my present employment. While it is unarguably a low, mean, base, and ignoble way to earn one's living, selling insurance is not so dishonest by general standards as to be punishable by fine or imprisonment. It's not comparable to drug smuggling, child pornography, prostitution, or some other similar form of organized crime, is it?

Neither is the divorce sufficient justification to elicit such disillusionment. It's not as though I've been singled out for some sort of cruel and unusual punishment. Hell, all you've got to do is look around you. Since serial monogamy has replaced traditional till-death-do-us-part wedlock, whose marriage hasn't failed nowadays?

You wonder, Gordon, what the explanation is for my despair? I'll tell you. In a nutshell, my writings remain as yet unpublished. It's as simple as that.

Yet I know—as even you, unsolicited, have said on numerous occasions—I'm damn good at what I do. However, I just can't seem to get a break. I'm always mailing off samples from whatever it is I'm working on, and all I get back are rave rejection letters, acknowledging my gift as a writer. Each letter tells me what a genius I am and how original my mss. are. But each letter, without fail, closes by saying that—even though the chapters I submitted for consideration were unique and obviously the works and the words of a genuine artist and a gifted wordsmith—my writings are not marketable. They're not targeted at a mass audience. And that's apparently all that interests those sharp-pencilled accountants and calculator-carrying, computer-accoutered M.B.A.'s who run the publishing houses.

I was so goddamned depressed earlier this month that I decided I ought to concentrate all my efforts on turning out a typical piece of topical trash—something that the masses would adore; something that would earn me megabucks in the marketplace. If this gambit works, I can tell my boss to take his sales brochures and insurance contracts, his annuity tables and his rate book, and reposit them where the sun don't ever shine, where only his proctologist can read them. I can retire to a life of reading and contemplation. I can devote all of my energies entirely to my serious prose. I can write. I can be happy.

A few weeks ago, on the spur of the moment—why even only a second or two of serious forethought would have nullified the implementation of such a patently ridiculous plan—I resolved to try my hand at writing one of those remarkably dull contemporary romance novels that are so very popular. You must be familiar with the ones I'm referring to, right? They're sold at drugstore counters, supermarket checkout lanes, discount-store cash registers, bus depots, railroad terminals, and airports—every conceivable place of commerce except for bookstores. Millions of them everywhere and all the stories the same: a nubile virgin meets a mysterious older man; she falls in love with him; she discovers, to her horror, that he has a questionable past; and she thinks she will lose him and forevermore be brokenhearted. However, in the last chapter, after overcoming obstacle after obstacle, she finds out that she was mistaken about him; his past is as pure as the driven snow. At the conclusion of each novel, the handsome prince is about to ride off into the sunset with his chaste princess, and everyone lives happily ever after. The end.

What realism! Too bad no one actually ever lives happily ever after in the world real people populate. The handsome prince turns, after the marriage has been consummated, into a frog with a grotesque infestation of warts; the chaste princess turns out to be either as frigid as the prioress of a Dominican convent or else she's as promiscuous as a nymphomaniac with VD or herpes. Welcome to reality.

So you know the type of books I'm referring to, right? You

can't enter a pharmacy or a grocery store without bumping into revolving carousels stuffed with these revolting romances. So what was stopping me from trying to add a title or two of my own to the volumes already displayed on these rotating racks? (Bad as the prospect of such hackwork seemed, it sure beat the prospect of selling insurance for the remainder of my life.) Basically, I didn't know shit about writing a romance novel. That glaring lack of knowledge was all that stood between me and prosperity.

I mulled over my predicament for several weeks but didn't meet with any success. Then the other day, in the supermarket, a solution came to me as if in a dream: an epiphany it was. I was pushing my cart down the aisle in search of generic trash bags. I can't afford Hefty's; I'm into generic brands nowadays. I've become extremely cost-conscious since I started living off the income generated from the sales commission of a product I scarcely believe in. Not really paying much attention to where I was going, I bumped into a display containing the ten best-selling romance novels of the month. One fell into my cart. An omen? (That wasn't the title, by the way.) The novel which landed on top of my groceries was written by June Featherstone.

For those members of the literati unfamiliar with her name—and I suspect you, Professor Douglas, would be numbered among those not conversant with her fictional world—a word or two of explanation: June Featherstone is the most widely read, which is not to say that she herself is well read, novelist in the world. Could she actually have been born June Featherstone? It must be a *nom de plume* that she felt her readers would not easily forget. And believe you me, Professor Douglas, even if you've read only one of her novels, it's highly unlikely that you'd ever suffer a lapse of memory when it came to the name June Featherstone.

Speaking of *noms de plume*—I know you'll appreciate that fluid segue, you old rhetorician—I had to come up with one for myself. (See the enclosed copy of a letter written on the first of May to Ms. June Featherstone from one Fiona Pilgrim.) If I'd have written June Featherstone a letter asking for help and signed it as

Joseph E. Leonard, she'd have known for sure that I was up to no good. No man in his right mind could ever buy one of her novels or ladle such fulsome praise upon her works as I did in my letter to her. Her audience is made up of thousands of American and British housewives who really believe there exists a Prince Charming who will really rescue the damsel in distress just as she is about to be ravaged by the taloned clutches, or incinerated by the fiery breath, of the most proximate dragon—be that dragon mythical, animal, or human.

So, in order to lend credence to my entreaty, I adopted a female persona and signed my letter to June as Mrs. Fiona Pilgrim, mother, housewife, and aspiring writer of romance fiction. I think that I must have been quite drunk the night I settled upon Fiona Pilgrim as my pseudonym. I vaguely remember thinking that the name struck me as being unusually feminine and quite odd and British yet Anglo-American enough to be believable.

At least with this ridiculous Fiona Pilgrim ruse, I've got a hell of a lot better chance that Featherstone will respond to my letter than if I had autographed it as Joe Leonard. But what if she answers it?

Holy Shit! I'll be in some fix then. That'd be a pretty pass, wouldn't it? Torn between wanting and dreading, I'd be a textbook example of ambivalence. Despite all my reservations though, I'd be more than glad to do it if I got the chance. I'd do anything to get my name, or Fiona's, in print. I'd put on Fiona's clothes—and I loath transvestites; the dresses simply never seem to hang quite properly—and crank out that romantic drivel.

Do you think I can do it? You know me. Can I ever master the cliché as June has done? Can I ever approach her level of incompetence? Some people are born with different gifts and aptitudes, and I know I could never turn a hackneyed phrase with her apparent ease. Will the editor within me allow me to constantly repeat key words, phrases, and literary devices? Why, there's more sighing in one chapter of Featherstone's shitwork than has been heard in the entire penal history of the Bridge of Sighs. And if there aren't at least two "sensuous lips" per page, readers might lose either

27

their interest or their place. Do I have the intellectual stamina needed to create the silly plot, the inane dialogue, the empty characters, and the predictable fairy-tale endings where everyone lives happily ever after that—taken all together—have made the romance novel so popular?

Why, this is a task that would test the skills of—of—of—faster than a speeding cliché! More powerful than an editor's pen! Able to leap tall stacks of rejection letters in a single bound! Look! Up in the sky! Flying through the air like an unsolicited manuscript winging its way over the transom! It's a bird! It's a plane! No, it's—*superwriter!*

Of course I can do it. Enough of this self-doubt. Hell, I can do anything just so long as it eventually allows me to devote my time, my talent, and my energies to my serious writing. (Can't I?)

Why then all this handwringing and soul-searching? Besides, I'll never hear from her anyway. So what have I got to worry about in this regard? More than likely, nothing will ever come of it. She probably doesn't even answer her own mail. I'll bet she employs some eighty-year-old secretary—possibly her former nanny who has raised her since she was just a babe in arms—to open and answer all her fan mail. By force of habit, June, the cold-hearted old hack, probably sends form letters to all her admirers.

Who knows though? Maybe she'll take pity on me, offer me some constructive suggestions, and—if what I produce meets with her approval—use her pull to help me find a publisher. It can't hurt for trying. Shit, Gordon, what have I got to lose? Nothing.

But whatever happens, or doesn't happen, I'll keep you posted—by post. In the meantime, I'll just sit here on my dead ass in Centreville and feel sorry for myself.

Thanks once again for taking the effort to reestablish contact after such a lengthy lapse and for allowing me to unburden myself of my worries and woes. You have always been a good listener and confidant. I must close. *Vielen Dank, Spacibo, Muchas gracias, Multumesc,* and *Merci beaucoup* for lending me such a sympathetic ear—or eye.

Down for the count but not out—not yet at least. I remain, groggy but still fighting, your old friend,

Joe

Joe Leonard

P.S. Here's some food for thought for you to chew on till you next hear from me. Do you, lover of Ovid, think that the Roman scribe who first put into print the maxim *Ars longa, vita brevis*—art is long, life is short—might have transposed the substantives during transcription? I think he must have erred. Everyone knows what a difficult language Latin is. The more I age, the more apparent it becomes to me that—at least as far as my own writing is concerned—the aphorism would be much more apt if the nouns were reversed and if it read: *Vita longa, ars brevis*; life is long, art is short.

P.P.S. Should you ever get disillusioned with academe, don't give it up for a career hustling insurance.

encl.: Letter from Fiona Pilgrim to June Featherstone dated May 1

12th July 1982
Harlequin House
Silhouette Lane
Fensucked-on-Strand
Ely, Cambridgeshire
England

Mrs. Fiona Pilgrim
2801 Hoosier Rd.
Centreville, IN 45480
U.S.A.

My dear Fiona,

I trust you will not be offended if I call you by your first name. I take this liberty only because your letter was so warm, so personable, and so full of genuine charm and native grace; indeed, I feel, if I may borrow an expression you yourself used in your letter of first May, as " . . . though I almost know you personally". What a smashingly good letter you pen, my dear!

Your comments concerning the amount of post I daily receive were very perceptive and quite correct. In fact, I am the recipient of so many letters that I rarely (indeed, never) have time to answer any of them. Were I to begin corresponding with my audience of readers throughout the world, I daresay I shouldn't have enough time remaining in the day, or strength left in my hand, to compose a single page of fiction. Therefore, I employ a personal secretary who handles all of my correspondence, so I seldom even read the letters sent to me, let alone respond to them. Perhaps you think this a disservice to my public, but all this fan mail serves, as the French say, only as a *divertissement* (diversion) which distracts me from the task at hand: to wit, the writing of my novels.

However, as good fortune would decree, on the very day your letter arrived from America, Nanny became indisposed and was confined to bed; thus did I fetch the post myself.

Fiona, you are, I should suspect, perplexed and wondering just who this "Nanny" creature is. Allow me to introduce this charming soul to you. She is Hortense Crimpet, my personal secretary. Nanny Crimpet has been with me for ages, having been governess here at Harlequin House for over thirty years. There are not at this time, nor have there been for many a year, any wee ones scampering about hither and yon. Children are wonderful, but they can do such damage to the flower beds and statuary, not to mention what havoc they can wreak upon the topiaries if the little scamps get their unsupervised hands on them. To maintain a formal garden is hard enough nowadays, and children can destroy in five or ten minutes what it might have taken Michener and Strickland (my gardeners) five or ten years to fashion. We no longer have youngsters to place under her care, so we had to find something to occupy the dotty old dear's mind and time.

Consequently, I appointed Nanny as my amanuensis years ago, and she has served me

capably in that capacity ever since. She
has, for longer than I care to remember,
tirelessly devoted herself to the charge of
corresponding with my readers. Goodness gracious but this has been a rather lengthy
excursus!

Because Nanny was unwell and incapaci-
tated, I, Fiona, rather than Nanny, read
your letter from start to finish. And I was
for some reason—perhaps it was the basic
honesty and naïveté of your appeal which so
impressed me—impressed. I've decided to lend
you a helping hand, something, in all my
years as a novelist, I've never before done
for anyone.

Let me begin by giving you some general
advice which you should heed if you are
truly serious about wanting to write a successful "romance" novel as you so aptly termed
it. At least I shall relate to you, Fiona,
the guidelines I have followed. And, believe
me, I've been—and I don't wish to appear the
braggart here and risk being accused of either hubris or pomposity, but it's true—
successful far beyond my wildest youthful
dreams. Once again, I must confide that you
are the first person with whom I've shared
the secret of my success, and I am just a
bit flummoxed at the prospect.

The casual reader of my books might think
them to be merely the products of a fertile
imagination: stories dashed off in a flash
of inspiration without a moment's thought
given to setting, plot, character development, et cetera. Well, nothing could be fur-

ther from the truth. The novels I write adhere to a set formula which the readers of romance fiction have come to expect and depend on. And this recipe for success—the ingredients of which I shall very shortly go over in detail—must be followed item by item or as closely as the narrative of your novel allows.

Depending on how your novel is progressing at a given moment, you do have a slight degree of flexibility. You might decide to substitute a dash of this for a pinch of that. But there is one essential ingredient which does not offer itself for substitution. And this is the leavening agent whose presence will make the story come to life and rise to great heights or whose absence, conversely, will make it fall flat and lifeless. I am speaking, Fiona, of *sincerity*. You must always be sincere. The instant you are not, your readers will immediately know you are being disingenuous. Without sincerity, you will be a horrible failure: your novel will fall as flat as a crêpe. With it, however, you will experience a jolly good success: your novel will rise as high as a soufflé.

Now to the remainder of the ingredients which, while not as indispensable to success as is sincerity, will certainly affect the final outcome of all your efforts. The story is always written in the third person, and the point of view is always that of the heroine who is young—twenty-one or twenty-two is a perfect age it seems to me—and beautiful. Perhaps she might have won some sort of beauty pageant and have been a Miss Something-or-Other. We in Great Britain are not big on beauty pageants, but you seem to have one popping up here and there every other week or so in the States. Were I setting the scene in England, I might have had her been elected the village May Queen three years running.

She must be unspoiled. To be quite frank, I mean here that *she must be a virgin*. She should also be a foil to the other women in the novel, women who are worldly and who have, may I use the expression, "been around". Pardon the crudity, but, if I speak in euphemisms, you might mistake my meaning and miss the point. These wanton women of easy virtue, whose characters are never as fully developed as is the heroine's, attempt throughout the novel to win the affections of the hero but to no avail because he is a good man in search of romance and true love sanctified by the marriage vows.

Your heroine should have recently finished university; do be sure that she has graduated with a First or an Upper Second—I believe such distinctions are analogous to graduating with honours from an American university or college. For example, Sarah Bellum, Oxbridge intellectual and luscious heroine of *Cogitating Hearts and Nobel Minds* (1969), had a 2:1 and eventually won a Nobel Prize. And she, Fiona, of all my heroines, was the one most well-received by my readers.

35

Additionally, your protagonist should have been elected president of her sorority. Thus, by endowing her with brains and personality to augment the allure of her natural beauty, she will then be an easy role model with whom our readers can aspire to relate to. Unlike in the United States, we don't have sororities at British universities, so, once again, if I were to set the scene for *Tempestuous Summer* in England, I should make her President of the Students' Union (although that office is more the result of politics than popularity) or President of some university society.

Also, she should have just started her career. For example, your heroine could find employment as a stewardess, working for an international airline. This would be an excellent device by which you could set your story in a foreign country where the action of the novel must take place. I shall elaborate on the subject of setting in a few moments. However, if you decided to make her a flight attendant, then you would have to spend half the novel convincingly explaining to your skeptical readers the paradox that she could be an airline stewardess and continue to remain a virgin. No, Fiona, if I were writing the story, I should definitely shy away from this type of employment. But you understand what I am driving at: the depiction of the heroine as young, beautiful, bright, unsullied, and in search of romance and adventure, love and marriage.

Let me diverge here for a moment because

it is precisely at this point—". . . love and marriage, romance and adventure"—that many aspiring authors go horribly astray and, consequently, fail miserably and have nought to show for their efforts. Do not, I repeat and underscore, <u>do not</u> allow your heroine to become soiled by any sort of dirty dalliance or—Heaven forfend!—sullied by a premarital relationship. And for God's sake, my dear, *do not* graphically render for the reader your heroine's amorous encounters; let the reader's imagination imagine!

Now, a word to the wise, Fiona. Never use a word in your novels to describe either an act or an emotion or a part of the anatomy or a bodily function that you would be ashamed to mention at dinner in front of Mr. Pilgrim and the children. Naughty words—words that Nanny Crimpet refers to as "no-no words"—and suggestive descriptions of the procreative act have no place in the world we are creating on paper.

Have I made myself perfectly clear? I have gone, perhaps, to excessive lengths to make this point, but—and please do not take umbrage at what follows—you are a native American, culturally bound, and the whole world knows how promiscuous the Colonies have become of late. By the bye, my remarks in this paragraph are certainly not directed at you; they are just general observations about the current sorry state of your debauched society and its sordid literature full of extraneous sexual encounters and potty-mouthed characters. I know I need not

37

belabour this issue any longer, for, as both a mother and a dedicated reader of my novels, you understand what I am trying to get across: namely, a view from afar—a view from a different culture—certainly broadens one's parochial perspective, don't you agree, Fiona?

Goodness me but I have rambled from the subject at hand. Where was I? Oh, yes. In a nutshell, when you broach the love scenes keep this in mind: the less explicit, the better. We never actually witness; rather we delicately intimate what actually passes in the intimacy of the bedroom.

You must have already discovered from reading my novels that the plots are always contemporary and that the settings vary with each novel. Yet, as I mentioned earlier—at which time I promised a fuller discussion of the topic of venues—the plot must always develop in a foreign land. It is simply much easier for our readers to escape to, and become romantically involved with, a place they've never been before: little do they stop and think that any place, once a residence and a routine are established, becomes as drab and humdrum as their current neighbourhoods.

But let that, Fiona, be our little secret. I'm absolutely delighted that you've set *Tempestuous Summer—The Hottest Season* in an exotic setting (". . . set . . . in an exotic setting" does seem a bit redundant, does it not?), for I find my readers love a little, may I term it, "armchair travelogue" as an added spice to enhance the flavour of the romance.

Once again, my dear, allow me to be unambiguously precise and not temper my words by beating around the bush about the skin tone of your male protagonist. I feel a comment, a strong word of warning, is in order concerning your "swarthy hero". I am neither an elitist nor a racist, but I should say that there can be "too much of a good thing". Or as some famous architect—I believe it was your own Frank Lloyd Wright—so tersely put it, "Less is more".

Swarthy is one thing, Fiona. However, too much swarthiness is a horse of an entirely different colour. Our audience must be able to "relate" to the hero. I put "relate" into quotation marks to set it off and draw your attention to it; when you are writing your novel and developing your characters, this word must—or you shall fail miserably—be uppermost in your mind. It is the *sine qua non* (the essential element) which will make, by its presence, or break, by its absence, your career as a writer of romance fiction. Our readers must be able to "relate" to the hero in the same manner and degree as does our heroine. So excuse my bluntness here, but do whiten him up a bit.

Good that he is an extremely wealthy man, for, as Nanny has so often said (she has a way with words), "It's just as easy to fall in love with a rich man as it is to fall in love with one who's poverty-stricken!" We all seem to be searching for a rich, hand-

39

some lover—or should I substitute "husband" for "lover"—who will turn our fantasies into reality. We spend our premarital lives looking in vain for the rich, handsome prince, and then, come the time for our nuptials, we end up marrying the penurious, ugly frog. Goodness me, Fiona, I certainly hope you're not sharing my letter with your husband. If you are, then I should direct a comment to Mr. Pilgrim: I was speaking in generalities, of course.

Ideally, the hero should be twelve to fifteen years older than the heroine. He may be a violent and passionate man—a hot-blooded lover. To a degree, that is. Again, as with the matter of swarthiness, passionate is one thing; too much passion is altogether an entirely different matter. Despite the fact that he is hot-blooded, he always treats our heroine kindly and with the utmost respect. He should be tall, be fashionably attired, and be an avid sportsman, virile in mien and suave in manner. Don't forget, the physical descriptions of the hero are extremely important, for our readers must be able to picture him in order to "relate" to him as does our heroine and also to fall in love with him.

He is never (*ever!*) married at the time he is courting our heroine, but he may be widowed or divorced. If you choose to depict him as being divorced, you must make it clear to your readers that his ex-wife has been solely responsible for the demise of their marriage. Make her out to be a shrewish "gold digger" (We have no word in English that so fittingly describes the type of woman she is as does this Americanism.), a greedy spendthrift who has misled him and who has married him for his money not for his love.

I myself much prefer a hero who has recently lost his spouse in some sort of tragic accident at a location where the moneyed aristocracy congregate. A spa, ski resort, or regatta are all excellent locales where you can do away with his spouse. Keep in mind, however, that car accidents and plane crashes have been overused and are, quite simply, much much too commonplace. I can't think of anything more pedestrian than to have my hero's first marriage come to a tragic end because his wife was killed while crossing the street against the light. People get killed in car accidents every day. Even if she were hit by a chauffeur-driven Rolls-Royce and killed on the streets of St. Moritz or Kitzbühl or Zermatt or Baden-Baden that wouldn't help. No, use your imagination.

If he speaks several languages, this sort of linguistic aptitude will give the novel a rather sophisticated sort of ambiance. However, be extremely careful in your employment of recondite expressions and foreign words and phrases. Our readers are not generally fluent in any language other than their own *Muttersprache* (mother tongue). Indeed, many of them seem to have much difficulty mastering the basic skills requisite for intelligent communication in English. I should suggest that you make minimal use of your hero's linguistic fluency.

But, Fiona, if you do decide to ignore my suggestion and employ in your writing sesquipedalian (long) words to develop a certain character's persona, or if you determine that your novel is in need of a cosmopolitan atmosphere best illustrated through the use of macaronic (an admixture of two or more languages) discourse, then that is, of course, your authorial prerogative. Just be certain that you provide contextual explanations or parenthetical elaborations for these esoteric words and foreign phrases.

The first chapter might consist of a few flashbacks providing detail about the heroine's background, but she should very shortly meet the hero. (Let the hero's history remain a mystery for as long as possible.) Then you can get on with the story—their developing romantic relationship—which should, for the most part, be simply sequential, moving to a happy resolution in wedded bliss. The history of their love affair, from meeting to marriage, should cover between seven and nine chapters; 100-120 pp. seem to me to be an ideal length for a first novel—a novella of sorts to test the (narrative) waters, so to speak, to ascertain if your literary efforts sink or swim.

Well, Fiona, I think that pretty well covers it. Let me iterate, however, my remarks about your treatment of the love scenes which are essential to the story but which, pay heed now, must be delicately treated. She and he can, after a suitable time, *almost* go to bed together—tease your reader; don't titillate her. But, mark my words, Fiona, they must never make love between the covers of your book. What they themselves do between the covers of the bed itself is something best left to the reader's imagination. We simply cannot permit our characters to make love before they are married. Before they consummate the act, they must be interrupted by self-doubt, mutual guilt, shame (especially on the heroine's part), a knock on the door, or what have you.

What need I tell you about writing in general? Your well-written letter provides ample evidence that you have an excellent command over grammar, punctuation, and syntax. I should only suggest that you keep your descriptions—which should be full of sensual details—short and your dialogue, which should be minimal, simple.

Well, now, Fiona, I hope I've been of some help to you. As I stated at the commencement of this missive, I've never before taken an interest in any writer's career (other than my own, of course), but I hope—as you yourself wished—that I may be instrumental in yours. Since you are so familiar with my *oeuvre* (the collected works of a writer), I'll wager that, probably by osmosis or capillary action or whatever the process, *Tempestuous Summer—The Hottest Season* already incorporates many of the suggestions I've given above. By the bye, I'm

2641-RUBA

absolutely mad about the title. Send me several chapters, and I'll be most happy to read them and comment accordingly.

I must soon bring this letter to a close, for it's time for me to take Nanny her tea and crumpets. The old dear waited on our family hand and foot for well over a quarter of a century, and now it's our turn to repay in kind and wait on her. I wish you could meet Nanny; she's such a love. Besides, I've already carried on to excessive lengths, but it's the first time I've ever written this sort of letter. And I did want to give you plenty of advice and cram in everything I thought could be useful so that you might be able to avoid some of the mistakes I made early in my own career. I look forward to hearing from you soon and reading portions of your manuscript.

Very sincerely yours,

June Featherstone

June Featherstone

P.S. Please give my best regards to Mr. Pilgrim and the children. Do send photos of the twins and your daughter if you have some to spare. Nanny loves to look at pictures of children. She can no longer tolerate having tiny tots around her—she gets so nervous when they're about and underfoot, disturbing her routine and trampling the flower

beds or mangling the shrubbery or threatening to topple a Ming vase from its plinth—
but she does enjoy snapshots of them. Yours,
J.F.

641-RUBA

July 18, 1982
2801 Hoosier Rd.
Centreville, IN 45480

Professor Gordon K. Douglas
Department of English Language and Literature
Warren House
Harvard University
Cambridge, MA 02138

Dear Gordo,

Holy Shit! Miracle of miracles!! Wonder of wonders!!! *Mirabile dictu*!!!! I had better pause and take a breather right here and now lest I break the exclamation-point key on my typewriter's keyboard!!!!! You wonder what earthshaking event could have occasioned such rampant joy on the part of your old friend? What monumental happening in the humdrum existence of Joe Leonard could possibly have elicited such an epidemic of exclamation marks to break out, blotting and blurring the page? Simple: Giddy Fortune's furious fickle wheel has spun anew, this time turning up some winning numbers—at long last—for someone dear to you, a person whom you know and love: me! I shall keep you in suspense no longer, Professor Douglas, lest you think my mind has become completely unhinged. Read the enclosed letter dated July 12 from June Featherstone to Fiona Pilgrim, (a.k.a. me, the Great Scribbler), and all your questions will be fully answered.

Not only did she write back, but she also generously volunteered to help Fiona with her ms. By God, Gordy, it worked. I've got her ear. Do you think she'd turn a deaf ear toward me if I wrote back, informing her that Mies Van Der Bauhaus said, "Less is more"? And before him, Robert Browning in *Andrea del Sarto*? I'd better leave well enough alone and keep my big mouth shut.

As you read her letter, pay particular notice to how she carries on about her beloved governess, confidante, and girl Friday, Nanny

Crimpet. Nanny Crimpet, indeed! Can you imagine that anyone could have suffered such a cruel fate as to have actually been christened Hortense Crimpet? I know the English are renowned as being a weird lot, but that eccentricity is no excuse for naming a kid "Hortense." Shit, it almost borders on child abuse. Picture this twelve-year-old nymphet strolling down the street and one of her playmates yelling at her, "Hi there, Hor!" Wonder how that sort of greeting affected her self-image or influenced her vocational aspirations?

The naming of poor Hortense Crimpet aside, it's awfully thoughtful of the famous June Featherstone to take time away from her writing and from attending to Nanny Crimpet to compose such a long and informative letter to such an importuning nonentity as Fiona Pilgrim. And such a kind and helpful letter it was, don't you think? I couldn't have hoped for more.

I can't believe it. What a shock! The old wordmonger actually answered Fiona's letter. Holy Shit! Who would have ever thought that—famous as she is—June would actually condescend to help a pestering fool like Fiona? (Not I, for one.) But she did.

And now the thought of the daunting task which lies ahead of me is almost too dreadful for contemplation, too degrading for words. Yet I'd better come up with plenty of words pretty damn quickly, for this may be my one chance in a million to break into print. Me, a writer of romance pulp fiction! Can you imagine? I suppose it's better than dying destitute and unknown and then watching from potter's field as my grandchildren reap the benefits of my posthumous fame.

Where in the name of the Muses on Mount Parnassus did I ever come up with a silly title like *Tempestuous Summer—The Hottest Season?* Enough temporizing. I'd better slip into Fiona's frock and set my shoulder to the wheel and my pen to paper.

Dammit, Gordo, how am I going to make this ridiculous exercise in banality believable? In addition to the novel, how am I going to continue a plausible correspondence with June throughout *Tempestuous Summer's* composition? Woe is me. I wonder if Steinbeck got started this way? I think he wrote advertising copy before he discovered, or was discovered by, his audience, but that's certainly not nearly so humbling and humiliating as this. Holy Shit!

Yours,

Joe

Joe Leonard

P.S. I'm toying with the idea of setting the novel in Romania (See June's advice about the absolute necessity of employing a foreign locale.) and using some of the information you mentioned when last we spoke. Write soonest or call me ASAP, and tell me more about your general observations concerning your stay there. Give me some specific details about the people, the customs, the manner of dress, the countryside, the political situation, the cuisine, the et cetera. In fact, supply me with anything and everything you think I can use to create the right atmosphere for *Tempestuous Summer*. Thanks, old buddy.

P.P.S. Should you ever get disillusioned with academe, don't give it up for a career hustling insurance.

encl.: Letter from June Featherstone to Fiona Pilgrim dated 12 July

August 5, 1982
2801 Hoosier Rd.
Centreville, IN 45480
U.S.A.

Ms. June Featherstone
Harlequin House
Silhouette Lane
Fensucked-on-Strand
Ely, Cambridgeshire
England

Dear Ms. Featherstone:

How could I ever—in mere words—thank you enough for your wonderful letter of July 12? Gosh, I could hardly believe my eyes when the mailman delivered it; when I opened the letter and read its contents, I was shocked beyond words. You are just too kind and thoughtful for words. In fact, I am at a loss for words—at least for the correct words—to describe just how much your letter has meant to me and how it has given me hope. Though I am realistic enough to realize that no amount of hope would ever be sufficient enough to allow me to attain your level of perfection (Yours, Ms. Featherstone, is a God-given talent.), your letter has given me hope that, with your help and guidance, I can make a small contribution to the genre we both love so dearly. Oh, Ms. Featherstone, thank you ever so much.

I have followed, to a T, the advice in your letter and have, accordingly, completely revamped and rewritten the first chapter of *Tempestuous Summer—The Hottest Season*. I do hope you'll like it. Your suggestions, incorporated in the segment of the novel I'm mailing you along with this letter, have improved *Tempestuous Summer* one-hundred percent. I think it's twice as good as it was before I revised it. I just love it, and I hope you will also.

Yes, I am taking you up on your generous offer, and I've taken

51

the liberty of enclosing the first chapter of *Tempestuous Summer* for your critical appraisal. I should never have been so presumptuous as to think, even for a moment, that you personally, Ms. Featherstone, would actually respond to my letter—let alone agree to read and critique my novel—but I shall forever be indebted to you.

Before continuing this letter any further, let me express to you how sorry I was to hear about Nanny Crimpet's illness. I can tell from the concern expressed in each line of your letter just how fond you are of her. Of course, we don't have governesses here in America—at least, very few of us do. Nonetheless, I know how close you two must be after all those years together and how attached you must be to her. My parents had a dog—her name was Buffy, and she was a wheaten cocker spaniel—and she lived with us for fourteen years, less than half the time Harlequin House has been served by your faithful servant, Hortense Crimpet. Buffy was like one of the family and a fixture in our home.

The last two years she was alive and with us, she became incontinent. And this inconvenience caused quite a fuss, for my mother was an immaculate housekeeper who, before Buffy began to soil everything in sight, kept a spotless house: silent butler, coasters on the end tables and coffee table, guest towels hung decorously in the bathroom, antimacassars and doilies crisply starched and pinned in proper place and position. You know the type, I'm sure.

Buffy's messes, deposited at random throughout the house, just about drove my mother stark raving mad. One never knew when one might come across—or, worse yet, step into—physical evidence of Buffy's incontinent presence in the house. We finally had to have Buffy put to sleep, and I can assure you there wasn't a dry eye in our home for weeks—even Mother was terribly saddened. Suffice it to say, I commiserate with you over the poor state of dear Nanny's health. I do hope she's getting along better by the time you receive this letter. Please give her my special regards and my best wishes for a speedy recovery.

Let me now reread your correspondence and respond directly to some of the comments you made in your most gracious letter. Yes, please, by all means do call me Fiona. I would be honored to be on a first-name basis with someone like you, Ms. Featherstone. Do I dare be so bold and ask if I may address you as June?

Once again, I'm so sorry about Nanny Crimpet's illness, and I hope she's regained her health and has resumed her duties at Harlequin House. Yet I try to look on the bright side of things: if she hadn't been ill, my letter would never have reached you. This situation reminds me of a saying we have here in America: "One man's junk is another man's treasure." It was a piece of bad luck (junk) that poor Nanny was taken ill, confined to her bed, and unable to function properly in her role at Harlequin House. But, at the same time, had she not been away from her desk—had she, in accordance with her normal routine, been able to fetch the mail the day my letter arrived—chances are you would have never read my letter (treasure) and would have never offered to help me.

As you can see from the first chapter, I'm writing *Tempestuous Summer* in the third person. Initially, I had written it in the first person, but, thanks to your advice, I rewrote the second draft in the third person, and it's much more powerful. This is perhaps the most obvious of your suggestions which I've incorporated in the present draft. Of course, within the first chapter you'll find much which I've unconsciously adopted from reading so many of your novels.

As per your recommendation, I've depicted Amanda West, the heroine, as a woman of high moral standards, and I've done this without having her march around the story waving a banner proclaiming, "I am a virgin." I propose to have her fall head over heels in love with Michael (Michael Kukiliko, the swarthy hero of my tale). Her relationship with him will be the closest she has ever come to losing her virginity. I shall take care, naturally, that she never does actually lose it or even come close to cheapening the value of that ". . . gift which once given can never be given again nor reclaimed from the recipient."

I placed the foregoing comment in quotation marks because

my father, when it came time to discuss "the birds and the bees" with me, put it this way: "Treat your virginity, Fiona, like a great treasure of extreme value and scarcity, one that, once given away, will forever be completely depleted. Once you part with it, it loses all the value it once held. So only give your great gift to someone who means an enormous amount to you and who will always cherish what you have given him. You can only give it away once, Fiona, so be sure the man to whom you give it is worthy of you. Treat your virginity like gold. Guard it from those boys who would wish to steal it from you, to cheapen its value. Treasure it. You would never give away something valuable, like gold, to someone who did not mean a great deal to you." My dad was a neat sort of guy.

Your comment about what Nanny Crimpet refers to as "no-no words" was well-intentioned, and the message was duly registered and followed. You are right about the permissive nature of contemporary American society. However, neither I nor my husband fits that decadent mold. We do not countenance blasphemy. In fact, Peter Paul is a member of the Holy Name Society at our parish church. Swearing or the use of gutter language around the children—or in any context, including my writing—is something that neither of us condone.

I picked, as you suggested, a foreign locale for my story: Romania and the Black Sea port of Constanta. My cousin—the very same cousin I mentioned in the postscript to my letter of May 1, the one who visited the Ely Cathedral several years back and sent me the picture postcard—actually spent several years in Constanta as a Fulbright scholar, researching the writings of Ovid. So I'm putting to good use—at least I have a good feeling that I'm putting to good use—some of the details she shared with me about that country (a country which she adores, by the way) and using some of the events which she witnessed and related to me.

I think my choice of Michael Kukiliko as the swarthy hero is ideal, for there is an inherent romantic allure about distant Polynesia—"Far away places with strange sounding names, far away over the sea," as the lyrics to that popular song of the late forties and early fifties, "Far Away Places," so aptly put it. And I don't believe the average reader would consider a native of Hawaii as being "too swarthy." Incidentally, it was most kind of you to share with me your feelings about this sensitive subject. I'm sure my readers will be able to "relate" to both the swarthy hero, Michael Kukiliko, and the strikingly beautiful heroine, Amanda West.

I'm toying with the idea of making Michael a widower whose wife was killed in a tragic accident—an avalanche—at Gstaad or St. Moritz. What do you think about that idea?

Oh, I've taken your advice to heart and tried not to use too many foreign words or phrases. But whenever I feel the insertion of a Romanian word or phrase will help the reader *be* there, I either define the terms parenthetically or else give the discerning reader contextual clues which will explain the meaning to her. At least, I certainly hope I have done this.

I am quite pleased with the way the initial chapter turned out—I mean in relation to your suggestion about providing the reader with enough information concerning the heroine's past in the first chapter. Henceforth, I plan to develop their relationship—she falls head over heels in love with him—in a sequential manner just as you've suggested. Of course, I plan to throw in a lot of obstacles which will make it appear as if they will never be able to settle all of their problems and reconcile all of their difficulties. But eventually they overcome all the problems and difficulties which threaten to thwart their union, and they "live happily ever after."

Well, Ms. Featherstone, that's my plan. I hope you like the first chapter. Peter Paul told me he thinks it's ". . . just great!" By the way, he wasn't at all upset by your remark about my marrying the ugly frog instead of the handsome prince. Actually P.P. is my Prince Charming and King of our household. (P.P. is my pet name for Peter Paul. Of course, when I was trying to toilet train the children, I had to desist in referring to him in this manner, for, invariably, there would be a mad rush to the bathroom the second after I called out his name.)

I must run. Paul and Peter (the twins) have a Little League baseball game. If I don't show up, they'll both mope around and be in a huff for the remainder of the day. Their teammates' mothers show up for every tedious game, and, if I were to miss even so much as a single boring inning, the children would take this as a sure sign that I no longer loved them.

I can't wait to receive your comments about the first chapter of *Tempestuous Summer—The Hottest Season*.

Anxiously yours,

Fiona Pilgrim

Fiona Pilgrim

encl.: Chapter I of *Tempestuous Summer—The Hottest Season*

TEMPESTUOUS SUMMER—THE HOTTEST SEASON

by

FIONA PILGRIM

Emma . . . found herself wishing that she had a man with her . . . . Some nebulous, comfortable—even handsome—figure suggested itself, which made her realise that even the most cynical and sophisticated woman is not, at times, altogether out of sympathy with the ideas of the romantic novelist.

A Few Green Leaves
—Barbara Pym

TEMPESTUOUS SUMMER— THE HOTTEST SEASON

dedicated to

JUNE FEATHERSTONE

2641-RUBA

The train from Constanta lurched to a sudden, but not unexpected, halt. It was—as it invariably was—late. The *Gara de Nord*, Bucharest's cavernous central train station, was—as it always was, no matter what the hour of the day or night might be—crowded. The depot was congested with seething clusters of colorfully attired peasants, madly rushing in one direction to board trains to the hinterlands or else wildly dashing in the opposite direction to catch buses, trolleys, or taxis to various destinations within the city. Whether departing or arriving, each visitor to the capital city wore clothing peculiar to his or her native province.

The crowd, a patchwork quilt of distinctive regional costumes, constituted a milling, variegated map of Romania, a veritable tapestry of a diverse people's native wear: fisherfolk from the Danube Delta; woodcutters from the Transylvanian Alps and the Carpathian Mountains; goatherds and shepherds from Moldavia; farmers from Wallachia; gypsies—mysterious in manner and exotic in appearance—from whichever village or town they had last struck their tents. And, scattered amongst this crowd, disguised and outfitted in brightly colored, handsomely embroidered folkwear representative of every nook and cranny of this charming country, were secret police and undercover agents from the dreaded *Securitate* (Office for Internal State Security) trying to trap either the unwary black marketeer or the covert Western sympathizer.

Yet the person whose mode of dress drew the most attention

61

that sultry summer morning was the strikingly beautiful American woman, Amanda West. To be sure, she was beautiful. And strikingly so with her long, slender, and very shapely legs; her tiny waist; her ample breasts; her neck, face, and arms tanned golden brown by the summer sun; and her silky blonde hair which she wore today styled in a sleek chignon. Possessed of an innocent and naturally beautiful face with the most sensuous lips, Amanda West would not have looked at all out of place were she strolling down the Boardwalk at Atlantic City representing her native state of Wisconsin in the Miss America Pageant rather than elbowing her way through the bustling crowd of travellers at the *Gara de Nord.*

Undeniably, this strikingly beautiful individual was a woman of stunning beauty. However, it was not simply her striking natural beauty that magnetically drew every eye in the station to her. No, there was much more to it than that. Here was no ordinary, extremely attractive woman. She was "different." She was, quite obviously, from the West: Germany? France? England? Perhaps America? She didn't look, nor did she dress, like her fellow travelling companions.

The heat had been so unbearable that morning that Mandy had decided to dress rather casually for the three-and-a-half-hour trip to Bucharest. She wore Nike low cuts with white sweat socks; the whiteness of her shoes and socks only served to enhance the tawny hue of her tanned and shapely lower limbs. Without much forethought, she had thrown on a paisley-print cotton number by Christian Dior, cut dirndl-like with the bodice's tasteful *décolletage* (low neckline) displaying only a modest portion of her ample womanly endowment. Here was a simple, yet highly functional, travelling ensemble which gave easy evidence to the fashion-conscious observer that Amanda West of the State of Wisconsin, U.S.A., knew how to dress.

She wore no jewelry whatsoever. (Her sapphire eyes were jewelry enough!) As a result of both her breeding and her own personal preference, Mandy felt jewelry to be ostentatiously ornamental in normal circumstances. And here, behind the Iron Curtain where there was little or no interest in displaying one's competence in accumulating material trinkets, she felt the wearing of jewelry to be in extremely poor taste.

She had stuffed her Aigner purse with the following items: her U.S. passport; her *legitimatie* (a Romanian I.D. card which granted her resident status and which, by Romanian law, had to be carried by her at all times); various *adeverinte* (official authorizations which permitted her to go to certain places at certain times to do certain things with certain people); the keys to her apartment and to her office at the university; some *lei* (Romanian money); and cosmetics and womanly things which might be needed at the most inopportune of times. She draped her purse nonchalantly over her shoulder and made her way through the pulsating throng.

As she exited the station, a stifling wave of oppressively warm air drowned her in heat—even though it was not yet past 10:00 in the morning—and Mandy wished with all her heart that she had stayed within the confines of her tastefully appointed and breezily cool apartment on the Black Sea. She had, for the past year, lived on the Romanian Littoral, and—though often extremely lonely for some sort of American companionship—she had become quite fond of her surroundings. However, periodically (today, for that matter) she had to report to the American Embassy and check in with the cultural-affairs attaché to let him know that she was alive, that she hadn't yet defected, and that she was making progress with her research on the Roman poet, Ovid.

Waiting for a taxi just outside the *Gara de Nord*, Mandy mulled over the fact that it just didn't seem possible that well over a year had now passed since she had first been notified that she had been nominated to be—and, as it later turned out, selected as—a Fulbright Scholar to Romania. At the time she first applied for the grant, she had just recently received her master's degree in Romance languages from the University of Wisconsin. Her major professor, who had also served as her thesis director, had urged her to put together a research proposal and submit it to the committee which awarded the Fulbrights.

Mandy, although a trained scholar and a serious student of Romance languages, was a romantic at heart. Therefore, she chose as her research topic an in-depth study of the romantic—some might uncharitably substitute "erotic" for "romantic"—writings of the Latin poet, Ovid. What better place to study his works, Mandy had suggested in her prospectus, than Tomis, the Black Sea port—and the oldest (some twenty-six centuries old) city in Romania? Here, Ovid had been banished, because of the amorous nature of his verse, by Augustus Caesar in 8 A.D., and here, nine years later and still in exile, he had died.

Thus Mandy requested a year at the University of Constanta—Tomis had been renamed Constanta in the fourth century A.D. in honor of the reigning Roman monarch of the time, Constantine the Great. Much to her great surprise, she was soon notified that her request was honored by both the Romanian Ministry of Education and The Council for the International Exchange of Scholars (the agency which administered the Fulbright program for the State Department). Amanda West's dream had come true: she was appointed Fulbright research scholar to the University of Constanta for the 1981-82 academic year.

Waiting patiently in the sweltering heat of the taxi stand as the queue slowly shortened and as she edged her way forward, Amanda West continued to muse upon her past and present situation. *How ironic it is,* she thought to herself, *that some 1,965 years after Ovid's death, I—a modest young woman of good breeding and strict religious upbringing—should travel halfway around the world to study the works of a poet banished from his culture because of the eroticism of his writings.*

In fact, it was just these very writings that had occasioned her visit to Bucharest, for Mandy was on her way to see the cultural-affairs attaché at the American Embassy. The purpose of her trip? To ascertain if he had received any word yet from the Fulbright-awards committee concerning her recent request for a year's extension of her original Fulbright grant.

"Gosh," she thought aloud as she considered her state, "the

road of life sure does have its sharp curves, sudden detours, and unexpected *cul de sacs* [dead-end streets]."

A Romanian gentleman immediately in front of her in the queue—a man who, by his response, obviously spoke no English—took Mandy's remark to be directed at him. He turned around and replied in his native tongue that he spoke no foreign language but that, if she would take a cab to the *Oficiul National de Turims Carpati* (the National Office of Tourism—the agency which handled all documents, hotel bookings, and travel arrangements for foreigners) on *Bulevardul General Gh. Magheru,* just across the street from the Ambassador Hotel, she would be sure to find an interpreter there who could answer her questions.

In flawless Romanian, an embarrassed Amanda West informed the gentleman that she had not asked him any sort of question but that she was actually going—if she ever caught a cab—in the general direction of the *Carpati* and that she appreciated his suggestion. She apologized for her babbling and resolved henceforth to keep her thoughts to herself.

In her mind's eye—in the best of all possible worlds—she saw the awards committee reappointing her to the Constanta position and granting her an additional year. Just two months prior to the expiration of her Fulbright, Amanda West had discovered a veritable treasure-trove of Ovidian documents at the *Muzeul de Istorie* (the Museum of History). The fact that the *Muzeul de Istorie* was located on *Piata Ovidiu,* the square named after Ovid, and that the museum's portals were guarded over by an imposing statue of the poet himself did not escape Mandy's notice. This find meant that she desperately needed an extension of her stay; she needed the additional time to study and to catalogue what she had so fortuitously stumbled upon.

After a wait of several more minutes, Mandy finally inched her way to the head of the queue and managed to catch a taxi. She instructed the cab driver to take her to the *Piata Universitatii* (University Square). It was here, close to both the University of

Bucharest and the American Embassy, that the Intercontinental Hotel was located.

Once at the Intercontinental, she went into the main restaurant and relaxed over a refreshing glass of *Borsec*, her favorite mineral water. Reinvigorated by the bubbly *apa minerala* (mineral water), she left the hotel, crossed the street, and walked the half block to 9 *Strada Tudor Arghezi* where the American Embassy was located and where, in a few minutes, her future would be decided. She passed through the Romanian state-police checkpoint, was questioned by the U.S. Marine security guards, and entered the embassy.

"Mandy! Mandy, what in the world are you doing here?" excitedly exclaimed Helena Corbiscu, the attaché's Romanian secretary. Helena was surprised and pleased by Amanda's unexpected visit. "I thought for sure you would be sunning yourself on the beach on such a day. If I had the pleasure of living in Constanta, I do not think—how do you say in English?—I do not think wild pigs could drag me to Bucharest on such an oppressively sticky day. What brings you here, Mandy?"

"Wild horses, Lena. I don't mean wild horses brought me here. I mean, the expression is, 'Wild horses couldn't drag me.' I actually came by the train. I just thought I'd come over for the day. Get out of the provinces and come to the big city and see how the movers and the shakers are getting along. How's it going with you, Lena? Any news yet about my application for an extension?"

"Mandy, I am okay, thanks. No, I have not heard anything at all about that from Mr. Allen." Hank Allen, the Cultural Affairs Officer, was Helena Corbiscu's boss.

"But I do know that he received some mail today in the diplomatic pouch from the Eastern European desk. And that is the section of the State Department which handles all the Fulbright awards to Romania. Should I ring him and see if he can see you now?"

"Oh, please do, Lena. I've only been in Bucharest for an hour and a half, but already I'm so darned hot I can't wait to get back to Constanta, slip into my bathing suit, dash out to Mamaia, and plunge in. As soon as I take care of my business with Mr. Allen, I'm catching the first train outta here."

"Oh, Mandy, how I do envy you. Living in Constanta in your beautiful apartment with its three balconies that practically overhang the Black Sea!" This observation was quite true. Amanda West lived directly on the Black Sea, on the coast road, in a lovely apartment.

"And being so close to Mamaia that you can run out there without a moment's notice. Is it not wonderful?"

Mandy nodded her assent, and her sensuous lips curled into a pleasant smile at the thought of her quite comfortable circumstances. Yes, it was wonderful, and Mamaia, the jewel of the Black Sea Littoral, was beautiful: mile after mile of sandy, well-tended beaches maintained by municipal authorities alternating with unattended pebbly shingles and punctuated here and there with luxurious sea-front hotels—luxurious especially to vacationers from the Communist world where drabness was endemic and drudgery an inherent motif which ran through the fabric of all Socialist societies. Mamaia was *the* resort where the beautiful people—important members of the *politburo*, that select group of a few top members of the Communist Party who were responsible for administering and overseeing the various government bureaucracies; lesser *apparatchiks*, those lower-level party members who put into practice the decisions of the *politburo*; and minor card-carrying functionaries—of the Warsaw Pact world congregated during the summer. Mamaia, the Romanian Riviera.

Yes, Mandy thought to herself, *I'm happy and lucky to live in Constanta—a city two-and-a-half millennia old. Why, I need only to open the balcony doors, and I look down upon Greek and Roman ruins. Yet, I'm only five minutes away from Mamaia, a resort city possessing every amenity that might be desired by a twentieth-century woman.*

Lena continued, "Just a minute, Mandy. I shall ring Mr. Allen. He has just hung up his phone, and I shall see if he is free to see you now."

2641-RUBA

Helena Corbiscu dialed Mr. Allen's extension and announced Mandy's presence. Hank Allen informed his secretary that he would see Miss West very shortly. Soon thereafter, he came out of his office and gallantly greeted Amanda in the Romanian manner, politely taking hold of her hand, bowing to kiss it, and saying, "*Sarut mana* [I kiss your hand]."

"Well, well, well. My dear Miss West. How good it is to see you again. How charming, as always, you look. Apparently you're none the worse for wear living all by yourself out in the sticks. Constanta, truly a charming city with that Old World ambiance; living there must be good for your blood. Yes, indeed, and to what, pray tell, do I owe the pleasure of this visit? I do hope it's not trouble with the authorities."

"No, no. Nothing of the sort. They treat me, at least within the university when it comes to academic matters, as though I were Ceausescu's daughter." Nicolae Ceausescu—a draconian autocrat much feared by Romanians of all political persuasions, be they party members or not—was the party boss and premier of Romania.

"Of course, once I leave the university I'm treated like a leper. No, no trouble with the authorities. Everybody in my department, in fact everyone at the university from the rector and the dean down to the maids and the janitors, has been most kind and helpful to me—distant but quite civil. I just thought I'd come to Bucharest for the day and do some shopping." This was an outright lie, for Mandy could buy anything she needed in Constanta. The things she really wanted were available neither in Constanta nor in Bucharest nor anywhere behind the Iron Curtain, for that matter.

"And, as I was already in the area anyway, I decided I might just as well stop by and see if you've heard anything."

" 'Heard anything'?"

"Yes, about my request for an extension to carry on with my studies for another year. Oh, Mr. Allen," Mandy pleaded, biting her sensuous lips, "I've put so much time and effort into my research. I'd be heartbroken if they sent me back to the States before I had a chance to wrap it up and collect all my data. Especially since unearthing all those new—well, really very old—documents."

"Ah, yes. Well, well, well. Of course, Miss West. Well, what a coincidence. 'Serendipitous' is the word, I believe, to describe the coincidence. That you should pick today, of all days, to trek in here on a shopping spree. It just so happens that this very morning, less than an hour ago in fact, I received word that the committee has okayed your request. You've got your stipend for an additional year. Congratulations, Miss West. Put it to good use."

Amanda West could hardly believe her ears. She jumped up and clasped her hands in a thankful, indeed prayerful, manner and shouted joyously, "Oh, Mr. Allen. Thank you! Thank you! Thank you ever so much. Oh, I'm so happy!"

"Good, I'm happy for you. I'm happy you're happy, one could even say.

"Now, Miss West," Mr. Allen said in a tone suddenly somber in nature—a tone which displayed none of the levity that had characterized his conversation up to that point—"you know perfectly well that my responsibility to all you Fulbrighters does not end with shuffling all the paperwork your presence in this country generates or making sure all your stipends arrive regularly and on time. I'm also interested in your well-being and how you're faring day-to-day. I'm old enough, my dear, to be your father—possibly even your grandfather. So with that in mind, Miss West, let me try to diplomatically phrase a somewhat indelicate question. And, please, my child, understand my motivation which is simply my concern for your welfare. How are you getting along and, perhaps even more to the point, how do you propose to get along for another year without—that is to say, have you—how long has—well, I mean how are you getting along romantically?"

"I beg your pardon, Mr. Allen. What *are* you getting at?"

"Oh, Miss West! Come now! You are an extremely attractive, I could even say strikingly beautiful and statuesque young woman." At this compliment, Amanda blushed and once again bit her sensuous lips.

"You are young and, I assume, quite normal. I don't question how you've coped this past year without any male companionship, but I do know for a fact that had you, excuse the indiscretion, seen any Romanian men, Internal State Security would have let me know first thing. You know how they feel about their people fraternizing with representatives of the Capitalist West."

"I didn't come here to marry a Romanian, or any other sort of man for that matter, Mr. Allen. I was briefed by the State Department in D.C. before I left America. I had a fairly good idea what was in store for me. They told me that it was absolutely against the law for me to ever spend even a single night in any Romanian's house—whether the occupants be male or female, married or unmarried, faculty members or students, or what have you. I believe a fine of 15,000 *lei*, three times the average Romanian's yearly income, was to be levied against the owner of the house if the law were ever transgressed.

"The briefing officer painted a pretty grim—and, as it turned out, a pretty accurate—picture of how I would pass the time. He told me that any Romanian who talked with me off the grounds of the university had to report the contents of his or her conversation with me to the security officer where he or she was employed. He said that I couldn't have any Romanian friends, male or female, because Romanians—having been ruled for centuries by either Ottoman Viziers or Hapsburg Archdukes, and now being surrounded by Warsaw Bloc countries—hated foreigners of all stripes: Capitalists or Communists.

"Well, I knew all this when I accepted the grant, and I was well aware of the situation I was stepping into. I didn't come here, Mr. Allen, to win a popularity contest or to find a husband. I came here solely to do original research on Ovid. And that is exactly what I've done, and that is exactly what I intend to continue doing!"

"Well, well, Miss West. Don't get testy, my dear girl. I fear you've missed the point entirely. I just don't want you—all alone over there by yourself in Constanta, without companionship of any kind—to do irreparable damage to your psyche, to your libido, and to things of a Freudian nature: boyfriends, dating, dancing, drive-in theaters. Things of that nature. A strikingly beautiful girl like you can't expect to spend her entire life reading Ovid. Why, if I were forty years younger, I'd—"

"Oh, that! That's what you're getting at, Mr. Allen." Amanda laughed as she suddenly realized the direction in which the conversation was headed.

"Well, I appreciate your concern for me, and I'm sure it's well intentioned. But, believe me, I'm perfectly all right. I've adapted and have learned to handle my—well, I've been able to sublimate my—my—why, yes, I'm able to channel all my energies into my research," Mandy haltingly replied, her cheeks suddenly flushed in embarrassment.

"And besides, whenever I get real lonely and want to see an American face, Bucharest and the embassy are only three and a half hours away. Anyway, I enjoy the train."

"All right, my dear. But I want you to know I'm here to help you in any way I can should you ever need a shoulder to cry on, a sympathetic ear to listen to your problems, or a helping hand if you ever find yourself in dire straits."

"I know that, Mr. Allen. It's reassuring, believe me. Thanks."

"Okay, young lady. Now that I've gotten that off my chest, and I've soothed my conscience, let me buzz Mrs. Corbiscu and have her type up a letter from me to the rector of your university. I'd better advise him now that your Fulbright has been renewed so that he can get the ball rolling on his end. You wouldn't believe the amount of time and the reams of red tape it takes to issue you people your visas, *Legitimatii*, et cetera. Come back in about an hour or so, and I'll try to have all the paperwork you'll need put together. Okay? And, Miss West, if you ever do need help of any sort, call me first thing. Just remember: your phone is tapped."

Amanda West assured Mr. Allen that she would unhesitatingly call him if she ever needed a friend or if she ever found herself in a difficult situation. She told him that her spirits had been lifted by his concern for her.

641-RUBA

Then she left the embassy grounds and—just passing time—
strolled through the quaint streets which surrounded the embassy.
That section of Bucharest had not been destroyed by the devastat-
ing 1977 earthquake, and it had retained all its Old World, Victorian,
fin-de-siècle (end of the nineteenth century) charm. She walked
over to the American Library on *Alexandru Sahia Strada* and
browsed through some of the weekly American magazines shelved
therein, catching up on what had been going on in America.

After the passage of several hours, Amanda returned to the
embassy to pick up the documents Mr. Allen was readying for her
to present to the rector of her university. Helena had just finished
typing the letter Mr. Allen had dictated to her when Amanda arrived. Mandy thanked her for typing it and engaged Lena in small
talk preparatory to taking her leave. Shortly, Mandy would have to
depart for the *Gara de Nord* and the return trip to Constanta.
Lena, who, like Mr. Allen, appreciated both the striking beauty of
the Fulbright scholar and the young woman's peculiar, isolated position as the only American in a city of 200,000 people (half of
whom most probably were men who, were they single and virile,
would be most interested in escorting Amanda West were she not
an American and were this not xenophobic Romania), put Mr. Allen's
letter in a large manila envelope with other papers intended for the
rector and handed the documents to Amanda.

As the papers passed from hand to hand, Helena commented,
and not at all casually but with intense interest as though she were
about to reveal information of great moment, "Oh, Mandy. I almost
forgot. It completely slipped my mind earlier. Guess what? You will
never believe it!"

"I haven't the vaguest idea, Lena. I couldn't even hazard a
guess. What on earth are you talking about? Give me a hint."

Lena warily looked around as though the embassy were bugged
(which, in fact, it was), put her hand to the side of her mouth as if
she were about to commit the most infamous act of espionage by
giving away the most sensitive and compromising of state secrets,

and whispered, "Mandy, there is going to be another American living in Constanta!"

This, indeed, was news. Mandy, a Capitalist pariah in Communist Romania, had been there alone—totally devoid of any companionship save for the company of Publius Ovidius Naso, and he'd been dead nearly 2,000 years—and the thought of another American to share some of the lonely hours cheered her. "Great! Really? Yippee! Whoopee! What in the world is she gonna be doing there?"

" 'She,' dear Amanda, is not quite the correct usage of the pronoun. In this case, the 'she' you refer to is a 'he.' And quite a masculine 'he,' I might add. What is that American expression you people use to describe an especially attractive gentleman? Ah, yes, I have it. Yes, he is what you would call a 'chunk.' Is not that the right word? No," Helena corrected herself, "that is not right. The word is 'hunk.' I saw him when he registered with the commercial attaché yesterday, and, I assure you, Mandy, he is a most handsome man. A most attractive hunk, I would say."

"Really?" Amanda answered quizzically. "What does he do, and what in the world could he be doing in Constanta?"

"I do not know exactly—some type of business venture, to be sure. I think he is a mechanic or something like that. He is here as some sort of technical advisor to the Ministry of the Interior; the Ministry is responsible for constructing the great canal they are building which, some day, will shorten by six-hundred kilometers the distance the Danube has to travel across Romania in order to reach the Black Sea. I think he is involved in this project in some sort of advisory capacity. But, of course, I am not certain."

"A mechanic? But what would I ever have in common with a mechanic?"

"Oh, Mandy. Do not be so negative. He is an American, and he is a man. And he is so handsome, so strong, so—so—he is from your state of Hawaii, if I am not mistaken."

"A Hawaiian mechanic! Lena, you've got to be kidding. Please say it isn't so. Of all people to come to Constanta! I'm allergic to pineapples, and I hate those luau lullabies—Don Ho and the ho-ho-

horrible 'Hawaiian Wedding Song.' Oh, this is too, too much. We simply won't have a thing in common."

"To begin with," Lena sapiently remarked, "you are a woman, a strikingly beautiful woman at that; he, a handsome man. That is enough of a difference to give you two quite a bit in common."

"What's his name? Not that I'm gonna look him up or anything like that. I've got enough to occupy my time already with just my research to do."

"His name is—" and Helena Corbiscu paused and skimmed down a list, the roster of those few Americans who had been issued permanent resident visas, until she spotted the stranger's name "—Kukilukoa—no that is not it. It is a real tongue twister, his name. It is Kukiliko. Mr. Michael Kukiliko."

And, sighing, she said, although she didn't need to underscore it again, "And he is a most handsome hunk."

"Well, I'm sure he is, and I'll probably bump into him sooner or later. Constanta is a large city, but an American stands out there like a sore thumb. So, I'll be on the lookout for him."

"Oh, you could never ever miss him, Mandy. He is so very large and so very swarthy. And, Amanda, such a handsome chunk is he."

5th September 1982
Harlequin House
Silhouette Lane
Fensucked-on-Strand
Ely, Cambridgeshire
England

Mrs. Fiona Pilgrim
2801 Hoosier Rd.
Centreville, IN 45480
U.S.A.

My dearest Fiona,

Thank you so much for your letter of 5th August and the accompanying first chapter of your manuscript. I do have some reservations (very minor) about *Tempestuous Summer*, but, on the whole, I loved the first chapter and found it absolutely engrossing. Your epigraph from *A Few Green Leaves* was an excellent way to introduce the reader to the theme with which you will be dealing. I simply adore Barbara Pym's writings. No one has yet captured the magic and thrill of the jumble sale as has she nor has anyone ever before made such jolly good thematic use of Ovaltine.

However, before discussing *Tempestuous Summer*, let me say a word or two about a certain matter which has caused me no small amount of vexation. I refer, Fiona, to your remarks about Nanny Crimpet's condition. I feel as though I should be less than honest if I did not register this one rather griev-

ous complaint with you. I strongly object to
your equating Nanny's illness with Buffy's
problem. I think it terribly insensitive of
you. Rest assured, Fiona, that Nanny is considered by the residents and the staff of
Harlequin House as an integral part of our
family and not as some mere pet that can
easily be dispensed with once it has outlived its usefulness. I for one certainly
did not appreciate your drawing the
unfavourable analogy between your Buffy and
our Nanny. What was the point? Could you
possibly have been suggesting, and none too
subtly at that, euthanasia for Nanny?

Well, perhaps I am overreacting, and rushing too eagerly to her defence, but I get my
dander up when anyone, even when uninten-
tionally, slights our dear old Nanny. She is
such a sweet. Although, in all honesty, Fiona,
living with, and looking after, Nanny is
taking its toll on me. With each passing
day, it's becoming more and more difficult
to deal with her and her strange antics. I
have shared the following secret with few
people, but I feel as though I can place my
trust in you: Nanny, poor dear, is rapidly
approaching senility.

Why, just yesterday she tied a lead around
the neck of one of the topiaries—in this
case, a yew pruned to look like a large dog—
and was trying to take it for a stroll. In
her defense, I should point out that, except
for the fact that one never sees a green
mastiff, the topiary looked just like the
real thing. At her age, her eyesight is

beginning to fail, so I'm sure she thought it had to be walked so it could do its "duty".

Still, that is no excuse. She had almost deracinated the obstinate evergreen before I convinced her that it was stationary and that—generally speaking—shrubberies require very little exercise. You should have seen her struggling with that adamant shrub as she tried to make it obey her commands. It just wouldn't budge. During an extremely violent tug—matched by an equally violent voiced command to get it to come to heel—a twig snapped her sharply in the calf. She insisted she had been bitten and needed to be vaccinated immediately against hydrophobia. Fortunately, I was able to convince her, but only after a most exhaustive exchange of words, that conifers, while admittedly homonymously somewhat similar, are not carnivores; that, although poisonous, the yew which had "attacked" her was not a carrier of rabies; and that she was not, therefore, in any danger of contracting the dreaded disease. Oh, it is indeed a trying time here at Harlequin House, Fiona!

If, like Buffy, the sweet old soul ever does become incontinent, I've already taken the necessary precautions. Long before I received your letter, I had spoken with Harlequin House's doctor, and he assured me that we can purchase either adult disposable nappies or incontinence knickers which, while inconvenient, will avoid the messes that so disturbed your poor mother. By the bye, Fiona,

I heartily sympathise with your mother, for I too like to keep a clean house. I'm sure the maids would all have had perfect fits had we ever had a Buffy and her accompanying excretory problems here at Harlequin House.

There! That's done with, and I feel much better now that I've fully expressed myself on this sad matter. You now know precisely how I feel about dearest Nanny. Let me turn my attention to your letter of 5th August and comment on it. Then I shall make some remarks about the first chapter itself.

Fiona, I would be delighted if you would refer to me as June. I think this sort of familiarity lends itself to the development of a candid and cordial friendship.

Yes, I am glad that you have rewritten *Tempestuous Summer—The Hottest Season* in the third person, for, truly Fiona, it would never have "worked" nearly so well as it does had you left it in the first person. You are certainly correct about one thing: there can be no doubt in the reader's mind that Amanda West is anything but what she is supposed to be. Jolly good for you! I found your remarks about your father's remarks about virginity remarkably well made.

Your choice of Romania is excellent. Few people have visited behind the Iron Curtain and far fewer have ever lived there. Thus, the reader will be able to learn about a new culture whilst enjoying the love story which takes place there. Was it not Horace in *Ars Poetica* who said literature should delight (*dulce*) and instruct (*utile*) the reader (*utile et dulce*)? Romania, a delightful choice.

Your cousin does seem to get around, doesn't she? She must be quite bright and very adventuresome, flitting here and there without a moment's hesitation or forethought. I should love to meet her someday and talk to her about the experiences she's had gadding about the globe. I do so enjoy talking with people who have had the gumption, at the drop of a hat, to pick up—or is it pack up?—and take off for "Far away places with strange sounding names . . ." if I may steal a delightful phrase from your letter of 5th August. I'm something of a homebody myself, and these Bedouin types appeal to me.

You think this statement ironic, Fiona, because of the cosmopolitan nature of my novels? I'll let you in on a little secret, my dear. My familiarity with the foreign locations where I set my novels comes from thoroughly researching *Baedeker*, *Fodor*, the *Michelin Green Guides*, and like guidebooks rather than from actually having spent any time in these strange and exotic lands. Despite the worldliness of my novels, I myself am very parochial. You see, there's the real me—the private me, the stay-at-home me who loves to putter in her garden. And then there's the other me—the public me, the cicerone who takes her readers to all sorts of alien locales and guides them through the cities and towns of foreign lands. And, Fiona, the two are in no way similar. My, how I've gone off on a tangent!

79

I absolutely can't wait to meet Michael. He sounds, already, very handsome—and with just the "right" (How does one ever know when there is too little or too much of anything?) tinge of swarthiness. Yes, Gstaad or St. Moritz would be a marvellous place to bury the first Mrs. Kukiliko. And yes, you have given the reader an excellent idea of what type of person Amanda is: where she has been; where, at present, she is; and where she is going. Capital effort on your part, Fiona. Capital!

So much for my specific comments about your letter and your plan of attack. Now to some observations about the first chapter as you have presented it to me and the remainder of the book as I envision it. As I said in the previous paragraph, I'm just dying to meet Michael, and I know he'll be a perfect match for Amanda. I'm sure he'll be swarthy enough, but, Fiona, will he be tall enough? And will he possess enough ambition and sufficient initiative to account for the fortune he has accumulated?

You are an American and know the "turf" (Or, in the case of Hawaii, should I have written "surf and turf"?) far better than I do. However, I have this image of Hawaiian males as being indolent, burly types: squat and compact Polynesian sumo wrestlers. Wreathed in leis and wearing nothing but machetes and native grass skirts, they lounge about beneath palm trees and play their ukuleles as they take a break from picking pineapples or cutting sugar cane. Though this stereotyping may be quite unfair to Mr. Kukiliko and his kin, this is the picture that comes to my mind when I think of Hawaiian Islanders. The point of all this?

Can Michael Kukiliko be rich enough to sweep Amanda West off her feet? To transport her, as it were, from her stepmother's sparsely furnished cottage to her "lover's" ancestral manor house? Let us never forget that our readers—living a bleak and boring life for the most part—are trying to *escape* from their surroundings. In order to transport them, the handsome prince must be able to afford a gilded coach drawn by four white chargers sumptuously caparisoned in trappings of fine silk and brocaded satin, a resplendent panoply that exudes aristocratic wealth. What sort of impression will he make if he arrives at the reader's doorstep in a rotten pumpkin begrimed with mud and pulled by four emaciated mice in tattered harness?

You understand, Fiona, what I am saying? We are talking about Cinderella. Yes, Cinderella! If the prince had not been who he was—if he had been, say, a fishmonger—neither the reader, nor Cinderella, nor he himself would have ever cared if he ever returned her lost slipper. Why? Because she would have merely traded scrubbing her stepmother's floors for scaling her husband's fish. Bluntly put, Prince Michael should reek of wealth not stink of fish. His wealth will serve as the vehicle that transports the heroine from charwoman to chairwoman.

And his wealth should be landed, aristocratic wealth not parvenu money. Perhaps he could be the son of some Hawaiian chief—they are like American Indians, are they not? Don't they have hereditary chieftains? Yes, make Michael the scion of the most royal of Hawaiian royal families, heir apparent to an entire archipelago. Make him a member of the nobility. Title him. That would give him some class, although certainly nothing of the *Burke's Peerage, Baronetage and Knightage* sort of class. (A hint for the next novel you write: *Burke's* has proven to be an invaluable source from which have come many ideas for the names and social positions of my heroes and heroines.) Without a doubt, Fiona, being married to a chief's son has much more appeal to the average reader than being married to a mechanic. Now that I've said it, I pray that Peter Paul doesn't make his living repairing motorcars. I seem to be always putting my foot in my mouth, being a bit too frank.

Let me turn away from Michael and focus on Mandy. Glorious girl. Charming. But! But here's a syntactical suggestion, Fiona. I love the characterisation of Amanda West, but, if I should ever again in the novel come across the phrase "strikingly beautiful" referring to her, I think I should like to strike Amanda dead. Use it once to describe her physical attributes and then drop it. Too much of the same thing is overkill. Strike that phrase from your vocabulary.

While I am on the subject of what annoys me in the first chapter, let me mention the clothing Amanda wore as she arrived at the *Gara de Nord*. I should think she would need a much sportier outfit to go with her trainers and sports socks than the Dior dirndl you describe her wearing. Actually, I cannot even imagine the House of Dior ever designing a dress in the dirndl style. It's peasant wear. It's hardly *haute couture* (high fashion or fashionable attire for women). A dirndl would be appropriate for a milkmaid in the Tyrolean Alps. No women of my acquaintance would want to wear such a tight-fitting dress in that kind of oppressive heat. How about a loose-fitting cotton-knit top and white culottes?

And do add a bit more detail when you are describing her wardrobe. Our readers can't afford to purchase the type of clothes our heroine is wearing. Think of your novel as being part romance, part fashion show. If you give your readers enough detail, they can identify with Amanda West and very soon they are vicariously wearing her luxurious apparel. So do try to work this into future chapters.

Once you've got her suitably attired, don't you think you should also give the reader more information about the "inner Mandy" than you have thus far provided in the first chapter? Fiona, I'm playing the devil's advocate here and being overly critical, but for a good cause: I want to improve a book which—need I say again?—I just adore. So keep that in mind if my suggestions begin to chafe and annoy you.

Don't you really think you should be inserting something about how—though virginal, to be sure—Amanda West has yearnings and desires to be loved completely as a woman and not just admired as a scholar for her mind? Thus far in the novel, it appears that the only man who has ever "turned her on"—excuse me for the vulgarity, but the expression seemed so apt in this context—is Ovid. By the bye, when I went up at Oxford, I was once called upon to write a quite lengthy treatise on Ovid. I perused sections of his *Metamorphoses*, but I couldn't—either in the original Latin or in the English translation—make any sense out of the pages I had been assigned to read.

So far, Amanda seems totally dedicated to her work. Fiona, my dear Fiona, you are a woman; you are quite familiar with these secret longings within each of us. Peter Paul—and I would never be so brazen as to pry into your conjugal relationship—must have awakened your desires. Forgive me if I trespass on sacred ground—and for mercy's sake please do not quote what I have just said to your husband; I should be so chagrined if we were to meet someday, and he knew how outspoken I have been in my letters—but what I am attempting to do is help you to write a better book. And I should be doing both you and your audience a disservice if I were not one-hundred percent frank about this matter. You must make Amanda come alive; you simply cannot be satisfied with a description of her intellectual life.

I'm not criticising everything you've done in the first chapter, Fiona, for you have given the reader an excellent idea of what Amanda *was*. Henceforth, your task is to tell the reader—or rather let Amanda herself *show* the reader—what she *is* and what, through the love and support of Mr. Kukiliko, she *can be*.

Give us some more of Amanda's emotions. The sensuous lips are nice but what about, just for one example, how she might feel when Michael runs his hands through her hair— how the heavy weight of it becomes almost buoyant when touched by his caressing fingers. One of my heroines, Linda, the lovesick young pharmacist in *Love's Potion—the Alchemy of Romance*, felt that the most erotic public act a lover could perform for his sweetheart was when, helping her on with her coat, he placed his hands upon the nape of her neck and gently untangled and released the hair caught beneath her collar.

What about the fleeting thoughts she must have, thoughts we all have, and perhaps sometimes shares with a friend, about her dream man's strong hands in her hair, pulling her to him, and so forth? Perhaps it would be difficult for her to find such a confidante considering her isolation and her social and political circumstances. Maybe she could have a pen pal and seek advice through an exchange via the post. Letters are a nice change of pace in a novel, don't you agree? But, on second thought, epistolary exchanges probably wouldn't work, for the authorities would more than likely censor her correspondence. Do give this suggestion some more thought.

You have the setting (you do have a gift for description); you have the premise; you have the attractive young woman; you have the handsome hero. Now let Amanda West live the story within the situation you have created for her. Let her discov—

Fiona, I have just been visited by the most eye-opening epiphany! Is it possible that Mr. Allen, the cultural-affairs officer, has secret designs upon Mandy's gorgeous body and that she will be saved from his rapacious grasp by the arrival of Michael just at the most crucial moment? Like your cavalry coming to the rescue just at the last minute as the Indians are about to raid the wagon train and rape the women.

One further bit of advice. Were I you, I should cut down on words that have to be translated either parenthetically or contextually. I know this is your first try at it—and an excellent one at that!—but the type of novel we write is meant for escape and enjoyment. And the overuse (not that you are by any means overusing them) of foreign words and phrases smacks of erudition. Furthermore, these interruptions distract our readers from the story line and lessen their emotional involvement in the story. You must keep in mind as you write that our readers, raised on TV and nurtured in poor schools, have quite limited attention spans.

Additionally, your employment of a language unfamiliar to the—excuse me, Fiona, but I must bring this letter to an immediate close. My major-domo, Hopkins, has just informed me that darling Nanny has had an accident in the butler's pantry, of all places! She has no business being there. The mishap is not life-threatening, however, so don't worry overmuch. Nonetheless, I must attend to her. Besides it's coming on tea time, and she leads such a precisely scheduled life. You'd actually think she was German, so preoccupied with regimentation and punctuality is she. If I'm five minutes late with tea, she thinks I'm upset with her, and she, in turn, becomes upset with me, and soon the entire staff at Harlequin House is in an uproar.

I can scarcely wait for the arrival of Chapter Two. Let me hear from you soon. A thought just occurred to me: could this Helena Corbiscu, so infatuated with Michael as she obviously is, be the "other" woman who threatens to steal Michael away from Amanda? I have a premonition that this might very well be the case. Keep a close watch on this Romanian hussy!

With fondest regards,

June Featherstone

June Featherstone

6th September 1982

P.S. Well, twenty-four hours have elapsed since I closed this letter, but I haven't posted it yet, so I thought I'd add this postscript. I told you Nanny had no business being in the butler's pantry—she hadn't. She just happened to pass out there as she was passing by, en route back to her bedroom from a lengthy visit to the wine cellar. She had no business being there either! It used to be that she was satisfied with her afternoon cordial, but of late she's developed the most unquenchable thirst. I don't know what's to become of her! She's all right but confined to bed with a severe headache and a sour disposition.

I reread, again, the first chapter of *Tempestuous Summer*, and an odd thought, which I felt I must share with you, kept running through my mind. It is, indeed, a strongly written chapter, but the general impression I am left with is this: it could almost—now please, Fiona, please don't misinterpret what I am about to say and become angered and upset with me and think me too captious—but it could almost have been written by a man. I have much trouble identifying with Amanda. She hasn't yet established her femininity. This is not to say she is not an admirable creation. I don't empathise with her yet though as I should. Perhaps that's it. This objection, of course, may be the fault of the present reader, but perhaps you might want to feminise her a bit more. Just allow your own womanly instincts to flow out of you naturally and capture them on paper as you work with Amanda's developing character. Don't be shy about it! What you are doing here is acting out your dreams—yes, *your dreams*—through the adventures of Amanda West. I must close. Duty and Nanny call. Cheerio! J.F.

November 16, 1982
2801 Hoosier Rd.
Centreville, IN 45480
U.S.A.

Ms. June Featherstone
Harlequin House
Silhouette Lane
Fensucked-on-Strand
Ely, Cambridgeshire
England

Dear Ms. Featherstone,

It seems ages since I last communicated with you. I'm sure you thought I'd probably passed away or dropped off the ends of the earth. But there are very good reasons which explain my tardiness in responding to your wonderful letter of September 5. I've been as busy as a bee—or is it a beaver? I forget which. I haven't had a moment's rest what with my writing (See enclosed Chapters II and III of *Tempestuous Summer—The Hottest Season.*), my motherly duties, and my community activities.

School has been back in session since early September, and I've been elected president of our local PTA (Parent Teacher Association). Believe me, it's turned out to be a responsibility I hadn't bargained for; it's very time-consuming. We've had membership drives, board meetings, and all sorts of fund-raising activities such as a bake sale, a school carnival, a magazine-subscription solicitation, et cetera. I'm gone from the house two or three nights a week—or so it seems.

And then there's Peter Paul's career to consider. He's in the insurance business, and he's convinced, beyond a shadow of a doubt, that my involvement in the community is essential to his success as a businessman. The more visible I am donating my time to Centreville's various civic clubs and volunteer organizations, the

91

more successful he'll be. At least that's what P.P. thinks. I myself think it's an absolute waste of valuable time which could be much better spent in another pursuit. And you know exactly just what that pursuit is. But, in the interest of family harmony, I keep my own counsel and volunteer for anything that he thinks will advance his career.

Thus, I'm chairwoman of the March of Dimes, an organization here in America devoted to preventing birth defects; I'm president of Centreville's Jayshees, a women's auxiliary of the Jaycees—I don't know if you have such an organization in England, but the Jaycees, the Junior Chamber of Commerce, are a group of civic-minded young businessmen devoted to community service; and I do volunteer work for our local American Red Cross chapter. I'm a Gray Lady at the community hospital. I loathe that term "Gray Lady"; I'm certainly not graying by any means. Apparently the term came from the gray uniform which the Red Cross volunteers once wore while on duty in military hospitals. My baby, Priscilla, also does volunteer work with the Junior Red Cross at Centreville Community Hospital. Her uniform is red and white candy-caned pinstripes, and we refer to Priscilla and her gang as "Candy Stripers."

I'm on the go from dawn to dusk, yet I can't ever seem to find enough time in the day to do all the things which need doing. Nonetheless, usually late at night after I've tucked the children in bed or early in the morning before I've fixed them their breakfasts or packed them their lunches, I daily steal an hour or two from my busy schedule for you know what! I secret myself away in the basement, where I've converted the utility room into a subterranean atelier, and write. Here, amongst the washer and the dryer, the hot-water heater and the furnace, and P.P.'s workbench and tools (not the most ideal of working conditions), I devote myself to the furtherance of my art. And the results of my efforts these past two months are what I'm sending, along with this letter, for your reading and comments. I do hope you like what I've written.

Let me now read over your letter and comment appropriately.

First and foremost, thank you, June, for allowing me to address you as "June." Before proceeding any further, however, let me clear the air regarding my ill-considered, but never ill-intended, remark concerning Buffy and Nanny's health. I was attempting to make the point that I know—even though I am not personally familiar with the experience, having never kept a retainer—how attached one becomes to a "faithful friend and servant of the family."

In retrospect, I see clearly that my analogy between Buffy and Nanny was poorly drawn. I assure you, I meant no harm by it. I never so much as meant to even imply that you treated her like a pet rather than a person. And I certainly was not suggesting that you either put her to sleep just because she's outlived her usefulness, or, if I may carefully employ here another animal analogy, that you put her out to pasture. If the whole truth were known, you would understand—as I'm sure you will understand after reading my letter—that my motivation was good, and my intentions were honorable. I feel nothing but genuine pity for Nanny, and I commiserate with you, June, for I know how upset you must be with the poor dear's deteriorating condition. It is obvious to me that Nanny Crimpet means as much to you as P.P. and the children mean to me. Enough said! I feel much better now.

Now that I've said what needed to be said, let's join Michael and Amanda in Romania. In order that you may better understand just what it is I'm up to in this novel, let me reveal the plot as I have roughly sketched it out. In the next several chapters, as Amanda and Michael begin to learn more and more about each other and as she becomes infatuated with him, I intend to reveal to the reader—probably during a candlelight dinner conversation at their favorite restaurant—that Michael is an extraordinarily wealthy man: the scion of a family which owns, in addition to much ocean frontage on Waikiki Beach, several gigantic pineapple and sugar-cane plantations. What do you think of that?

I shall most likely—at the same time as he is revealing the secret of his family wealth to her—also have him come clean about his mysterious past and have him tell Mandy about the loss of his beloved spouse. I have as yet not decided on how and where to get rid of her. (Possibly I should have phrased the preceding sentence in a more genteel fashion.)

Sometime late last spring or early in the summer, there appeared in our local newspaper the saddest article about a man in Southern Indiana; he had been attacked and been done in by a huge, upwards of fifty pounds, swan. I swear this story is the God's honest truth, June; I should have cut it out and sent it along with this letter and the accompanying chapters of my manuscript. Apparently, the male of the species is extremely protective of the nest during mating season. And when this man, an elderly gentleman who had been fishing in the area, encroached upon the swans' territory and ventured too near to the spot where the female had been nesting, the protective male attacked the boat and overturned it. Beating the hapless fisherman with his powerful wings and pecking at him with his huge beak, the swan actually caused the old man to sink to the bottom of Van Bibber Lake and drown. What a sad and ignominious end. I mean, there are ways to die, and, then again, there are more fitting ways to expire.

My cousin—the world traveler—has told me that the town of Bruges, the capital of Flanders in Northwestern Belgium, is famous for its handcrafted lace and its flocks of gorgeous swans. I was toying with the idea that Mrs. Kukiliko could be in Bruges on a buying trip, stocking up on lace tablecloths and napkins for their mansion in Hawaii and their chalet in Kitzbühl/St. Johann. Michael could be in nearby Ghent touring the castle when they brought him the bad news. She could rent a dinghy or some similar such smallish boat and come to such a sad fate as befell the ancient angler of Van Bibber Lake.

Do you think such fowl play an appropriate swan song for Mrs. Kukiliko? It may seem a bit bizarre to you, June, but the demise of the old fisherman is not at all apocryphal. And if such an event could happen in Indiana, then it could happen anywhere in the world! We here in Indiana lead routine, rather commonplace lives, and nothing bizarre has ever occurred within the state's borders. Let me know your feelings about this, please.

In Chapters II and III, I tried to let the reader experience some of Mandy's sexual yearnings for Michael's abundant masculinity. Of course, I guarded against the danger of becoming too explicit. This was easy, for I'm not the type of woman given to the use of "loose language" or to the discussion of matters "of a prurient nature." Nonetheless, I tried to put on paper some of Mandy's sensuous—may I go so far as to say "sensual"?—feelings. I think I succeeded, but I'm not one-hundred percent sure. However, when rereading Chapters II and III, I was embarrassed on five separate occasions, and I blushed twice. So I think I must be doing something right. I'm anxious to hear your reaction after you've finished reading the latest installments.

Please give my regards, and best wishes for a speedy recovery, to Nanny. I dream of someday visiting Harlequin House and meeting you both. I would be embarrassed to the nth degree if you ever shared my comments concerning Buffy and Nanny with the individual concerned.

A word or two about your postscript. The fact that you felt the first chapter could have been written by a man and that I should "feminise" Amanda a bit can, I think, be quite fairly attributed to my lack of experience. After all, this is my first "serious" attempt at writing a novel, and—by the very difficult nature of the task— I'm bound to make some false starts and to commit many errors. However, because of such constructive criticism as that voiced in your postscript, I can correct my mistakes. I believe, thanks in large measure to your good and perceptive suggestions, you'll find Chapters II and III much easier to "relate" to. How shall I ever be able to repay you, and thank you enough, for your guidance?

I guess that just about wraps up what I've got to say. I'm waiting on pins and needles to hear how you like the two chapters accompanying this letter. Write soon.

Warmest regards,

Fiona

Fiona Pilgrim

encl.: Chapters II and III of *Tempestuous Summer—The Hottest Season*

After a relaxing journey through countryside made richly verdant and bountifully fertile by the irrigating waters of the Danube and its tributaries, Amanda West arrived at the *Gara Feroviara*, Constanta's main train station. Stimulated by the exciting events of the day, Mandy decided she would walk along the Black Sea coast the mile and a half to her apartment on the *Bulevardul Carpati* rather than take a taxi as was her habit when returning home from a visit to Bucharest.

Before beginning her journey, however, she crossed the street in front of the train station, entered the lovely wooded park, and followed a pebbled path to its center. She found an unoccupied bench and sat down to watch the watery workings of Constanta's famous artesian landmark, the lovely *Orga de apa*, the water organ. As she rested there, enjoying the coordinated eruptions of a dozen different spurting fountains, she reflected on how happy she was to be back in Constanta, a city she loved so much. After watching the fountains complete their computerized routine several times, Amanda got up, exited the park, and walked home.

Worn out from the long walk, Mandy felt she needed to freshen up with a brisk shower and a change of clothes. It chanced to be Thursday, and the prospect of a shower on a Thursday in Constanta could indeed refresh the most lifeless and invigorate the most lethargic, for the old quarter of the city in which Mandy's apartment was located was allotted hot water only on Wednesday afternoons and Saturday mornings. She went into her bedroom, sat down at her vanity, looked into the mirror, and began to remove the pins which had held her chignon in fastidious order and proper place. She shook her head frivolously—as might a frisky young filly kick up her heels and shake her tail on a spring day—and watched her golden tresses tumble out of the chignon and cascade, an aureate waterfall, over her shoulders. She ran her comb through those gilded strands, and the late afternoon littoral sun, streaming through the louvered windows of her balcony door, enriched the naturally metallic luster of her glossy locks.

She undressed, went into the bathroom, and—bracing herself with a tiny shriek—stepped into the shower and let the icy water run its cold course over every inch, every curve, and every crevice of her beautifully proportioned body. Grateful that she hadn't frozen to death, she jumped out as quickly as she had jumped in, checked her body for signs of frostbite, and toweled herself dry. Looking in the mirror, Amanda admired the toned firmness of her perky breasts. She was at that age—lucky young woman!—when they still held their firm shape and had not yet yielded to gravity and had yet to develop the sagging, pendulous contours of mature womanhood.

Shivering, she dusted herself with Christian Dior bath powder, stepped into a pair of white bikini panties by Lily of France, and slipped on an Olga-Plus-with-Lycra bra for the full-figured woman. Dressing casually for what promised to be a casual evening, Mandy put on her favorite Izod-Lacoste polo shirt, magenta in color with the trademarked alligator in a bold yellow. This color combination, certainly daring if not out-and-out audacious, would have raised eyebrows and certainly would have been considered garish in some conservative circles were it not an Izod-Lacoste product. She wore her favorite pair of Calvin Klein jeans, prewashed and prefaded with reinforced seams. Not expecting any visitors—in the year that she had lived in her apartment, she had never entertained any guests—Amanda West neglected to put on any shoes or socks. This oversight would very shortly beget unexpected consequences.

Allowing her hair to dry naturally, she combed it out and then went into her tiny kitchen to prepare herself a light meal. The entree was *iaurt* (yogurt).

How the Romanians can make yogurt so good must be a state secret, she thought to herself, *but if I could ever get the formula, I could become a millionaire overnight, for there's nothing any better anywhere in the world than Romanian iaurt.*

In addition to the *iaurt,* she also had several slabs of *cascaval Dalia,* her favorite cheese, and poured herself a glass of *Borsec. Boy, Americans just don't know what they're missing, not having mineral water that tastes so good,* she mused. Mandy had just wiped the last crumb of *cascaval* from her sensuous lips when the doorbell rang. Startled, her heart skipped a beat! So unusual an occurrence was this interruption of her normal routine, she first thought that someone had most certainly rung her bell in error, for no one had ever called on her. She went to the door and squinted through the peephole.

The tiny sight which greeted her eyes made her heart skip several more beats and her blood run several degrees warmer. Standing there, all three inches of him, his actual figure shrunken to Tom Thumb-sized proportions by the constrictive lenses of the Judas hole, was absolutely without doubt the handsomest, albeit tiniest, man she had ever seen. As she eyed him up and down, Amanda noted that he was dressed in the following manner: black Florsheim wingtips; neatly pressed McGregor slacks, gray in color, with BanRol waist and a color-coordinated belt; a crisply starched white oxford, button-down dress shirt by Ralph Lauren; a subdued Vanner's of England 100% pure silk tie, knotted in a tight half-Windsor, in muted stripes of blue and gray; and a two-button, navy-blue blazer by Bill Blass. Attired as he was—his clothing undeniable evidence of ready money, good breeding, and high fashion—the stranger could just as well have been modeling for an ad in Sunday's *The New York Times Magazine,* representing one of Manhattan's tonier menswear stores rather than standing there in the hallway of Amanda West's apartment in Constanta, Romania. But here he was!

Mandy had been taken aback by the thoroughly Western appearance of her visitor. Although obviously a fashion plate, he, or rather his sartorial appearance, would not have provoked any stares or fixed any glances in a more capitalistic setting or in a free-market economy. This same observation, however, could not be made about the handsome facial features of this dark stranger. His well-proportioned face would have stood out in any crowd, any place in the world, and drawn the onlooker's attention. Amanda, her pulse quickening, gazed at his face. Truly, this gentleman was the handsomest person she had ever seen.

He looks just like a movie star, she told herself.

His skin was tanned as brown as Mandy's own; it appeared almost golden. He had a very strong chin, sensuously shaped lips, and high prominent cheekbones. His nose was broad—in an American Indian manner. And his eyes, kind and understanding she judged them to be, were cappuccino brown, almost too effeminate for that manly face. His wavy black hair, graying now around the temples and over the ears, was modishly cut so that barely over half the ear was exposed.

Mandy, at a complete nonplus and not stopping to think that her caller could be none other than the "most handsome hunk" or "most handsome chunk" of Helena Corbiscu's description—and, obviously so, an American whose native tongue was English—asked him in Romanian, as though such a visit were an everyday occurrence, "Yes? What can I do for you?"

Although she was not, Mandy certainly should have been dumbfounded when this American at her doorstep replied, through the locked door, in flawless Romanian, "I am looking for the apartment of an Amanda West. She is an American, doing research at the university. Do you perhaps know where she resides? I am led to believe that she lives either in this apartment building or in this block somewhere. Have you ever seen an American woman in this neighborhood, and might you know where she lives?"

In response to this query, Mandy unlocked the door and opened it. One can easily imagine her initial shock seeing Michael Kukiliko live in the flesh for the first time. She had appraised him, and very carefully at that, through the reductive lenses of the Judas hole and—though full-figured—he had appeared thumb-sized. She opened the door and looked down, unconsciously expecting to find an extraordinarily handsome three-inch elf. Finding herself staring at her caller's Florsheim wingtips, Amanda quickly looked up, and up, and up, until she was gazing at the handsome face of the stranger, he who had quite swiftly been transfigured: the tiny Lilliputian now transmogrified into a mammoth Brobdingnagian. The quarter-foot leprechaun of the peephole had shot up and was now a six-and-a-half-foot giant.

That her caller could only be the "handsome hunk" Helena Corbiscu had mentioned earlier that day at the American Embassy did not yet register with Amanda. Perhaps had Lena said "huge handsome hunk," then Mandy might have recognized him immediately. She replied, still using Romanian and still not sure of his identity, "Why, I'm Amanda West. What can I do for you?"

Michael, breaking into English, said, "Hey, Mandy." Then he put forth his hand in the most gallant and genteel Romanian manner and took Mandy's in his. Kissing her hand, he said, "*Sarut mana.*" And, as an afterthought, he needlessly translated it for her, "I kiss your hand." But he did not drop it as was the custom. He continued gently shaking her hand in his huge grasp—firm and strong, warm and friendly, it was.

"Close your mouth, or the bugs'll fly in," Michael jokingly remarked. Mandy was stunned and stood there agape, her expression accurately reflecting her shock. "I'm Mike Kukiliko. I'm an American, and I just moved here yesterday and have already discovered that the natives aren't all that friendly. The folks at the embassy gave me your address and—"

Just then, Michael happened to look down, and he immediately interrupted his animated and ebullient discourse. "—and—Lord! I hope to shout! Mandy, let this be our secret. Share it with no one. I've got a foot fetish, and you've got about the most attractive set of toes I've ever laid eyes on."

Mandy, embarrassed and feeling half naked, curled her sensuous toes, bit her equally sensuous lip, and tried in vain to voice a complete sentence. "Gosh—well—gee—I'm—ah—um—you see—"

"Not only beautiful, but also highly intelligent. I like loquacious, well-informed women who can readily express themselves on a variety of topics and speak what's on their minds. I like the way you carry on a conversation. You've got a real way with words, Mandy West. Hey, you do speak English, don't you? Or should we go back to Romanian? What's your pleasure, Mandy? You are, as Jack Bailey used to say on his radio and TV show of the same name, *Queen for a Day*."

"Um. Well. You see, Mr. Kukiliko, I'm just a little startled. I mean I've been here a year and never had a single visitor, and then—all of a sudden from out of the blue—you show up. Hey, how's it that you've only been here a day or two, and you already speak such fluent Romanian?"

"It's a long story, and I'll tell you. But only if you invite me in. Not a word more shall cross these lips till I cross this threshold." Mandy had been so surprised by Michael's visit that she had forgotten her manners and had not yet invited him in.

"Oh. Excuse me. How rude of me. Oh, please do come in. I'm so excited you're here. Another American. Just think of it. I can't quite believe it. But how'd you learn to speak such excellent Romanian, and what in the world are you doing here, a million miles from no place?"

"I'll answer all your questions in due time, Miss Mandy." This was the first time he referred to her as "Miss Mandy," and she warmed immediately to the sound of it. "But first let us sit down and start this relationship off on the right foot. With a drink and a toast. Look what I brought along."

Michael had been carrying—in a mesh shopping bag typical of the Romanian marketplace—a large selection of packages wrapped in throwaway plastic sacks. Taking the packages out of the bag and looking for a place to set them down, Michael said, "Let's sit down at the table and check out these goodies I bought you. Beware, Amanda West! I'm sure your mother told you on countless occasions: beware of tall, dark strangers bearing gifts. I'll bet she also told you never to talk to strangers, too, didn't she? Is that why you're so reticent?"

"Are you always this animated, Mr. Kukiliko?"

"Only when talking with pretty girls. Upon first meeting people, I'm terribly inhibited, but—after breaking the ice—I usually warm to the occasion and loosen up. As the time passes, as you get to know and love me, you'll find that I'm not at all the stuffy type. Come on. Enough if this inane conversation. Let's get down to some serious business and some serious guzzlin' and look over this stuff I bought—and brought—for you."

Then Michael turned his attention to the packages he had set on the kitchen table and unwrapped one. Mandy was surprised to discover that his get-acquainted gift to her was a large bottle of cherry syrup. He continued, without a word, unwrapping the other packages until he had lined up on the table six bottles of syrup, each one containing a different flavor.

"Now, Miss Mandy, I know you've lived here for a year or so. Right? So in that time you must have discovered the nectar of the gods?"

"*Borsec?*"

"Precisely! What else? Makes that bottled water they're drinking in America—Perrier—taste like sulfur water. I didn't buy any *Borsec* because I was sure you stocked up on it. No Romanian home would be complete without it. Right?"

"Right. As you say."

"Okay. I've got the syrup. You've got the *Borsec*. I'll bet if you opened that cabinet, there'd be at least two glasses inside. That's all we need. I'm ready to party. How 'bout you?"

Mandy opened the cupboard, took out two glasses, and handed them to Michael who said, "Okay, Mandy. Here's a little touch of America right in the very middle of the Communist heartland. What's your pleasure, Lady? Lime rickey? Cherry phosphate? Sarsaparilla? You name it, Miss Mandy, and I'll mix it up for you—only two drinks per customer, though. Don't want nobody gettin' drunk here, and out o' hand, cuttin' up and givin' this place a bad reputation. Don't want some boozer causin' a ruckus just cause she can't handle her liquor. Don't want no one phonin' the local gendarmes and reportin' a noise violation, a breach of the city ordinance that'll cause the establishment to lose its liquor license and go outta business, do we? So what're you gonna have? What'll slake your thirst tonight?"

"Now why hadn't I ever thought of that?" Mandy questioned aloud, suddenly seeing that by mixing *Borsec* and the flavored syrups she could concoct any type of phosphate she desired.

"You hadn't thought of that, if you'll excuse my frankness, because you're a tad slow on the uptake, Missy. Just joshin' you, Miss Mandy. Now, you and me, representing the land of the free and the home of the brave—to clarify, I speak of the good ol' U.S. of A—have gotta become fast friends and stick together through thick and thin, agreed?"

"Well—yes, I guess," Amanda hesitantly acquiesced.

"Don't commit yourself so wholeheartedly to my proposal, Miss Mandy. Well, time will tell. Nonetheless, we've got to build a sound foundation for this friendship and set it off on the right foot—footing for a foundation as it were. So let us drink to what the Germans call '*Brüderschaft*,' and then we'll become friends for life."

"I'm sorry. I'm only familiar with the Romance languages. I don't speak a word of German. What's this *Brüderschaft* mean? And you never did answer my questions: 'How come you speak such excellent Romanian and why are you here?' "

"All in good time, Miss Mandy. All in good time. '*Brüderschaft*' is a word which describes the most wonderful of German ceremonies which, very shortly, we shall perform. Sit down, please, and let me mix you a drink. I myself am goin' for a raspberry phosphate. How 'bout you? What's your pleasure, Little Lady?"

"The same, bartender," Mandy laughingly replied, coming under the spell of her guest's infectious personality and easygoing manner.

Michael opened the bottle of rich raspberry syrup and poured until about an inch of the viscous red extract covered the bottom of the glass. Then he filled the glass to the rim with *Borsec.*

"Hey, Pretty Lady, have you got a swizzle stick I can use?"

"A swizzle stick? In Romania? You've *got* to be kidding."

"Okay, Mandy. We'll just have to make do and improvise then as best we can with what we've got at hand. This will undoubtedly detract from the flavor, but I'll stir our drinks with a spoon. Hand me one, please."

Mandy did so, and, swirling the syrup and *Borsec* together, he mixed her what would soon prove to be a phosphate that surpassed any she had ever enjoyed at the soda fountain of her neighborhood Rennebohm Rexall drugstore in Madison, Wisconsin, USA. She was about to take her first swallow when Michael unexpectedly stopped her just as lip was about to touch rim.

"Hey, Miss Mandy. Hold it. Wait just a darn minute. We're talking about our budding relationship and about *Brüderschaft.* You can't drink drop number one until we first drink to *Brüderschaft.* Now German, just like Romanian, has two forms of address: the formal and the familiar. Just like English once had. We've lost that distinction in English, but the Germans haven't. So when people first meet, they always address each other using the formal pro- nouns and formal verb endings. It's only after some time—some- times years, sometimes decades—that they'll use the informal forms of address. And when the time comes that people of the opposite sex and of a similar age decide that they should greet one another and exchange pleasantries in the familiar, rather than the formal, form of address—that is, as fast friends rather than as casual ac- quaintances—then they drink to *Brüderschaft,* to brotherhood."

"Okay. I'm game. I guess we two have got to stick together, representing the American presence as we do."

"I hope to shout, we do! Now, Mandy, copy everything I do, and we shall drink to *Brüderschaft.* First, we pick up our glasses." Which they did.

"Then, without spilling a drop of these expensive drinks, I put

105

my arm around yours and vice versa, and we interlock elbows so to speak." Which, with arms entwined, they did.

"Then we lightly touch our glasses together and say, '*prosit*,'—which is really untranslatable but probably means 'cheers' or 'to your health'—and look each other earnestly in the eyes." Which they did. Amanda had never felt so warm. She practically melted as she looked deeply into his soft, brown eyes.

"Then we each take a drink out of our own glass." Which they did.

"And then, finally, before we unlock our elbows and set our drinks down," and Amanda was totally unprepared for, and completely surprised by, what happened next, "we kiss one another." Which they did.

Michael's lips, made sweet by the syrup, gently pressed against hers, and Mandy, emotionally shaken, gasped, "I can't believe this! I've known you for all of ten minutes, and I've already kissed you! It's beyond belief!"

"Well, now you can call me 'Mike' instead of 'Mr. Kukiliko.' And I won't have to wait till I take you home from our first date and kiss you goodnight to wonder how it will feel to kiss you goodnight for the very first time. And now you know firsthand all about *Brüderschaft*. A nice way of getting to know one another, huh? I'll drink to that. *Prosit!*" Then he took several large drafts of his raspberry phosphate.

"Okay. Now I know about *Brüderschaft*. But I don't know a thing about the man who just kissed me. I just can't believe you—another American—are here. I don't mean you as you, Mr. Kukiliko. I mean—"

"You mean me as 'Mike,'" replied Mandy's new friend.

"Yes, Michael, I don't mean you as you. I mean you as another American here. Why? And how'd you learn to speak Romanian so well?"

"Well let's start at the very beginning. 'In the very beginning was the Word, and the Word was with God; and the Word was God. He was in the beginning with God. All things were made through Him, and without Him was made nothing that has been made.' Thus spake St. John about the very beginning. Whoops, wrong beginning.

"Don't mean to be irreverent or sacrilegious, Mandy, but I promised you I'd start at the very beginning. You might have noticed— that is, if you're the observant sort, possessed of an inquisitive mind— that my surname, combined with my Polynesian complexion, indicates that I'm from Hawaii. So, *Aloha.* The first twenty-one years of my life are really boring, so I won't go into that period except to say that I attended a private prep-cum-boarding school—the Kamehameha School. It used to be affiliated with the Congregational Church, but now it's completely nonsectarian; it's endowed by the Bishop estate. Perhaps you've heard of it?"

" 'It'? Do you mean the Bishop estate? The Congregational Church? Or the Kamehameha School?"

"The Kamehameha School."

"Can't say that I have," Amanda answered. "Do go on."

"Well, I picked up my high-school diploma and a good, sound academic background at Kamehameha. Despite four years of partying and revelry, I graduated with a civil-engineering degree from the University of Hawaii. My family decided that I should do post-graduate work, so they packed me off to the mainland. I always had an aptitude for things of a mechanical nature, and I love to tinker; yet, my real love has always been language and linguistics. So for the sake of my family I continued my studies and got a master's in civil engineering from MIT, the Massachusetts Institute of Technology in Cambridge. And for my own sake, while I was there in Cambridge anyway, I enrolled and took various language courses, including Romanian, at Harvard. Indeed, I earned enough credits to pick up a degree from Harvard while I was working on my major course of studies at MIT. So there you have it, Miss Mandy. A simple tale, yet true."

"Well, I commend you, Michael, on your excellent grasp of Romanian. They certainly taught you well. But you haven't explained how you ended up here."

"Listen up, Mandy. I've got a ready explanation. The Romanian government is engaged in a mammoth construction project; they're building a canal of massive proportions. It'll take 'em about eight years to complete the job. When it's finished, it's going to divert part of the Danube and cut out a lot of mileage that the barges will have to travel to get to and from the Black Sea. Plus, it'll irrigate thousands upon thousands of hectares.

"And, Mandy, think of the geopolitical significance of such an undertaking. Since the Danube forms part of the common border between Russia and Romania, all the Russkies had to do to make the Romanians toe the party line—at least prior to the building of this canal—was to threaten to bottle up traffic on the Danube. However, when the canal is finished, the Russkies can blockade the Danube till hell freezes over, but it doesn't matter. By then, the Romanians will have unimpeded access to the Black Sea via the new waterway. You've heard talk about the project, haven't you?"

"Sure. I've heard much about it. In fact, every time I go to Bucharest, the train has to slow down when we come to a construction site."

"Okay. Well, I'm here in an advisory capacity, helping the Romanian government build it."

"How long do you suppose you'll be here?"

"Oh, for at least a year, Miss Mandy. So that should give us a great opportunity to become good friends or a good opportunity to become great friends."

"Michael, I'm truly happy you're here," Mandy practically gushed. "I think we'll have a lot of fun together."

"I hope to shout, we'll have fun! Look, Miss Mandy, I've got an appointment with one of the project directors in charge of the Dobrugea section. [Dobrugea was the name of the district in which Constanta, the county seat, was located.] I've got to meet with him very shortly. It shouldn't last much more than an hour. What say I come back here after the meeting, pick you up, and we go out to dinner and a night on the town? You can introduce me to your favorite haunts and give me a moonlight tour."

"Michael, I'd just love that," Mandy said, without, for the first time in over a year, a thought about Ovid or his writings.

"Okay, Amanda West. But only on one condition. We've drunk to *Brüderschaft*. Right? So stop calling me 'Michael.' Call me 'Mike,' or 'Hey, you,' or 'Pineapple Head,' or 'Kanaka,' or any term of endearment which comes to mind except 'Michael,' 'Sir,' or 'Mr. Kukiliko.' "

"Yes, Sir! As ordered Mr. Kukiliko. Okay, Mike."

"That's better. See you in an hour or so."

Then Michael picked up his glass, raised it in a toast to his hostess, and said, doing a perfect imitation of Bogart in *Casablanca*, "Here's lookin' at you, kid."

He emptied his glass, and, without asking her permission, he rose from the table where they had been sitting and went around behind her chair. He put his huge sensuous hands gently on her shoulders, nuzzled her hair with his chin, and gave her a brotherly kiss, on the crown of her head, along with the admonition, "If you break this date and go out with another man, you and I are all washed up, Lady!"

He then said in Romanian, "No need to get up. I can find my way out. Finish your *Borsec* and syrup. See you in an hour or so."

And before she had time to tell him that she had enjoyed meeting him, or that his visit was the most wonderful thing that had happened to her since moving to Constanta, or that she looked forward to being with him that evening, Michael Kukiliko had left. In thirty minutes—the duration of his short visit—the regimented, scholarly life, with all its clockwork regularity, she had lived for the past year had, higgledy-piggledy, been completely turned upside down. For the first time in her adult life, Amanda West did not feel in command of the situation. She had only to look at him, and her heart started to beat a bit faster and her legs started to tremble ever so faintly.

She sighed, looking into space and thinking of *Brüderschaft*. It had been but a wisp of a kiss, yet it had deeply branded her heart and had left its smoldering mark! For, even though the kiss itself

41-RUBA

was not erotically intended, it stirred within Amanda West—for the very first time in her life—the most romantic yearnings.

Could I be that lonely? she questioned herself. *Why does his presence make me want him in a way I've never wanted anyone? Why does his nearness make me crave him in a way I've never craved any man? Why?*

She felt, when she thought of his lips touching hers, a warmth growing from her loins and radiating throughout her entire body. She seemed, as she recollected the events of the past half hour, to have lost her ability to think and to have found her ability to feel.

I'm being foolish, she said to herself. *I've only known him for ten minutes. Love at first sight—especially at my age—is something that only happens in fairy tales and poorly written love stories.*

But he's so charming, so uninhibited, so spontaneous, so handsome, so literate, and so much fun to be with. And so present—so here and so now in Constanta! And no Romanian authority to intervene and report our involvement to the embassy. He's an American. Neither of us could get arrested for fraternizing with foreigners since we're both foreigners!

I'd better hurry up and change clothes, or I won't be ready. Gosh, is he a neat guy, she thought, quite happily, to herself.

Slightly over an hour after his departure, Michael Kukiliko re-
appeared at Amanda West's apartment. A delightful surprise awaited
his return. He rang the doorbell, and the beautiful girl who greeted
him was garbed in a discreetly provocative V-necked dress in a
subdued leopard print by Norma Kamali. Mandy had purchased it
at Bloomingdale's while in New York just prior to coming to Romania. The plunging, scalloped neckline of the dress revealed a broad
expanse of tanned skin bisected by a robust and declivitous cleav-
age.

The garment was cinched at the waist with a wide suede cum-
merbund, solid tan in color. Matching the belt were her Christian
Dior—Tailorette Pinstripe-sheer-to-the-waist pantyhose in French
taupe. The hosiery she had discovered in Lord and Taylor's inti-
mate-apparel department. She knew, from the moment she spotted
them, that she just had to have them—her calves and thighs became all atingle the minute the pantyhose had first caught her notice! Her dainty feet were now shod in Corelli snakeskins.

She had, solely because of Michael's earlier remarks about his
fondness for her toes (she did not know at this time if he were
serious about his foot fetish or merely toying with her emotions),
chosen a provocatively open-toed, high-heeled pump, tan in color,
which had been marked down 20% at Saks Fifth Avenue.

Not visible to Michael's naked eye were the Delectables by
Maidenform which she had selected to wear that evening: an el-

111

egant seamless bra with a flexible underwire and matching bikini underpants of silky satin tricot with antique-lace scalloping, highlighted with just the slightest touch of shirring. She had mail-ordered her underthings from the lingerie section of her Spiegel Catalog.

Mandy had, prior to dressing, anointed her body with her favorite fragrance: *L'Interdit Parfum* by Givenchy of Paris. As was her custom, she wore very little makeup except for a wisp of mascara and a touch of eye-shadow, both by Estee Lauder. Mandy, feeling both nervous and frivolous, had decided to wear her hair in a pony tail and thus, insouciantly coiffured, did she greet her guest.

"Hi, Mike. That didn't take too long. How'd it go?"

"Swell. My, my, my, Miss Mandy. I must say you look as though you'd just stepped out of the pages of *Vogue*. What a classy outfit—very chic."

"Oh, thanks. It's really nothing. Where would you like to eat?"

"You're the boss. I only know enough about Constanta to find my way home. If I get off the main drag, I'm lost."

"Where actually are you living?"

"At the Victoria."

"The Victoria! You've got to be kidding. The Victoria on *Bulevardul Republicii?*"

"The one and the same! There can't be more than one Hotel Victoria in Constanta, can there?"

"Why, Mike, do you realize that the Victoria is only a block away?" Mandy astonishingly observed.

"Yes, convenient isn't it? It's almost as though someone's planned it that way. Weird, that we two Americans—strangers in a very strange land indeed—should wind up as neighbors living only a block apart from one another."

"I'll say. But the Victoria's a second-class hotel. Why didn't you stay at the Continental or the Palace? They're both first-class hostelries."

"True. But they're both expensive, catering exclusively to Western tourists. And if I were only here on a two-week vacation, I'd check in at either one without a moment's hesitation. But since I'm here for at least a full year, I wanna squeeze the most outta my money and lavish it on more important things—like you. Money's no object tonight. Where to, Miss Mandy?"

"Well, that depends. I don't even know how we're going to get there once we decide where we're going. I mean, I haven't got a car. Have you?"

"To be sure. I've rented a nice little Dacia from the *Automobil Clubul Roman* [Romanian Auto Club]."

"Oh, how nice. I haven't really felt the need for a car here like I did back in the States. I mean, practically everything I need is within a stone's throw. I just take a tram, a bus, or a taxi whenever I have to go any place or run an errand. Or else I go by foot; everything's so close at hand. How do you like it, so far?"

"So far, it's given me no problems. Of course, I've had it less than a week. The Dacia seems to be a solidly built little car. Even though it's assembled here in Romania—hey, here's a bit of trivia: Did you know, Mandy, when this land was part of the Roman Empire 2,000 years ago that it was known as Dacia and the inhabitants as Dacians?

"Anyway, even though it's assembled right here in Romania, the Dacia's design and equipment are either Renault's or Peugeot's, I forget which. So it should prove to be a pretty dependable little machine."

"Yes, I'm familiar with the history of Romania, Mike. I hope you don't have any trouble with your Dacia; it's a cute little car.

"Well, as long as you've got a car, I suppose we can splurge and drive out to either Mamaia or Eforie and dine at one of the fancy hotel restaurants. Or we could just go native and walk to one of the cafés close by. I've got a special favorite within easy walking distance. It's near the *Piata Unirii* [Union Square]—that's where I do all my shopping. It's by far the nicest *Piata* [square] in town. And after we eat, we can browse around the *Piata Unirii*, and you can see for yourself what's available. They've got an open-air flower, fruit, and vegetable market that's open till dusk. And it's very good and very capitalistic. I think you'd find it interesting."

"Sounds great to me. Let's go, Miss Mandy. The evening's young. Let's show the flag. Let them Romanians know that we Americans aren't stick-in-the-muds and wallflowers. Off we go for a wild night on the town."

Michael offered Amanda his strong and steady arm—which she readily accepted—and they walked along the millennia-old cobblestoned streets of Constanta. These ancient roadways were as old as recorded time itself. Older even. Legend had it that the Argo had dropped its anchor in Constanta's harbor and had paused here in its quest for the Golden Fleece. Jason; Castor and his brother, Pollux; the mighty Hercules; the nimble-fingered Orpheus—these legendary soldiers of fortune and the other Argonauts had walked these same streets where, tonight, Amanda's and Michael's footfalls fell.

Other adventurers, more real than mythical, had paraded through Constanta in search of conquest and glory as they marched into history: the phalanxes of Alexander the Great, the legions of the Caesars, the hoards of Attila, the knights of the Crusades, the janissaries of the Sultan, the hussars of the House of Hapsburg, and the infantrymen of both the Allies and the Axis.

The bloody boots of each successive generation's conquering army—the martial history of the civilized world passing by in internecine review—slogged through these same streets that Amanda West and Michael Kukiliko, two Americans alone and isolated among thousands of gypsies and Romanians, now peacefully and happily traversed.

They stopped to watch the dying sun work its wonders on Constanta's landmark—the Casino, a delicately crafted and painstakingly sculptured marble monument. A daintily layered and ornamentally frosted wedding cake of a building, the Casino, built originally to entertain the card-playing aristocrats of Victorian Europe's royal families, now seemed incongruous in this drab socialist country. It should have been located in the forested hunting preserve of some stupendously wealthy and desperately mad European prince, this Neuschwanstein on the Black Sea.

The happy couple watched the façades change from their native white to gold then orange then purple, the shades of nightfall, as the sun burned out and sank into the enveloping horizon. Mandy, silent and pensive, thought of stories she had read about the Taj Mahal and about how its native white marble also took on differing hues as the setting sun gave place to the rising moon. She recalled that the Taj Mahal was a lover's monument built by a great Maharaja and dedicated to the memory of his beloved wife.

They walked on and, turning these romantic thoughts over in her mind, Mandy unconsciously squeezed her escort's arm and felt quite happy. She sighed blissfully.

"I beg your pardon," Michael said, breaking the silence. "Did you say something?"

"Why, no!" Amanda West replied, blushing because she was frightened that her sigh might have provided Michael with an indication of how she felt about him.

They passed by the domed mosque, abandoned now by its Turkish builders but maintained by the city as a tourist attraction. Its attached minaret resembled a missile ready to rocket toward Heaven and Allah, carrying as its payload the prayers of the muezzin and the faithful. Crossing the huge square in front of the Museum of History, Mandy didn't even stop to point out to Michael the magnificent statue of Ovid and translate for him—in the unlikely event, gifted linguaphile (lover of languages) as he was, that he was unfamiliar with the dead language—the Latin inscription on its plaque.

En route to Mandy's favorite café, the couple passed by numerous shops, all awninged in gaily colored stripes, and kiosks, each of which specialized in a particular item. In America, a single grocery store would have stocked all of these various goods, but here, in Romania, each vender sold a product peculiar to his or her shop or kiosk. And always in the background, distant but yet near, the sounds and the smell of Constanta: the laving murmur of the Black Sea breaking in whitecaps over the embankments; the cawing bleat of the gulls and the screeching caterwauling of the cats; the incessant haggling of the gypsy rag pickers and bottle collectors, old women shrilly practicing their centuries-old trade and voicing the start of their evening rounds; and the sea scent, pervasive and pleasant.

They ate their meal—salad, soup, pork cutlet, French fries, black bread, *Borsec* (of course!), and a delicious Black Forest torte to conclude the meal, the dessert an ethnic reminder of over seven hundred years of German influence in this Latin land—which Michael, as well as Amanda, enjoyed very much. They talked of nothing and of everything: TV commercials they hated and movies they loved; novels not worth finishing and records worth replaying; most embarrassing experiences and most enjoyable vacation spots; hopes frustrated and dreams fulfilled. They talked about all the minutiae which, if never dwelt upon seems so inconsequential but which, if once shared, breaks the barriers of the unknown and transforms strangers into friends.

After dinner, they walked leisurely through the *Piata Unirii*, stopping here and there whenever Amanda wished to show Michael where she purchased a certain item. They drew looks and stares; but the scrutiny was not of the idle-gawking or the mean-spirited glowering type. Rather the looks were of a curious nature, not displaying any animosity whatsoever. It was only natural that Amanda and Michael should arouse such interest, for here was a couple, obviously from the West one could easily tell from their dress, mingling with the populace rather than staying inside their hotel and eating in its first-class dining room. Why were they window-shopping at stores frequented by the proletarians rather than shopping in dollar shops, those stores where commodities hard to come by in Communist lands could be had—but only in government-controlled stores and only if one could pay in Western currency?

No wonder Mandy and Michael were the subjects of such curiosity. What could two Westerners be doing hundreds of miles behind the Iron Curtain, shopping not at the tourist shops but at the markets and kiosks where the Romanians purchased their own meager foodstuffs and scant household supplies? Why should they

116

be eating at a restaurant popularized by Romanians rather than one exclusively reserved for the tourist trade? But all the eyeing and the interest went unnoticed, for the objects of all this attention were blind to it: they had eyes only for each other!

Arriving back at her doorstep, Mandy, fumbling for her key in her Aigner purse, wanted to invite Michael in but felt it would be too forward of her and might possibly invite a compromising situation that could very easily and quickly get out of hand. After all, she had known the tall, dark, and handsome stranger less than half a day. All the same, she felt something for him that she had never before felt for any man. *Can "love at first sight" be more than an empty cliché mouthed by love-struck adolescents?* she thought to herself. She did want to invite him in, but she didn't want to send him a false signal; she certainly didn't want to give him the impression that she was a loose woman.

Her ambivalent predicament was soon resolved by Michael who announced, as if he had taken it for granted that Amanda was about to invite him in, "Well, Miss Mandy, I've had a lovely time this evening. But the hour's late, and I've got a very early appointment in Tulcea first thing tomorrow morning. I'll have to be up and outta here by 5:00. This truly has been one of the most enjoyable times I've ever spent with anyone. And I really don't use that line with every girl I take out. I sincerely mean it."

"Oh, me too, Michael, I mean Mike—I—I—truthfully, until we went out tonight, I never realized how lonely I had been and how much the sound of another American voice meant to me!"

"Well, you'll be hearing much more of this particular American voice in the near future. How 'bout tomorrow night for instance? Dinner again? When I get back from Tulcea?"

"Oh, Mike," Mandy replied, sighing, "I'd just love to."

"Great. It'll give me something to look forward to. Make the day pass quickly. I've gotta run. It'll be time to get up and hit the road before you know it. Till tomorrow then? And sweet dreams."

And then—without a word of warning; without asking her permission—Michael Kukiliko bent his huge, swarthy frame down, took Amanda West into his strong arms, pulled her body tightly against his, and pressed his hard, yet gentle, lips against her sensuous and warm mouth. His hands, wrapped around her tiny waist, massaged the small of her back and gave Mandy a great sense of safety. She felt secure in this gentle giant's arms.

As his firm lips, acting in concert with his hands, massaged hers, Michael's tongue ever-so-gently moistened her lips but did not cool them. Indeed, it seemed to have just the opposite effect: his tongue, like some great bellows, kindled a passionate longing deep within her, stoking what had, heretofore, been a dormant fire in her erogenous zone. Fueled by his lips, her warm body began to react in ways she had never experienced or anticipated. She didn't want him to leave, didn't want him to release her from his embrace; yet, at the same time, she was terrified of the consequences if he didn't soon depart. She was not *that* kind of girl, but, for the very first time in her life, she could easily understand how *that* kind of girl could happily be *that* kind of girl.

As Michael embraced Mandy, her tumescent breasts pressed tightly against his massive chest. He continued kissing her as she unconsciously ran her fingers through his graying hair. It was fleece soft. She could have spent the remainder of the evening, if not the remainder of her life, blithely twining skeins of it.

After several minutes of this mild petting—which seemed to Amanda, inexperienced as she was with the conduct of her raging libido, like several hours of wildly passionate love making—she pulled herself, albeit reluctantly, from his encircling arms. Michael gently relaxed his hold of her the moment he realized she wished no more of it. Breathing unusually heavy, almost to the point of panting, she sighed, "Oh, Michael—I mean, Oh, Mike—I don't—I've never—I've—well, I'm just not the type that—oh, Mike, I had an absolutely wonderful time. I can't wait until tomorrow night. G'night."

Then, in Romanian, she thanked him, "*Multumesc* [Thank you], Mike."

And in response, Michael gallantly bowed and said, also in

Romanian, "*Cu placere* [You're welcome]. See you tomorrow night then, Miss Mandy. Had a great time."

And then he was gone, and Mandy was alone again and miserable, wishing she could have been *that* type of girl and could have taken advantage of the opportunity and could have invited him in. Her body ached now, as it never had before, for close contact with a man—certainly not any man; only one man could ever satisfy her passionate longings. She thought of his tongue gently moistening her mouth. She pictured his tongue flitting about her sweet lips as a hummingbird darting about a field of flowers sucking nectar from stamen. She wanted to draw Michael near; she wanted to hold him; she wanted him to lie near her, to make love to her, to father her children, and to be her provider and protector, her escort for life. Amanda West had, for the first time in her twenty-one-and-a-half years, fallen, head over heels, hopelessly in love.

641-RUBA

December 8, 1982
2801 Hoosier Rd.
Centreville, IN 45480

Professor Gordon K. Douglas
Department of English Language and Literature
Warren House
Harvard University
Cambridge, MA 02138

Dear Gordy,

Merry Christmas, Happy New Year, Season's Greetings, and all the rest of the Yuletide bullshit. This could very well be the merriest Christmas I've ever had, for June appears to love Fiona's novel. (See the attached letters from June to Fiona dated September 5 and from Fiona to June dated November 16 plus Chapters I, II, and III of *Tempestuous Summer*.) At least she loved the first chapter. The reception *Tempestuous Summer* has received from her is due, in large measure, to all the background info you've sent me about Constanta and your stay there. Thanks. Please keep it coming!

I've tried to incorporate into the second and third chapters all the suggestions she made—at any rate as I interpreted them. Of course, I might be on the wrong track. I'll just have to wait patiently until I hear from her. I hope she'll be able to discern that, thus far, Fiona has conscientiously followed her lead. All in all, I'm shocked that Featherstone has actually taken the time to read, and has commented so carefully upon, Fiona's writing. At heart, June can't be all that bad even though her writings certainly are.

I wonder what prompted her to start turning out such shitwork? Perhaps she had secret designs about someday becoming a serious writer and used her gift as a prolific purveyor of romance fiction to further that end. Wouldn't that be ironic if she found her books as tediously annoying as I do? What if she wrote them merely as a prelude to some worthwhile literary endeavor, much as a pianist practices scales to limber up his or her fingers prior to performing? She's intelligent enough, for her advice rendered to this point has been editorially sound. She must realize how bad the stuff she grinds out is. Well, who am I to judge her works or her motivation? Certainly, her writing another silly novel is no worse than me writing another worthless life-insurance contract.

What do you suppose that old biddy is really worth? She's loaded for sure. She's written over twenty titles, each of which has sold in the millions. In the millions! Can you imagine that?

Her novels are somewhat like perennial plants. Every year, with unfailing regularity, the same plot blooms again but in a slightly mutated form: a name change here; a change of venue there, et cetera. Her romances are about as transparent as SARAN Wrap. (Goddamn, that kitchen simile reads like something Fiona Pilgrim might have penned on a particularly bad day.) Featherstone seems to be able to produce a novel every other month, and they all become immediate best sellers. I write highly literate, well-researched, absorbingly interesting, and very entertaining novels—the composing of which occupies five years of my life, ruins my academic career, and busts up my marriage—and all I get to show for my efforts are piles (no, not hemorrhoids) of rejection letters. Shit, will my work ever see the light of day? Is there a light at the end of the tunnel? Is there a tunnel? Will I ever get published?

Gordy, it's enough to make a grown man cry. Well, one lives in hope, and I can only hope June continues to love *Tempestuous Summer*. As you'll discover when you read her letter, she thinks, with some reservations, that it's gotten off to an excellent start. It's certainly as bad as anything June's ever written, so maybe this portends that it'll be a smashing success. It makes sense in a perverse sort of bass-ackward way: it's pretty bad prose which means, considering the genre, it's pretty good writing.

Wouldn't it be something if, one day, Fiona Pilgrim's prose were as prominently displayed in the drugstores and the supermarkets as June Featherstone's? That'd be great. Just so long as I could keep my identity under wraps, and none of my friends, save for the obvious exception of you, knew that the prim and proper Fiona Pilgrim was, in fact, the lewd and lascivious Joe Leonard.

Oh God, to be rich and famous! Let me be more precise: I want to be rich and anonymous as Joe Leonard; I want to be rich and famous as Fiona Pilgrim. What could I produce if I had the time to write and to think, uninterrupted by the needs of the children and undisturbed by the demands of the job?

Yes, always the demands of the job looming over me like some sort of Biblical plague. Who would have ever thought my life would have come to such a sorry state? Divorced and, of all things, reduced to selling insurance and working twenty-five hours a day trying to make my monthly quota and quarterly goals. It seems the upper-ups in the home office have nothing better to do all day but sit around, twiddling their thumbs and thinking up new ways to motivate the sales force to sell a product few people need and far fewer want—except the stockholders of the company who get richer and richer every time some poor sucker signs on the dotted line. Their solution?

Let's have another contest: sell so much life insurance and win a trip to Acapulco; sell so many dollars in fire premiums and receive a color TV; sell so much volume in commercial insurance or workers'-compensation insurance and earn a set of luggage; beat your quarterly quota by twenty-five percent and be the recipient of a superduper Cuisinart. My next book ought to be about my experiences as an insurance agent. I could entitle it *The Contest* and tack on the subtitle, *How to Win a Seat at the Million-Dollar Roundtable*.

Who could have guessed, fresh out of grad school with a tenure-track position and a promising academic career ahead of me, that my life would have turned out as it has? Of course, I could see when I started to write that I couldn't serve—or in this context "service"—two mistresses at one time, but I never expected that the Muses would seduce me like they did. But they did, and Betty left me. I don't blame her a bit though, for I was fully at fault. A bigamist of sorts, I was married to her and to my art, and I loved my art much much too much.

But why bitch? I made my bed, and now I've got to lie in it. What galls me, though, is the idea—indeed, the fact—that I've ended up selling insurance. (Life insurance is going to be the death of me yet.) A man of my talent and training! How can I rationalize this so it doesn't appear to be a rationalization? In his essay *Of Great Place*, Francis Bacon said, "It is only through indignity that man rises to dignity." I presently suffer much of the former, so maybe I'm due for some of the latter. Only time will tell.

I suppose I could justify my failure by reminding myself that, unless to the manor born, every writer had to do something demeaning to sustain himself until he was discovered. Of course, one could work forever in a custom house, like Melville, or spend a lifetime in the post office, like Trollope, and never be discovered—at least never be commercially successful till late in life. Even worse, some artists never found either a market for their work or jobs that would provide even minimal sustenance. So they were buried in potter's field, like Poe, or dumped into unmarked graves, like Mozart. Enough of this morbid musing.

I've got to look on the bright side of things. Franz Kafka and Wallace Stevens were both employed all their lives by insurance companies, yet Kafka and Stevens somehow managed to produce highly commendable works. If they could do it, then so can I. (Can't I?) Wouldn't it be great if I bought my own independent insurance agency? I could incorporate as "The Kafka-Stevens Agency, Inc." Then I could use this great slogan on the letterhead of my company's stationery: "The Kafka-Stevens Agency, Inc. Let Us Write Your Life." Of course, my insureds would think I was referring to writing them their life insurance. Only I would know the truth, but that would be some small recompense. So I'll sell insurance until I get a book published or start drawing social security—whichever comes first. If June continues to be enthusiastic about *Tempestuous Summer*, publication might very well come first.

What do you think of her letter? And how about that postscript

"... it could almost have been written by a man ...."? She's sure as hell pretty perceptive. It's been written by one hell of a man because it takes a lot of balls to try to pull off a hoax like this one. I've got to establish Mandy's femininity, the old bat says. Let my "... womanly instincts flow out ... on paper ...." What, exactly, is she suggesting? Short of having Mandy run out of Kotex or Tampax at the worst possible moment, I don't know how to make her any more feminine—except to follow, to the letter, June's suggestions.

By so doing, I've managed to get the prim and proper Amanda West to Constanta and into the swarthy arms of Michael Kukiliko. Boy has now met girl, and girl has now fallen in love with boy. Were it not for her virginal innocence, they'd be in the sack before the end of Chapter IV. But she's not, as the reader knows full well, *that* type of girl.

Despite what seems to be a strict Victorian veneer, I'll bet that, beneath that goody-goody exterior, Mandy's a real tigress in bed. Those prim-and-proper types usually are. Appearing barren of emotion and models of rectitude, they erupt with a lava flow of emotion once you hit their hot button. That's the way it was in high school. All the prick teasers looked as if they'd take you to bed and fulfill your wildest fantasies no matter how kinky your night thoughts might be. Yet once you took them out on a date, if you tried to give them a goodnight kiss or a fraternal peck on the cheek, they'd slap your face; if you tried to cop an outside feelie, they'd cut off your hand.

Then the prissy ones who looked like they might become nuns— the ones you were sure would turn you over to the principal and accuse you of molesting them if you held their hand; the ones you were positive would cry rape if you tried to dance close with them during a slow dance at a sock-hop—those girls would suddenly disappear for a nine-month interval during their junior or senior year. They'd drop out of school, enroll—not for the academic year but the gestational year—in the Florence Crittenton Home for Unwed Mothers, have their babies, and come back to school a year behind

125

their classmates, looking as if they were still planning to take the vows and veil and enter the convent. I wonder what Mandy's really like?

Hey! Wouldn't it be hilarious if the chaste Miss West gave the worldly Mr. Kukiliko a bad case of crabs or a good dose of the clap? Or better yet, she could infect him with VD, and, like Pangloss' in *Candide*, Michael's nose could fall off. But then my readers couldn't "relate" to him, for he'd no longer be in possession of his nose, a situation which would obviously distort the natural symmetry of the face of this "handsome hunk." Who could fall in love with a swarthy hero with no nose or a Panglossian tin-plated substitute?

All things considered, Featherstone is probably right; I need to put some warm blood in Amanda's veins. And I can do it, for I'm creating this world and peopling it as I see fit. I'm omnipotent. I've never had such power. Now I know how God felt.

So I've formed my Adam and Eve in the image and likeness of June's heroes and heroines. I'll shortly hear how she liked my latest effort. I can't wait to see if she picked up on Fiona's forced and clumsy allusion in the swan anecdote to Browning's poem, "How They Brought the Good News From Ghent to Aix." She'll probably not even notice Fiona's juxtaposed wordplay with fowl play (sic) and swan song. Well, she loved Chapter I and wanted me to send her more. She must be a real glutton for punishment. I think Chapters II and III pretty well follow suit, so I hope they'll also meet with her approval.

What do you suppose June Featherstone's really like, Gordy? The stern picture that graces the dust jacket of her novels reveals a very matronly sort of woman, sixtyish I would guesstimate, staid and schoolmarmish, with gray hair pulled severely back in a tight bun. Her lips fixed in a defiant grimace, she stares contemptuously at her adoring public. Perhaps her writing has turned her into such a sourpuss. Perhaps she was having a particularly bad day the day the photo was shot. Or perhaps she's painfully camera-shy, hates to have her picture taken, and is, out of its range, a sweet grandmotherly type. I don't know.

I do know, however, what writing's done to me. It's turned me into an insurance salesman. Could Fate have dealt me a harsher hand? Come to think of it, I believe she certainly could have. I could have been an insurance salesman, or a banker, or a realtor, or a doctor, or a lawyer, or a butcher, or a baker, or a candlestick-maker who was complacently satisfied to be nothing but an insurance salesman, or a banker, or a realtor, or a doctor, or a lawyer, or a butcher, or a baker, or a candlestick-maker.

That sort of acquiescent acceptance of my lot in life would have been much much worse than my present situation, for then I would have been intellectually dead. I would have been condemned, as penance for my worldly success, to pass the remainder of my purgatorial existence mindlessly attending Kiwanis Club luncheons, Shriners' parades, Chamber of Commerce meetings, Junior League Christmas bazaars, country-club foursomes, and assorted fish fries and pancake suppers sponsored by the various fraternal clubs and civic organizations I had to join in my wretched life in order to make contacts (networking, the very lifeblood of a healthy and prosperous insurance agency) so that I would have been a very good and very successful insurance salesman or banker, or realtor, or doctor, or lawyer, or knaves all three.

Sure as shit, things could have been worse: I might not have realized how miserable I was. Well, I've sold my artistic birthright—not for bread and pottage as did Esau but, rather, for policies and premiums—and now I've got to bust ass and sell some insurance to another unsuspecting victim.

Actually, I might not have to push this insurance very much longer, for I've got June on my side, and her support may be the answer to all my prayers, a genuine godsend! She thinks I've got great promise as a fledgling writer, and she's taken me under her wing. Now that's an auspicious stroke of luck that augurs well for my future.

This is my big opportunity to finally break into print. If I just follow her suggestions, maybe I'll have a novel published before the passage of another year. All I've got to do is sit tight, wait for her letters, and then follow verbatim her directions. It's almost as if she were ghost writing *Tempestuous Summer*. She really has been such a big help—offered me so much good advice.

Despite the fact that I so dislike her books, June Featherstone must be a rather dear old soul. Think of the time it must have taken her to read my ms. and then to offer such detailed criticism. I wonder what she'll have to say about Chapters II and III? They're so horribly written—so unconscionably bad; so blatantly melodramatic—that she'll quite likely think they're great. She'll probably nominate me for a Pulitzer or a Nobel. What will her response be? What pearls of wisdom will she drop before this swine?

I'll let you know. Once again, thanks for all the Romanian info. And, once again, Merry Xmas.

Yours,

Joe Leonard

P.S. Should you ever get disillusioned with academe, don't give it up for a career hustling insurance.

encl.: Letter from June Featherstone to Fiona Pilgrim dated September 5; letter from Fiona Pilgrim to June Featherstone dated November 16; Chapters I, II, and III of *Tempestuous Summer— The Hottest Season*

16th December 1982
Harlequin House
Silhouette Lane
Fensucked-on-Strand
Ely, Cambridgeshire
England

Mrs. Fiona Pilgrim
2801 Hoosier Rd.
Centreville, IN 45480
U.S.A.

Dearest Fiona,

I am in receipt of your letter of 12 November and the chapters (Two and Three) which accompanied it. My dear, you have a gift! I do have some very minor reservations about *Tempestuous Summer*, but, all in all, I'm mad about it. I just love it. Bully for you, Fiona! Of course there are those rough spots which we shall have to polish smooth and burnish through our joint efforts, but, after two or three revisions, you shall have a final draft that I myself would be proud to call my own.

Before commenting on your latest instalments of *Tempestuous Summer*, I should relate to you the good news concerning Nanny since you so thoughtfully expressed an interest in her condition. She is presently back at work and functioning effectively. Just how long this blessed remission will last, however, the doctor will not say. But since he has doubled the dosage of her medicine, she has not once tried to take any of the topiaries for a walk or attempted to claim that she had been bitten by a vicious branch or had been mauled by an intractable twig. Now that Nanny is somewhat sedated and not running madly about causing such an uproar in her wake, Harlequin House has, once again, thankfully become a tranquil retreat whereat I have much peaceful, leisurely time to think, to write, and to read.

And, rereading your letter, I would be remiss if I did not congratulate you on your election to the presidency of the PTA. Your devotion to the children and Mr. Pilgrim is admirable. Wonderful that Peter Paul (Dare I refer to him as P.P.?) is so supportive of you in your endeavour to become a writer. How invaluable it must be to have a spouse who reassures you in those moments of self-doubt and uncertainty that, at one time or another, plague every writer. Nanny has been, for me, the person who has picked up my spirits when I've been down and encouraged me to go on and complete the sentence, the paragraph, the page, the chapter, the book, or whatever it is I'm working on the moment writer's block obstructs my progress or misgivings about my purpose stay my pen.

Now about Mrs. Kukiliko's passing. The swan story, while interesting, reads like a canard, and *we must be sincere with our readers*. It's simply too bizarre for fiction even though it actually happened in Indiana. No, Fiona, return to your original design and do away with her in some Alpine chalet.

I should think it would be abominably humiliating for one to be flogged to death by
a swan—a déclassé demise, to be sure. I
myself should be utterly embarrassed to expire in such a manifestly ridiculous manner.
Were you to opt for her to exit life in this
manner, the reader would say to herself,
"What kind of man is this Michael Kukiliko
anyway? What sort of hero would marry a
woman whose death was caused by a bird?" No,
no, Fiona. This bird business is a bad idea.
Abandon it.

Besides, a swan attacking someone brings
immediately to the reader's mind the violent
and perverted union between Leda and Zeus.
And the women who read our novels do not
need to be reminded about the opposite side
of the gentle romantic love we depict in our
works. Rape has *no* place in the type of
novels we pen.

Well, well, my dear, I should almost label Chapters Two and Three as being unquali-
fied successes. Brilliant! Enthralling! You've
done it. Capital effort on your part, save
for one major criticism. I have little to
comment on except to commend you for a job
well done. My prime concern in Chapters Two
and Three is that—perhaps through no fault
of your own; I can see now that you have too
literally followed my suggestions—you have
been carried away by, and taken to extreme
lengths, my comments concerning your first
chapter's dearth of sartorial description.

Fiona, allow me to put it bluntly: you
have exceedingly overcompensated for this

failure in the second and third chapters. I meant that you should give us a little more description about the clothes Amanda is wearing, but good heavens! The reader doesn't care to know where Amanda purchased her outfit or whether she paid wholesale or retail for it. We don't need to know what size dress she wears in order for us to picture her. And we certainly don't need to know the manufacturer of her brassiere or the brand of knickers she was wearing that day.

Truly, Fiona, you've gone to extreme lengths in describing her wardrobe. However, the responsibility for this excessive description is partially mine because of the ambiguous comments I made after reading the first chapter. Let me rectify my error with the following ultimatum: never mention either Amanda's measurements or the type of undergarments she is wearing, for such information only serves to distract the readers and prevent them from readily identifying with your heroine.

If I might be a little risqué and a bit unrefined (just between us two girls), in Chapter Three—when you were telling the reader about Amanda's Maidenform bra and matching knickers—I was suddenly horrified. I thought for sure you were next going to inform the general public what brand of sanitary towel she used. Excuse me if I have offended you, but the point must be unequivocally made: enough can be too much!

And, while we're discussing things of a personal nature, this discussion brings to mind another related criticism: isn't it a bit suggestive, in the shower scene at the beginning of Chapter Two (p.16), to have the water ". . . run its cold course over every inch, every curve and crevice of her beautifully proportioned body"? To what else but the intergluteal fold, that crease which bifurcates the buttocks into two hemispheres, and the other orifices in that general area could you be referring? This is simply too graphic an image for the delicate eyes of our readers. You will have to do away with it when you write the next draft. You are not writing a dirty book, Fiona.

And then, in the very same scene—I do not like this section at all!—you describe Amanda jumping out of the shower and admiring ". . . the toned firmness of her perky breasts" (p.16). Fiona, my dear misguided Fiona, just what, exactly, is this "perky" breast business all about? I have read innumerable romance novels over the years, and I have yet to encounter the adjective "perky" as a modifier of the noun "breast". Where in the world did you come up with such a bizarre juxtaposition? "Perky breast", indeed—an ill-chosen choice of words as I have ever come across!

One further point about this horrid shower scene. You conclude the scene as follows: ". . . they still held their firm shape and had not yet yielded to gravity and had yet to develop the sagging, pendulous contours of mature womanhood" (p. 16). Fiona! Tut, tut, Fiona! Through our prose, we want to enable our readers to *escape* reality not be reminded of it. Why write something which can only remind the reader of the effect of time and gravity on her bustline? This shower scene will have to be deleted from the next draft. That's all there is to it.

That concludes everything I've got to say about *Tempestuous Summer*. I've nothing else to relate to you except to encourage you to keep at it. You're on the right track. You've baited the hook with just the proper amount of information about Amanda and Michael and their budding relationship. You've caught the reader's attention; now merely continue in like manner and reel her into your story.

The difficult part of the novel is done with. You've given the reader a good idea about Michael and Amanda's backgrounds, and you've got your hero and heroine together in a romantic setting. The rest of the story is, actually, beyond your control. It's now up to Michael and Amanda. Remember Fiona, *show* don't tell. Let your characters' actions and speeches and thoughts reveal to us their inner passions, how they feel about each other. In short, let Mike and Mandy show us, rather than you—as the intrusive author—tell us. Keep up the good work and write, write, write!

Fondly,

June

June Featherstone

P.S. Nanny has again asked me to ask you about a picture of you, Mr. Pilgrim, and, especially, the children. She has read everything you've thus far sent me—with the obvious exception of the Buffy comments which I excised from your letter the moment I read them—and has been quite approving in her remarks relating to *Tempestuous Summer*. In fact, she just loves your novel, and I interpret this as an extremely good omen. The old dear is a genius when it comes to forecasting what will and what will not sell.

Judging from her enthusiastic response to Chapters One, Two, and Three, I'd venture to say, Fiona, that if you can continue to write with such competence—and I personally have no doubts about your capabilities—you'll have a bestseller on your hands. As I mentioned in the last sentence of the preceding paragraph, my Nanny has never yet failed to be an accurate barometer of the marketplace.

Incidentally, when you were discussing the method by which you proposed to make Michael a widower, did you consciously allude to Robert Browning's wonderful poem, "How They Brought the Good News From Ghent to Aix"? Or was the allusion merely a fortuitous and felicitous grouping of words? If consciously intended, I congratulate you on a brilliant display of wordsmanship! If it were merely an accident, let me encourage you to read Browning's poem about Ghent and the death of poor Roland, gallant steed. (My favourite Browning poems remain the much

anthologised "Meeting at Night" and "Part-
ing at Morning". They are both so romantic!)
Do send along the next chapter or chapters
as soon as you've got them written. Nanny
and I are so anxious to see how Michael and
Amanda are getting along. Yours, J.F.

P.P.S. An afterthought: Something amorphous
troubled me about Chapter Two, but I just
couldn't quite put my finger on it; then, at
dinner last night, Nanny mentioned in passing a tiny reservation she had had about
Chapter Two, and it became as clear as a
bell, if you will pardon the cliché. I refer
to that section of the novel where Amanda
has been squinting through the peephole,
sizing up—quite inaccurately as it turns
out—her visitor (Chapter Two, p.19): "The
quarter-foot leprechaun of the peephole . . . ."

Well, my dear, that description just
doesn't work—for Nanny or for me. Mention
the word "leprechaun" to us and up jumps a
little man dressed in green top hat and
tails with a shamrock in his lapel. He has
carrot-red hair, a face flecked with freck-
les, a grin that stretches from pointed ear
to pointed ear, and he's wearing court-jester
shoes with a bell on their scimitar tips.
He's always saying something like "Sure and
begorra", or "Erin go braugh", and there is
a distinct odor of Guinness emanating from
him. He's Irish from head to foot. No, "leprechaun" simply will not work in this context.

You need something small and brownish. Perhaps a dwarfed Buddha might work. Michael is abundantly swarthy, and Amanda must not look through the peephole and espy a ruddy face awash in a sea of green. Rather, she must discover, I should strongly suggest, a tiny Hawaiian figure—a miniature Tiki god of sorts. You might think this a mere quibble, but—since it struck both of us as being incongruous—I would take heed.

While I am dealing with this particular paragraph, let me put several questions to you, my dear: Was your employment of the majuscular "S"—in the clause, ". . . he who had quite Swiftly been transfigured"—deliberately crafted and deliciously clever etymological wordplay? Or was it, rather, simply a case of accidentally depressing the shift key, a typographical error resulting in a jolly good Swiftian *bon mot* (a witticism)? If it be intentional rather than inadvertant, I congratulate you. Bully for you, Fiona!

P.P.P.S. One last thought (I promise!), another nit-picking observation to be sure, about Chapter Two: You wrote, "As she eyed him up and down, Amanda noted that he was dressed in the following manner: black Florsheim wingtips, et cetera". Well, Fiona, it seems to me that if Mandy is eyeing her visitor ". . . up and down", she might want to start at the "up" rather than direct her glance at the "down": i.e., at her caller's Florsheim wingtips. Just something to think about for revision. J.F.

January 4, 1983
2801 Hoosier Rd.
Centreville, IN 45480

Professor Gordon K. Douglas
Department of English Language and Literature
Warren House
Harvard University
Cambridge, MA 02138

Hey Gordo,

You sobered up yet from welcoming in the New Year? Here's some good news that's got my year off to a promising start. (See June's letter dated December 16.) June continues to be in love with *Tempestuous Summer* and continues to offer good advice. So far the only problem I envision with this correspondence is that the mailman might have a loose tongue, and, before long, everyone on his route is going to know that Joseph E. Leonard is shacking up with some broad named Fiona Pilgrim. Shocking! With me receiving all these letters from England addressed to a Mrs. Fiona Pilgrim, I'm sure he's convinced I'm keeping a mistress.

Ms. Featherstone's really taken an interest in Fiona, hasn't she? Her postscripts are something else. Fiona's leprechaun is too green for her; she wants something shaded in a more appropriate hue. I'd like to see the color of June's face if a leprechaun ever dropped his drawers and flashed his green pizzle at her. I bet she wouldn't be able to recollect if the pizzle in question were green, brown, ruddy, Irish, or Hawaiian.

The ending of her first postscript is enough to induce a fit of writers' block. She tells me that she and Nanny Crimpet are anxious to see how Michael and Amanda are getting along. Just think how anxious I, their creator, am. I don't have the vaguest notion what they're up to. Who knows what's going to happen next in this ridiculous story? I, for one, sure as shit have no idea, not even an inkling. If you have any suggestions, Gordy, pass 'em on. Do you realize just how ridiculous that last sentence is? I, the author of *Tempestuous Summer*, am asking you, the reader of *Tempestuous Summer*, what's going to happen next in *my* novel. I hope Amanda and Michael know what's going to transpire, for someone's got to tell their story.

I wonder if writing *Tempestuous Summer*—in conjunction with writing all these letters to June—hasn't addled my mind a bit. I think I'm slipping; I must be losing my grip, for I'm actually looking forward to putting pen to paper each morning and discovering what Amanda and Michael are up to, what they're going to do that day. It's almost like automatic writing: once I began to tell their story, they took over, stole the pen from my hand, and told it their way, regardless of my wishes or design. I no longer exercise any control over them.

Isn't that weird? They're doing the same thing Adam and Eve did to their Creator, damn them. I've created this world and peopled it with folk made according to my (well, really, June's) specifications, and—just like Lucifer and all the other fallen angels and Adam and Eve—my creations have turned against me, have exercised their free will, and are doing whatever the whim of the moment dictates. Yet once again, I know how God felt.

I'll tell you one thing I've learned from writing this book: there's a hell of a lot more involved in composing a romance novel than first meets the eye. I thought I'd breeze right through it from start to finish without so much as pausing to take a breath. As it's turned out, nothing could have been further from the truth. I'd probably be stalled on page one of Chapter I if June hadn't been there, offering suggestions and giving me encouragement. This experience has been a real eye opener.

Well, what are Michael and Amanda going to do next? I'll never find out unless I stop musing and start authoring. I'll send you the results when I've got some.

Yours,

Joe Leonard

P.S. This Featherstone is no dummy. Her reference to classical mythology took me completely by surprise. I hadn't even thought of it. Did you ever read a short poem by Yeats entitled, "Leda and the Swan"? It's an interesting piece.

P.P.S. Should you ever get disillusioned with academe, don't give it up for a career hustling insurance.

encl.: Letter from June Featherstone to Fiona Pilgrim dated December 16

January 20, 1983
2801 Hoosier Rd.
Centreville, IN 45480
U.S.A.

Ms. June Featherstone
Harlequin House
Silhouette Lane
Fensucked-on-Strand
Ely, Cambridgeshire
England

Dear June,

Thanks so much for your last letter (dated December 16) and the as-ever-and-as-always good advice contained therein; I have, as you will soon discover when you read Chapter IV, followed your suggestions to the letter. (Incidentally, I'm delighted Nanny Crimpet is getting along so well with her increased medication. Surely that is a heavy load you no longer have to carry on your shoulders. Give the old dear my warmest regards, please.) For example, I've gone over Chapter IV with a fine-toothed comb and gotten rid of every objectionable reference to Amanda's wardrobe; by this, I mean I've struck every mention of where she had purchased her clothes and how much she had paid for them. I had a wonderful sentence about how she had purchased her U. S. Army fatigues shirt marked down twenty percent at the Army-Navy surplus store, but, out of deference to your advice, I deleted it.

Also, as you so strongly suggested, I've avoided mentioning her unmentionables. I'm amazed at how much your good editorial eye has improved the look of *Tempestuous Summer.*

Following your lead, I am attempting—with some degree of success, I certainly do hope—to allow the characters to *show* how they feel toward, and respond to, various people and circumstances rather than *tell* the reader from the perspective of the omniscient author. I really do hope I have succeeded here. I think I have achieved my objective, for I had nothing in mind when Mandy awoke the morning after her first date with Michael. I mean I had nothing to "tell" the reader. Yet before I knew it, she and Dr. Sibescu had accidentally met. You'll have to read Chapter IV (attached) to find out about this mysterious Sibescu character. I have no idea what he's doing in the novel, but he seems to be up to no good! All the dialogue that ensued *showed* certain things about their characters and the type of people they are. Don't you think so?

Actually, June, their meeting one another in *Piata Ovidiu* was as big a shock to me as it was to Amanda. I had no idea this was going to happen. Yet it did happen, and the results of this meeting and the subsequent conversation will *show* something about Amanda and Michael and their budding relationship. I don't know yet what it is that makes Dr. Sibescu so hateful towards Michael, but when I put pen to paper again and let Amanda and Michael and Sibescu have a free reign to work towards the final resolution of the mystery, then it will all become quite clear. At least I hope so, or all my effort will be for naught.

Well, this has, indeed, been a short missive, but I've much to do today. Papa Pilgrim—Peter Paul's father—is making his annual pilgrimage to "get to know" his grandchildren. He arrives tonight for a short stay, and I must get the house in spic-and-span order. He's a fastidious housekeeper and a real stickler for cleanliness. The last time he paid us a visit, I actually caught him running his forefinger over the mantel—and along the mullions in the kitchen window—measuring the depth of the dust which had accumulated and layered there since his previous visit. Can you imagine that?

He also harbors fears that I'm starving P.P. and his grandchildren, so, whenever he comes, I have to put on a real "spread." We "pig out" (That's a popular expression here in America, a term which means to eat an enormous quantity of food.) in order to prove to him that neither am I suffering from anorexia nor am I endangering the health of those near and dear to him.

Alas, I'm up to my elbows in potato peels; I'm preparing mashed potatoes to accompany a rump roast and lima beans. After Papa Pilgrim has departed, we all suffer from indigestion for at least a week until our digestive systems have had time to recuperate from my culinary efforts.

With that said, I'll bring the potato water to a boil and this letter to a close. I am nearly a month tardy in saying this, but I do hope you and Nanny had a joyful and happy Christmas. I wish both of you a prosperous and healthy 1983. Happy New Year!

Love,

Fiona

Fiona Pilgrim

P.S. P.P., Paul and Peter, and Priscilla send love and kisses: xxxx and oooo's.

encl.: Chapter IV of *Tempestuous Summer—The Hottest Season*

145

After a very restless sleep, a tired Amanda West awakened and regretted that Michael Kukiliko had not stayed the night. She had, the entire night long, dreamt of nothing but him. Her night thoughts were sensuously filled with the feel of his huge hands wrapped securely around her tiny waist; the texture of his soft, wavy hair as she curried it with nervous fingers; and the delicate touch of his lips and tongue as they ever-so-gently, but nonetheless diligently, traced and probed the contours and depths of her own mouth.

She brewed herself a pot of chamomile tea—a Romanian cure-all guaranteed to calm a queasy stomach and ease a case of jittery nerves—drew open the drapes, unlocked and pushed ajar the French doors which opened onto the balcony, and found herself a comfortable chair which afforded her an excellent panorama of the coast. Sitting there and sunning herself in the warm morning air, she watched the easy wash of the Black Sea as it timelessly lapped against the embankment surrounding the Casino. And all the while, she turned over in her mind thought after thought about Michael.

Why didn't he invite me to accompany him to Tulcea? It's not a long trip, and he probably knows that my schedule is flexible. I'm certain that he enjoyed my company as much as I enjoyed his. So why didn't he ask me to share the ride and break the monotony of the trip?

How could it be that such a handsome and cultivated man

wasn't married? Or hadn't been married? He wore no wedding ring, and he hadn't mentioned, in his short discourse on his past, any type of romantic involvements in his life. Of course, he couldn't very well discuss such matters with me, a virtual stranger, anyhow.

But what does it matter, anyway? she continued to muse. *I don't care about what he has been—or even what he will be. All I care about is what he presently is. If I've learned nothing else from studying Ovid and his contemporaries, I've learned that the Latin maxims which served the Romans so well—*Carpe diem! Carpe rosam! *(Seize the day before it is spent; gather the flowers before they wilt)—are just as relevant in my life as they were in theirs. So I'm not going to dwell on his past or day-dream about his future. I'm going to seize the opportunity that presents itself today and grab hold of Michael and enjoy our time together. Right here! Right now!*

And Mandy resolved, then and there, to do just that.

Having drained her pot of chamomile tea, she was relaxed now, the calming effect of the tea having worked its soothing influence. But her troubling questions remained unanswered. Amanda decided that a change of scenery might distract her from that which so preoccupied her at the present moment. She would go to the university. There, she thought she might be able to unearth from the detritus of history some new information about her long-buried subject. Actually, her decision to go to the university that morning was motivated more by a desire to take her mind off Michael than by a need to carry out any pressing Ovidian research.

Since it was neither Wednesday afternoon nor Saturday morning, she heated some water on the stove, poured it into the basin, and took a quick sponge bath. Knowing that both the rector of the university and her department head—the distinguished scholar, Dr. Nikoli Sibescu—were away for the week attending the annual Party Congress in Bucharest, Amanda decided to dress casually. She put on a pair of brown Bass Weejuns penny loafers, beige gabardine slacks, and a khaki-colored, U.S. Government Issued (G.I.), short-

sleeved fatigues shirt; the name tag above the left-breast pocket
had been removed, but the tag above the right-breast pocket was in
place and boldly announced, to anyone who cared or dared to look
there and who could read English, "U.S. Army"—a provocative
label in this staunchly Communist country.

She brushed her lustrous hair and then plaited it into a single
braid, a style which always made her look years younger than she
actually was. Why, with her hair coiffured in such a manner, one
might have easily mistaken her for a freshman in high school rather
than a mature young woman engaged in postgraduate research.

Her clothes and her hair in place, Mandy tidied up the apartment, did the dishes, and was now set to leave her quarters for the
university. Walking briskly along *Strada Karl Marx* in the direction
of the *Piata Unirii*, she intended to purchase some yogurt, cheese,
and black bread for lunch. Just as she was rounding the corner
where *Strada Karl Marx* bends into *Piata Ovidiu* (the square
named after Ovid, her *raison d'être* [reason for existing] for being
in Constanta at the present moment), Mandy collided head-on with
a passer-by hurrying in the opposite direction. Absorbed in thought,
she had been reflecting upon the introduction of Michael into her
life, how a relationship with him could exercise a negative effect on
her scholarship, and had not been minding her way.

"Oh, excuse me," Mandy said apologetically in Romanian.

The person whom she had nearly upended responded in Romanian, "Oh, it was really nothing. Nothing at all. My fault,
actually. I was not paying any attention to where I was going. I
was—" and then he suddenly stopped conversing in Romanian
and began to speak in letter-perfect English with just the slightest hint of accent. "Why, Miss West! What a coincidence bumping into you—literally and figuratively—this morning. On your
way to the university? Making any headway with the latest
Ovidian material you've exhumed?"

"Why, yes. Yes," Mandy replied in stunned disbelief coupled
with monumental embarrassment. The individual whom she had
nearly knocked to the pavement as she careered into *Piata Ovidiu*

was none other than the remarkably handsome head of her department, Dr. Nikoli Sibescu.

A number of questions, like a covey of quail exploding from cover, shot through her mind: *Could it really be he? Is he not supposed to be in Bucharest at the annual Party Congress? What in the world is he doing back in Constanta a week early? And what will he think, loyal apparatchik that he is, of me wearing a khaki-colored fatigues shirt with the legend "U.S. Army" stenciled over the breast pocket?*

Amanda West felt about two inches tall. Here was the archest of the arch-Communists at the university, and he had caught her, red-handed, clothed in U.S. Army fatigues. *I might just as well have fashioned a sari out of the U.S. flag, wrapped it around me, and paraded to the Piata Unirii whistling "Yankee Doodle Dandy,"* she thought to herself. *This is bound to have disastrous repercussions. Of all the people in the world I didn't want to meet this morning, he's number one on my list.*

"But—but Dr. Sibescu—but I thought you and the rector were in Bucharest—at the annual Party Congress?"

"We were, Miss West. And our dear rector remains there, attending to official party business. However, I was called back to Constanta to rectify some personal problems at the university; I had to leave the session early. Nonetheless, the rector is representing Constanta well, and the city and the university will have a prominent voice at the Congress. May I walk with you to the university? If indeed that is where you are headed?"

"Yes, please do; by all means. However, I've got to stop at the *Piata Unirii* first and buy something for lunch. You don't mind a slight detour, do you?"

"No, not at all. I am delighted to be in your company, Miss West. Certainly is a beautiful day, is it not?"

"Yes, Dr. Sibescu, it is. And Constanta is so lovely with the sea, the ships at anchor in the harbor, the parks, the *fin-de-siècle* [end of the nineteenth century] architecture, the mosques and minarets, the churches and campanile—the perfect blending of East and West. I just love it here!"

"I am truly happy for you, Miss West. You have adjusted remarkably well to the tempo of Romanian life. Some of the Fulbrighters who preceded you certainly did not make the transition so easily from life in America to life in Romania. Many of them went back to your country disillusioned with our Socialist experiment."

And as they walked to *Piata Unirii*, Dr. Sibescu talked on and on about the effects of the Socialist experiment in Romania and about the changes made in his country since the Communists overthrew the Monarchy after World War II. Mandy, having had the successes of the proletarian revolution in the Balkan states enumerated on countless occasions, was prepared to ward off the party propaganda and diplomatically changed the subject of conversation without offending her companion. She brought up his newly published monograph on indigenous wild mushrooms; he asked her about the progress she was making with her research. They talked about the infighting within the department, and, before long, they had arrived at the steps of the *Piata Unirii's* largest vendor of dairy products and foodstuffs.

He remained outside while she went inside to stand in one of the interminable lines, lines endemic to Socialist economies. A good half hour had passed before Mandy emerged from the store with her luncheon supplies. She thought her escort might have deserted her, but Dr. Sibescu was waiting patiently when she exited the store. He had been a Communist for as long as he could remember, and, for him, waiting in line or waiting for someone—or just simply waiting—was as normal for him as ordering a Big Mac and fries at the neighborhood McDonald's would have been for Amanda.

"I hope I haven't kept you waiting too long. I'm sorry."

"Do not give it a second thought. Let us walk along the sea, Miss West, and take the back route to the university."

"Fine with me; I love to walk along the cliffs. Oftentimes, I picture Ovid standing in the exact spot where I'm standing, looking

151

out over the Black Sea and wondering if he'd ever board a ship and set sail back home to Rome."

"Yes. Well, unlike Ovid, you will some day very soon leave our country and fly back home to America, will you not?"

"Oh, no! I haven't seen you since I got the good news. I've been granted a year's extension. The Fulbright committee has given me one more year. I'm just thrilled!"

"Wonderful news, Miss West! Ah, yes! Wonderful news, indeed! Let us walk this way then, along the cliffs, for I wanted to talk privately with you. And there is little risk that anyone will detect us conversing if we take the back route."

"Oh. Okay, Dr. Sibescu," Mandy replied, extremely puzzled by his secretive manner.

What in the world could he want to talk to me privately about? she pondered. *Oh, dear Lord, perhaps he's going to give me some flak about wearing a U.S. Army fatigues shirt in the very middle of a Warsaw Bloc country. Why did I have to bump into him, of all people, today, of all days?*

"Miss West, you are no stranger to Romania. You have been here for a time that is fast approaching a year, and all of us in the department are charmed by your personality and honored by your presence. And you are not the first, nor will you be the last, Fulbrighter we have had in residence here. Therefore, we know a good deal more than some people in the American Foreign Service give us credit for.

"For example, I know that, when you were briefed at the State Department in Washington prior to your departure for Romania, you were told that every conversation you had outside the classroom would be reported to the Intelligence Officer at the university. That all your movements would be monitored by the Internal State Security apparatus. That your apartment would be bugged and your phone would be tapped, no? Is this not true?"

"Why—well—" Amanda hesitated, not knowing in what direction this particular conversation was headed. "Well, I'm not at liberty to respond to that sort of questioning, Dr. Sibescu. Besides, I don't see how it has any bearing on my research or—"

"Oh, come, come. Miss West," Dr. Sibescu heatedly interjected, "I have always been honest with you and completely above board. I should wish that you would deal with me in a correspondingly candid manner."

"Okay. You've gone out of your way to be kind and honest with me from the day I first arrived in Constanta. What you said about my briefing is true. But I don't see how or why that affects me. I've never done anything wrong! I mean, golly, I'm not with the Central Intelligence Agency or anything like that, if that's what you're hinting at. In fact, I've never even met anyone in the CIA. Honest, Dr. Sibescu."

"Do not be too sure of that last statement, Miss West. But my point in having this frank discussion with you is not to accuse you of anything; rather, my point is to alert you to a situation that could have the gravest consequences vis-à-vis the success of your research. I very recently became privy to certain information which may be of inestimable value to you."

"I see," replied Mandy, not seeing at all.

"You see," said Dr. Sibescu, giving her a conspiratorial wink, "I am the Intelligence Officer at the university, that individual to whom all the reports concerning foreigners associated with the institution—and their contacts and movements within Romania—are turned in."

Mandy gasped, and her cheeks flushed, so surprised was she at this revelation.

Dr. Sibescu continued, "I am the man responsible for processing these intelligence reports and then recommending the appropriate action to be taken by the *Securitate* [Office for Internal State Security]. As you can easily surmise, Miss West, I have taken a great risk and compromised my position by revealing this information. I have completely overstepped the bounds of my authority by sharing all this with you."

"Well, of course, I realize that, Dr. Sibescu. And I'm very grateful to you, I think, for taking me into your confidence. But I don't know why you're telling me all this. I fail to see its relevance. I mean, I haven't done a thing wrong. I've never slandered President Ceausescu. I've never stolen any state secrets. I've never tried to infiltrate any university societies. I've never bought or sold anything on the black market. In fact, I've done nothing the last year except mind my own business and carry out my research."

Dr. Sibescu looked angrily at Amanda and then coldly replied, "Until last night all that you have said was quite true, Miss West."

Stunned by this news, Mandy could hardly believe her ears. A deluge of questions flooded her mind: *Did he really say that? How could he have possibly known about last night? What business of his was it anyway? What I do with a fellow American has not a thing to do with Internal State Security matters. Michael's an American, not a Romanian, so what right does Dr. Sibescu have to spy on me and pry into my affairs?*

Of course, she never gave voice to any of these thoughts. She had not the courage to ask him how he dared do anything. It was his country, and he was in a position of absolute power over her.

"But how did you find out about me and—and—about me and my friend?"

"You will recall, when I first bumped into you at Ovidu Square, you were surprised to find me back in Constanta. I told you, because of personal problems at the university, I had to return prematurely from the Party Congress."

"Yes, I remember."

"I came back late yesterday and resolved the crisis. I went home, did some paperwork, and retired rather early. I arose this morning at the break of dawn and went straightaway to my office. The very first report to receive my attention was a lengthy transcription of what transpired last night between you and your—your—how shall I phrase it—your newfound compatriot. I took the liberty of investigating the background of this dissembler who identifies himself as a Mr. Kukiliko and—"

Mandy, overwrought by Dr. Sibescu's disclosure, and stunned

by his knowledge of her activities, rudely interrupted the man whose continued cooperation she desperately needed if she were to continue to gain access to the Ovidian materials which were indispensable for her research. She actually shouted at him, "What? You even know his name?"

"Miss West, when one is surrounded—as we in Romania are—by, if I might use the expression, hostile powers, then one makes it his business to know everything there is to know about everyone who has crossed our borders—be that everyone an American, a Russian, a Turk, a Bulgarian, a Hungarian, or a Whatever. Why do you think we do not allow the other Warsaw Bloc countries to send their troops on maneuvers into Romania or conduct war games on our soil? History has been a harsh, but a good, teacher, and we have learned our lessons well. Our survival as a nation depends on our xenophobia.

"But you know all of this. So do not act the part of a naïve little waif. Did you not know, or at least suspect, that even you yourself, Miss West, are presumed by some within the department to be an agent of the hated CIA? So you can see the risk I am taking revealing all of this information to you. You could ruin my career if you so desired."

"Well, if that's the case, then why have you been so forthright with me and jeopardized your position?"

"Why? Because of your exceptional scholarship and the progress you have thus far made with your research. I have come to admire beyond measure the intellectual gifts you have brought to the study of Ovid—a god at whose altar I also worship. You have truly, Miss West, shed some significant new light on his writings and his life. And I never believed, not even for a moment, that you had any connection with the CIA."

"Thanks, Dr. Sibescu, for that vote of confidence. That's reassuring, I can assure you. And believe me, I've never even been approached by anyone from my government—or from yours, for that matter—asking me any questions about my involvement with the university or about the progress of my research or about anything connected with my stay here."

"I believe you, Miss West. But mark my words, Mr. Michael Kukiliko, or whatever his real name is, is not what he appears to be. He is a very deceptive man, this blackguard. And he will lead you astray and into compromising and dangerous situations."

"Oh, Dr. Sibescu. Don't be silly. He's an American engineer from Hawaii, and he's over here at the request of *your* government to help them design the new Danube Canal."

"That is his story, Miss West. Do not be so gullible. I have my sources. I know all about this so-called Mr. Kukiliko. Avoid him and his kind at all costs. Don't become a pawn in his dirty little game, for, if you do become involved with him and you find yourself in an unpleasant predicament, I shall be powerless to help you. Watch your step with this individual; if you allow him to mislead you, you will be treading on dangerous ground, I assure you."

"Oh, come now! Be serious. Oh, I don't know what to make of all this—this—this innuendo. I think you must be mistaken. Michael is a wonderful man—I'm dead sure. I'm absolutely positive, Dr. Sibescu; he's neither deceitful nor dangerous."

"You, of course, must determine that. I have given you fair warning, and you have been made duly aware: 'A word to the wise is enough,' as the saying goes. Just remember: your relationship with this individual who goes by the name of Kukiliko could very easily affect your ability to carry out your research. If this scoundrel, wittingly or otherwise, involves you in his intrigues and incriminates you in some underhanded espionage trick or other such similar subversive activity—"

"Espionage? Subversive activity?" Amanda incredulously shouted.

"Yes, in some espionage trick. I shall not be able to do a thing to help you; the matter will be far beyond my control. Think it over, Miss West.

"I think I should perhaps take a different path now. To my knowledge, no one has seen us walking and talking together, so no sense in taking any unnecessary risks. Let us not tempt fate. I shall take my leave now."

And then he took her hand in his, bent at the waist to kiss it, and gallantly said, "*Sarut mana.*"

He turned on his heel without a further word and departed, leaving Amanda alone on the cliffs overlooking the Black Sea. She stood there, transfixed, for the longest time as she gazed uncomprehendingly into the waters of the sea. She tried to sort through the menagerie of allegations Dr. Sibescu had made and attempted to make some sort of sense out of it all.

What could be so dangerous about my relationship with Michael? What sort of man is Michael Kukiliko—if that's actually his real name—anyway? What are his true intentions? Could he have lied to me? Could the end result of my relationship with him be my expulsion from Romania?—or something even far worse? A huge fine? Imprisonment? Death by firing squad? What are this handsome and mysterious stranger's true intentions? Good grief, what have I gotten myself into?

41-RUBA

February 1, 1983
2801 Hoosier Rd.
Centreville, IN 45480

Professor Gordon K. Douglas
Department of English Language and Literature
Warren House
Harvard University
Cambridge, MA 02138

Dear Gordy,

Before I inform you that I have finished another letter (January 20), that I have completed another chapter (Chapter IV), and that I have sent it off to June for her perusal and editorial advice, I should be remiss if I did not first offer you congratulations on getting your book published. The book was, in my opinion, an intellectual *tour de force*, and the five or six reviews I have read have—to a man—been exceptionally enthusiastic. I don't think you could have wished for a more positive reception. And, of course, thanks for the kind words about me on your acknowledgments page. With the sort of laudatory reviews it's earning, I'll bet you'll soon be put up for full professor. Again, congratulations!

So how do you think *Tempestuous Summer* is developing? Personally, I've suffered an aesthetic change of heart. I know, intellectually, that all romance novels (my own included—let me reword that: Fiona's included) are shitwork. But, viscerally, I'm beginning to get interested in Amanda and Michael; I'm beginning to enjoy their relationship.

What is it, I wonder, that Dr. Sibescu has discovered about Michael's past that makes him think Michael presents such a noxious threat to Amanda's well-being? Damned if I know. Hell, I don't even know who this Sibescu character is. Who is this guy? In all your letters, you never mentioned running into any villainous character named Sibescu, did you? How'd he sneak into my story?

These characters of mine are behaving like recalcitrant children: I've given them life and raised them, but now they don't respect my authority; they won't mind me anymore. They've grown up, and they're beyond my control.

I'd sure as shit like to get on with the next chapter, but I had better wait till I hear from June. Absent benefit of her guidance and her experienced hand to guide my (read Fiona's) pen, I'd get started out on the wrong track and end up lost in some unmarketable piece of trash. With her assistance, at least I'll end up with a lucratively marketable piece of trash. Nothing to do at the moment except patiently wait till the next mail from Harlequin House arrives. Until that time, I'll occupy my days reading some more romance novels. I love reading them because they're so interesting and induce such easy zzzzzzzzzzzzz's. Good night. Sleep tight. Don't let the bedbugs bite.

Best regards,

Joe

Joe Leonard

P.S. Should you ever get disillusioned with academe, don't give it up for a career hustling insurance.

encl.: Letter from Fiona Pilgrim to June Featherstone dated January 20; Chapter IV of *Tempestuous Summer—The Hottest Season*

11th February 1983
Harlequin House
Silhouette Lane
Fensucked-on-Strand
Ely, Cambridgeshire
England

Mrs. Fiona Pilgrim
2801 Hoosier Rd.
Centreville, IN 45480
U.S.A.

Dearest Fiona,

Excuse me, my dear friend, but this letter promises to be the most disjointed and incoherent correspondence I've ever penned. I'm at my wit's end. I'm almost to the point of ringing up the doctor and asking him to phone the chemist at Boots so that I might get some powerful sedatives. Well, I told you I was upset. And, first thing, I employ language with which I'm sure you're not familiar. Forgive me. "Chemist" is our word for your "pharmacist", and "Boots" is the name of our largest chain of chemists—what you Americans call "drugstores".

As you can readily see, I'm in an absolute dither. Let me, before going on, calm your fears: my agitation has nothing at all to do with Chapter Four of *Tempestuous Summer*. I've read it, loved every page, and have hardly a suggestion to make. Keep at it! You're on the right track. The introduction of Dr. Sibescu and the mysterious information to which he is privy is a stroke of real genius. Not only will his presence in the novel (I'm sure he'll be a perfect foil for Michael!) provide a test of the strength of Mandy and Michael's commitment to one another, but also the mystery of it all can only serve to encourage your readers to read on to discover, as the French so aptly put it, the *dénouement* (final resolution).

If I could make one general comment about the shape the novel is taking—rather than narrowly limiting myself to comments about Chapter Four—I should suggest that you try, in every chapter, to include Michael. I felt the most delicious thrill when he entered the plot, and he is—quite obviously, for you have created him thus—a perfect match for the magnificent creature who is Amanda West.

I do have some additional constructive criticism about the book; however, don't become overwrought with anxiety! On the whole, *Tempestuous Summer* is excellent. But all this must wait for a future letter.

I am presently in the very middle of the most awful muddle here. If you are standing as you read this letter, Fiona, sit down, for what follows might very well undo your equilibrium. Brace yourself for a shock. Nanny Crimpet (our very own Nanny!) has gone and got herself into serious trouble—a terribly sticky wicket—and may even be held for treason. Yes, *treason!*

Oh, Fiona, it is beyond comprehension and almost too distressing to relate to you. But

you've grown so close to us over the past
months that we consider you one of the family. I feel I must share this with you. My
fingers quake as I type these words: Fiona,
Nanny has struck the Queen!

You are saying to yourself that June must
be jesting. Oh, would that were the case.
This situation, however, is no laughing matter. I must tell you how the whole regret-
table affair came about.

Recently, Nanny developed an intense desire to see Buckingham Palace once again.
Since the poor dear has had such a devil-
ishly difficult time of it the last several
months—what with her rabies fright and all—
I set out at once to make arrangements for a
trip down to London.

Well, the day of our departure soon arrived. With Nanny bathed, brushed, and shining—she wore her blue suit with the
Valenciennes lace jabot and the velvet lapels, tiny gold earrings, and a Queen Mother
hat (Her wearing apparel the very model of
matronly fashion, she looked just precious.)—
we set off in the Rolls with James, Harlequin House's chauffeur, at the wheel.

She was unusually sullen during the trip
down. At the time, I attributed her morose
nature to either the effects of her increased medication or, perhaps, motion sick-
ness although riding in the Rolls is like
riding on a cloud. Well, we arrived safely,
parked the car, and stood watching the changing of the guard. In retrospect, I can't
fathom how it happened that we became sepa-

rated, but, in the crush of rude tourists (Please, don't take offence, Fiona, but the rabble was composed mainly of Americans on holiday.), dear Nanny suddenly vanished: gone without a trace! Disappeared into thin air did she.

I was simply frantic, in a terrible tizzy not knowing where in the world she had disappeared to. She is not at all well, you know, and had been, throughout the entire length of the trip from Ely to London, acting so thoroughly dyspeptic. And I was fearful that something dreadful might transpire. And, sure enough, it did! My fears were borne out.

I frantically searched the crowd and tried to enlist the aid of several tourists (Americans, the entire lot of them!), but I couldn't get a soul to take me seriously. Imagine that! Suddenly, there was the most frightful commotion. I ran over to see what was causing such a fuss, and there was Nanny: the picture is embedded forever in my mind. Each time I recall it, I become nauseated. She was stubbornly clutching a sheathed sword of great heft and furiously striking out at a band of bobbies who had surrounded her and who were, at that very moment, in the process of rushing her to an awaiting police van. They disarmed her, pushed the poor woman into the van, and, without so much as a word of explanation, off to gaol they sped!

I immediately summoned James, and we gave chase, following them to the very portals of Scotland Yard. It was here that I finally found the tale out—at least pieces of it. Apparently Nanny, without so much as a word to any of the attendant officials (security at the Palace is notoriously lax), had simply walked past the guards and slipped by the security officers watching over that particular entrance to the Palace. Once inside, she proceeded to walk upstairs and, as confused as she is, wandered about unescorted on a privately conducted tour.

Even on her best days, the old dear remains a bit dotty and has terrible problems controlling her bladder (the Buffy Syndrome). Well, Fiona, you can easily imagine how she acts on her bad days! And, as it happened, the day we chose to visit Buckingham Palace turned out to be the worst day she had had since the doctor had doubled her dosage.

Shortly after her entrance into what later proved to be the private quarters of the Royal Family, she desperately needed to relieve herself, so she found a bathroom. Thank goodness for that timely discovery, or she would have certainly spotted a palace carpet or stained the royal parquetry. When she had finished her business therein, she emerged from the door opposite the one she had entered and discovered herself right in the very middle of the Queen's own private chambers!

The Queen had been sickened with a touch of the flu that day and had been reading in bed at the time of Nanny's visit. Her Majesty was, the story goes, most irritable with, and condescending to, our Nanny. The

Queen—she must have been in a real royal
snit, for Nanny, one of her most loyal subjects prior to their meeting, could not possibly have presented any sort of threat to
the royal presence—very rudely commanded
Nanny to leave the royal suite immediately.

Well, one simply does not address Hortense
Crimpet in such a peremptory manner, no matter what that individual's station in life
might be. Nanny, a sensitive person who does
not bear up well under criticism of any
sort, simply could not brook such an arro-
gant show of disrespect from a person half
her age.

In order to teach this impertinent young
woman what Nanny thought was a much-deserved
lesson in proper manners and to impress upon
her the need to show a little respect for
her elders, she snatched the nearest thing
at hand: a scabbard sheathing the sword—once
belonging to Her Majesty's late father King
George VI—which the Queen uses to knight
personages being so honored at various In-
vestitures. With great energy, Nanny rapped
the Queen a good blow across the knuckles.

Piecing the story together as best I could
from Nanny's discursive mutterings, I gather
that the Queen, whose disposition was already soured due to her bout with the flu,
had been rehearsing her role in the ceremony
surrounding the bestowal of awards for those
honoured on The Queen's Birthday Honours
list or The New Year Honours list. Her Majesty had been brushing up her dubbing tech-
nique using her late father's sword and had

sheathed it in its scabbard and laid the weapon aside prior to retiring to her bed to read.

They say the Queen will bruise and will be unable to use her hand for several weeks. Nanny is in a cell at Scotland Yard, and it makes me weep to think about it. Yet, I must collect my wits and forge some plan of action to get the old dear released before her trial at the Old Bailey (that's London's criminal court), a trial which, God forbid, will undoubtedly attract much notoriety and much bad press.

I am allowed to see her twice weekly, but, from one day to the next, she seems more and more despondent. I am forever trying to raise her flagging sprits but, alas, to no avail. Why, just yesterday, I forthrightly confronted Nanny and, in no uncertain words, told her, "Nanny Crimpet, you must keep your pecker up! This is certainly not the time to quail in the face of adversity!"

And what did I earn for all my efforts? Her only response was a vacant stare accompanied by an unintelligible grunt.

I must close, for I am too disturbed to write anything resembling coherent correspondence. Penning these lines has brought it all to the surface again. I had thought I had it repressed and under control, but I was mistaken.

Do keep writing, Fiona. Write, write, write. And I shall try to write you again in a bit when I am not quite so agitated. In my next correspondence to you, I hope to report that the situation has been resolved and that Nanny has been released into my custody. Keep us in your prayers.

Love,

June

June Featherstone

February 20, 1983
2801 Hoosier Rd.
Centreville, IN 45480

Professor Gordon K. Douglas
Department of English Language and Literature
Warren House
Harvard University
Cambridge, MA 02138

Dear Gordy,

Read the enclosed dated Feb. 11 from June to Fiona. The letter speaks for itself. Such strange goings-on. What a weird pair they are: one wacky writer looking after one feeble-minded old ninny of a nanny. Someone ought to write a book about those two eccentrics.

Speaking of eccentricity, what about that curious sentence, "Nanny Crimpet, you must keep your pecker up!" I had to read it three times to make sure my eyes weren't playing tricks on me. I was wondering if there might not be some sort of bizarre anatomical anomaly affecting Nanny. Most, indeed all, of the women I've dated in America were never endowed with a pecker—either a recumbent one or a drooping one much in need of shoring up. Worried that there had been some sort of serious miscommunication— I mean, males and females in England are, as far as I know, of the same genus and species as males and females in America, so you'd expect them to be equipped with similar instruments of procreation. Wouldn't you?—I checked with my *vade mecum*, my invaluable *The American Heritage Dictionary*. Here, I discovered that, in British English slang, "pecker" means "courage" or "pluck." Weird, eh?

My misinterpretation of June's sentence reminds me of that saying attributed to G. B. Shaw, "England and America are two countries divided by a common language." Enough about Nanny and her problems with keeping her pecker up. What about QE II's health and safety?

I haven't read a single word about Nanny's breach of Buckingham Palace's security and her assault upon the Royal Presence. Have you? Yet remember last year when that Fagin fellow broke into the Palace? Holding a broken ashtray (a potential weapon were the intruder bent on regicide) in his hand, he sat himself down on the Queen's own bed! They nabbed him without a struggle, and no harm came to Her Royal Majesty. However, before the coils of the royal mattress had time to spring back into place, evening out the wrinkles Fagin's backside had left in the royal bedspread, news of his intrusion had made banner headlines throughout the world.

But not a word about Nanny's assault upon Her Majesty's person and privacy. And it's been over two weeks. Something's amiss here. Perhaps they're trying to hush this up so as not to embarrass one of England's great national treasures, the eminent writer, Ms. June Featherstone. I wonder?

Well, wondering about June's and Nanny's problems sure as shit won't contribute a single word, thought, scene, or whatever to the number of pages that will eventually make up *Tempestuous Summer—The Hottest Season.* I've got to get down to some serious writing here and get to the bottom of this mystery concerning Michael's intentions and his plans for Miss Mandy. I've got to follow June's well-meant advice: write, write, write. I'll write you more when I've written more for June to critique.

Best regards,

Joe

Joe Leonard

March 10, 1983

P.S. Sorry I haven't mailed this letter sooner, ol' Buddy, but I got carried away with Chapter V of *Tempestuous Summer*. I'm sending it along, so you can peruse it and give me some feedback, some constructive criticism. Any words of wisdom you can send my way would be greatly appreciated. Chapter V's got some rough edges, but June'll polish them down. J. L.

P.P.S. Should you ever get disillusioned with academe, don't give it up for a career hustling insurance.

encl.: Letter from June Featherstone to Fiona Pilgrim dated February 11; Chapter V of *Tempestuous Summer—The Hottest Season*

After Dr. Sibescu's abrupt departure, Mandy proceeded along the path to the university. Once in her office, however, she couldn't keep her mind on Ovid or off Michael. She kept thinking about Dr. Sibescu's comments concerning Michael and the dangers inherent in the situation. What were these dangers that Sibescu found so threatening to her well-being?

After less than an hour at her desk, during which time she accomplished nothing, Mandy put aside the papers she had come to review, for she just couldn't concentrate. Feeling that the fresh air would do her good and that the walk might clear her mind, she decided to return home by foot. She walked along the *Bulevardul V.I. Lenin* until it intersected the *Bulevardul Tomis*. She then followed the latter seaward until it terminated in *Piata Ovidiu*.

She stood in front of Ovid's statue for the longest time, hoping to recall some words of wisdom from the poet, words which might help her understand the intense emotional attachment she felt for Michael Kukiliko—a man who, only a day ago, she did not even know existed. But the sage was extremely close-mouthed that day and was not dispensing any advice. She could not recall a single aphorism of his which might have helped her understand her feelings.

Suddenly, her vigil was interrupted, and her reverie, shattered! Someone had silently approached her from behind and—as she gazed at the statue and thought about the Latin inscription on the plaque affixed to its base—placed a huge hand on her shoulder. Startled, she quickly turned around, grimaced her sensuous lips, and gasped, "Hhhaaa!"

"Hhhaaa! yourself, Miss Mandy," replied the voice of the man whose hand had just scared the wits out of her.

Michael then took his hand off her shoulder, reached down and took her hand in his, brought it gently to his lips, and lightly kissed it, saying, "*Sarut mana.*"

"Michael! I mean Mike! I thought you were scheduled to be in Tulcea all day and not due back in Constanta till late this afternoon?"

"I was. But I managed to conclude my business there early. And I was so eager to see you again that I rushed back the very moment I was done. At least you could say you were delighted to see me."

"Oh, Mike, I am; I am. Really. I'm just so surprised! How did you know I was here?"

"Blind luck. I didn't know where you were. I stopped by your apartment, but—obviously—you weren't there. I figured you'd be at the university, so I was driving out to see if I couldn't talk you into taking a long walk along the beach. And as I was driving by Ovid's statue, I saw the most beautiful girl standing in front of it. What were you doing? Translating the inscription?"

"No, I was just thinking about things, trying to recall something he had once written. Nothing at all important, though. Look Mike, I'd love to go for a walk. Wanna drive out to Mamaia? It's only three or four kilometers away, and it's got a splendid beach. You haven't been out there yet, have you?"

"Yes and no: yes, let's go out to Mamaia; no, I haven't been there yet. We'll go anyplace you want to go, Mandy; do anything you want to do. Just ask, and you shall receive. I'm at your beck and call. Anything your heart desires—that is, within reason—is yours for the asking. You see, Amanda West, you're dealing with an uxorious man."

"A what?" said Mandy, feigning perplexity but, Romance-language scholar that she was, being fully aware of the term since it had a Latin root, and she was quite familiar with the tongue. She was, though, quite pleasantly surprised with Michael's easy use of such an esoteric word. And then, hoping to score a point in this game of verbal one-upmanship, she added a risqué afterthought which caused Michael to chuckle. "It sounds to me," she said, "like some sort of Romance-language venereal disease."

"An uxorious man is," said Michael chuckling, "as you know very well with your background in Latin scholarship, a man who is excessively devoted to the wishes of the woman whom he—whom—whom he is presently—ah—ahem—squiring."

"Well, if you're so uxorious, Mr. Michael Kukiliko, and so interested in catering to my every whim and fulfilling my every wish, what say we drop by my apartment first, so I can change into something more suitable for a stroll along the strand?"

"But of course. Whatever you wish. However, I do think you look beautiful dressed just exactly as you are."

Amanda blushed, and Michael gallantly escorted her to where he had parked his car. Like a valet, he opened the door for her. She was thrilled by his manners, his kindness, and his obvious concern for her well-being. They circled the square and drove to Mandy's apartment. Michael waited in the car while Mandy ran in and changed into white footies, Adidas tennis shoes, cut-off jeans, and a loose-knit pink-boucle pullover with romantic butterfly sleeves and a scoop neck which modestly bared the rising swell of her magnificent bosom. Feeling that her outfit was too drab, Mandy wrapped—babushka fashion—a gaudily striped red, pink, and white scarf around her heavy hair. She smiled at herself in the mirror, tweaked her cheeks to make them flush with color, sighed heavily twice, and dashed down to the car and to her patiently waiting suitor.

Michael, dressed in the suit—dark blue and pinstriped in a shade which perfectly matched his graying temples—he had worn to his appointment in Tulcea, suggested that they stop at the Victoria on the way out of town. A walk along the seashore called for a much more leisurely outfit.

While he went to his room to change clothes, Mandy remained downstairs in the lobby and browsed in the hotel's dollar shop—a shop catering exclusively to vacationers from the capitalist world, tourists who had Western currency to spend. Michael entered the shop just as Mandy was paying the salesgirl for the several small things she had purchased. He was dressed in white Converse high tops, calf-length white sweat socks, white tennis shorts, and a white 100% cotton polo shirt which had been Sanforized and prewashed to reduce shrinkage. His huge brown legs, so sturdy and long, looked like two massive oak trunks, and the whiteness of his tennis togs against his naturally brown skin emphasized his tawny masculine nature; here was a magnificent mahogany specimen of a man!

He offered her his arm—which she readily accepted—and they got into the car and started off for Mamaia. They hadn't driven more than a block up *Bulevardul Tomis* when Michael commented, almost offhandedly, but with a detectable degree of annoyance in his voice, "I hadn't noticed that you smoked."

"I don't," replied Mandy.

"Oh? Strange? I don't want to pry, but I am quite curious. I couldn't help but notice that you purchased several packs of Kents and Marlboros in the dollar shop. I just assumed automatically that when one purchased cigarettes, one generally smoked them."

"Not this 'one.' I don't. Do you? I find them terribly disagreeable."

"I'm ashamed to admit it, Mandy, but, like most dumb kids who never consider the cancerous consequences down the road, I got hooked on cigarettes when I was in high school. And I had a pack-a-day habit for several years. Say, am I being too nosey if I ask for whom you're buying them then?"

"Not at all. Ask away. It's a free country—that was a joke, Mike. Ha, Romania's the furthest thing from a 'free country' as we both know only too well. I'm buying them for me."

"I see," replied a puzzled Michael. "Might you perchance elabo-

176

rate a little—fill me in on some tiny detail I might have missed in the course of this conversation? I guess I'm a little dense today because, if you yourself don't smoke and you're not buying them for a Romanian acquaintance, why do—?"

"Oh," Mandy said, interrupting him, "I can see how confusing this all must seem to you." And then she burst out with a rich, hearty laugh. "I just keep forgetting—probably because you speak such excellent Romanian—that you're not entirely familiar with the culture, customs, and local habits of the natives. You know Romanian; you don't yet know the day-to-day cultural idiosyncrasies of the folk who speak Romanian.

"Mike, if you ever want anything done in this country; if you want your car serviced at the garage; if you want calling cards made; if you want a doctor's appointment at a set time; if you want to go to the head of the line at the post office or the grocery store; if you want a maitre d'hotel to seat you and a waiter or waitress to serve you—if you want anything done in Romania, you've gotta have plenty of Kents or Marlboros.

"You see, they're kind of like an alternate form of currency. Romanians love American cigarettes, but the locals are unable to buy 'em in Romanian stores because commodities from the West can only be purchased with Western currency; cigarettes from America and Europe are simply unavailable unless you happen to have Western currency and are an outlander who can shop in the dollar shops and pay with real cash rather than this Monopoly money the Warsaw Pact uses."

"Well, I've never heard of such a thing in all my travels," Michael interjected.

"Yes. It's probably unique to Romania. So, anyway, figure you purchase a pack of Kents or Marlboros in the dollar store for seventy-five cents or a buck at the most. Out on the *strazi* [streets], Kents will be worth about five dollars—that's five dollars a pack, not a carton—and Marlboros are going for about four dollars a pack.

"But, Mike, you never ever sell them, for that would be black

1-RUBA

marketeering. And people who traffic in the black market and get caught get sent to jail or shot. So what you do is use them to bribe people to wait on you in a store or to move you to the head of a line when you're queuing up for something or to serve you in a restaurant the day you're seated rather than three weeks later. Once the help knows you've got Kents or Marlboros, they'll treat you like royalty—or like *politburo* functionaries in this Communist country—and fall over one another trying to win your approval. They figure if they give you good service, you'll frequent their establishment more often, tip more generously, and give 'em some more cigarettes."

"Sounds rather strange to me, Mandy. How does one subtly go about this business? I mean how do you let them know you've got the hidden treasure? And then how many do you relinquish? Are there any unwritten codes one needs to follow?"

"Oh, no. It all depends on how you feel and how many cigarettes you happen to have on you. For example, suppose you've heard there's a good restaurant in a certain section of town, but you've never been there. You go to the place for the first time, and the first thing you do is open a pack of Kents and offer several to the maitre d'. Then, after dinner, you inconspicuously leave the remainder of the pack on the table. Why, next time you go into that place for dinner, they'll treat you as though you were Nicolae Ceausescu himself. I swear, it works."

"It does? No kidding?"

"No kidding, Mike. Or say the first time you're standing in line for an hour at the post office, waiting to buy one airmail stamp to send a postcard back to the States. Well, when—after an endless wait—you finally get to the front of the line, and it's your turn, drop a pack of Kents on the counter. I guarantee every time you enter the building from that moment on, you'll get a reception which surpasses even that given to the Inspector General of the Romanian Post Office. They'll wave you to the front of the line before you've even taken the first step to queue up."

"Really? I'll have to try that. I'm glad you don't smoke. As I said, I once did but kicked the habit long, long ago. It leaves the most awful, horribly stagnant taste in one's mouth, don't you think so? Not to mention the mephitic [foul smelling] stench it leaves on your breath and clothes."

And before Mandy could affirmatively respond to his question, Michael suddenly swerved to the side of the road as if he were avoiding a head-on collision, pulled up to the curb, placed his huge hands behind Mandy's neck and, drawing her close to him, gave her the most passionate of kisses. "Oh, Mandy. I don't know what's come over me. I don't know what's happening between us. But I've never felt so much, so quickly, and so ardently for any woman in all my life. So help me, God. I want you!"

Mandy, her pulse quickening and her sensuous lips quivering, was shocked. Before having time to utter a sigh, she shouted, "Good Lord, Michael! Not here! Not in broad daylight, right in front of everybody in Constanta! It's the middle of the afternoon on the busiest thoroughfare in town, and here you are practically molesting me. Take you hands off me, and put them back on the steering wheel where they belong, and drive us to Mamaia. What's gotten into you? Are you mad?" she said sternly as she rebuffed his advances. But in her heart, she wished that he would have ignored her protestation and spent the remainder of the afternoon kissing her lips and holding her tightly against him.

"Sorry, Miss Mandy. Guess I got carried away there. Let's go to Mamaia and stroll along the strand and talk."

And they did just that. They walked and talked for over two hours. They collected shells which the Black Sea had cast upon the shingle; they tried, and failed, to catch the tiny, scurrying hermit crabs which, in search of empty snail shells to call their home, briefly appeared between the receding of one wave and the onrush of the next; they counted pelicans and sea gulls; and they talked: of things they would do together in Romania and of things they would do much later, after they had returned home. They talked so freely because they knew, out here on this beach, that no phones were tapped, and no apartments or hotel rooms were bugged.

Yet this freedom of expression did not in any way allow Amanda West to bring up as a topic of conversation the one vexing question that troubled her the most. All the while they talked, they never once talked about what Mandy really wanted to discuss.

How can I ever broach the subject to him? Amanda thought to herself. *I mean, I can't very diplomatically tell him that Dr. Sibescu, the chairman of my department at the university, warned me emphatically to stay clear of one Michael Kukiliko. He had sneered and used the phrase, ". . . as the person who identifies himself as a Mr. Kukiliko," which meant that Michael was someone else entirely. Sibescu's convinced that Michael's a disreputable character bent on causing me nothing but trouble.*

I can just picture the course of the conversation we'd have to have in order to get to the bottom of it all:

"Okay, Michael, or whoever you are, let's you and me have a little talk before we get too involved. Nothing really all that important to discuss. I just want to know if you're with the CIA and how many men you've killed working for the Company? And, for starters, I'd like to know what your real name is? And what is your true purpose for being here? Tell me, so I don't inadvertently blow your cover. And while we're on the subject, have you ever been—or are you, in fact, currently—married?"

But there's no way—not in a million years—that I could ever give words to these thoughts and voice them. Oh, but I so desperately need my questions answered. What ever am I to do?

What they did was talk of other subjects of little consequence, and the time quickly passed.

"Hey Mandy, we've been walking for a couple of hours now. I've worked up a huge appetite. Let's stop in one of these restaurants and get us a bite to eat. What do you say?"

"Fine with me, Mike. I'm practically famished. But we don't dare go in there dressed like this, do we? I think they must have some sort of dress code."

"Don't be so self-conscious. This isn't a fashion show. They're not at all interested in what we're wearing—only what we're paying with. The color of our clothes interests them not a whit; it's just the color of our money that interests them, and I'm paying in greenbacks—or plastic money if they'll accept my Visa or American Express Card or MasterCard. Besides, no matter how you were dressed, you'd be the most beautiful woman in the room—in any room, anywhere in the world."

Mandy blushed at the compliment and, averting her eyes, studied the highly uninteresting Bauhaus façade of the Hotel Riviera, the structure in front of which they had stopped. The Riviera was one of Mamaia's most luxurious hotels. Motioning toward it with his arm, Michael grandly announced, "Well, the Riviera looks like as good a place as any. What say we give it a try?"

"Oh, let's do. I've heard the food here is just great and the atmosphere inside is simply divine."

They entered the hotel and found the restaurant. With Amanda conspicuously flashing her pack of Kents, they were seated immediately—to the obvious displeasure of a vacationing Bulgarian couple who had been waiting several hours for a table.

The meal—which consisted of salad, *corba de pui* (chicken soup), vegetable medley, French fries, and freshly caught fish from the nearby Danube Delta—was superb. The wine, which Michael drank straight but which Amanda mixed half-and-half with *Borsec* as was the Romanian custom, was a Pinot Noir with an excellent bouquet from the Murfatlar vineyards.

Halfway through the course of the meal, Michael remarked, "Do you ever, Mandy, get used to these people staring at you all the time?"

"Oh, sure. After a while. You've just got to understand their mentality. They're not being rude. It's just that history has taught them to be suspect of strangers, and, since they've become a Communist country, they've been taught to be watchful and wary of people from the West. You'll soon not even notice everyone's watching your every move."

"Perhaps. I hope so. You know—I have the strangest feeling. Everyone in this room is staring at us; yet, and don't look now, there's a gentleman—a handsome devil at that—at the table directly behind ours who, and maybe I'm paranoid, has been glaring, rather than staring, at me since we were seated. He's given me a positively menacing look all evening long."

"Maybe," Mandy lightheartedly replied, "you ought to get up and go over and offer him a Kent. Perhaps he's having a nicotine fit."

Michael, not appreciating the humor of Amanda's remark, continued, "It must be my imagination playing tricks on me. I don't know a soul in Romania whom I could have offended to such an extent that it would occasion such rudeness."

"Well, then, it must be, as you said, just your imagination playing tricks on you, Mike."

"Perhaps it is," Michael uneasily replied. "But if looks could kill, I'd wager you'd be eating dinner with a dead man right now. Oh, Mandy!" Michael suddenly said. "He's talking to the maitre d'. Turn around quickly now and see if by any chance you recognize him or have seen him following us. Maybe he's our tail. I understand we've all got one, trailing us around the country and reporting our every move to Internal State Security."

Mandy turned around, expecting to find just another nameless, nondescript plainclothes security officer who had been assigned to monitor their movements. What she saw, however, was not at all what she had expected to see. She immediately recognized the man who had glared at Michael with such an inimical look. Taken aback, she gasped and, in the process, lodged a French fry in her trachea.

As soon as she began to turn purple, Michael—by nature, a very perceptive man—immediately sensed the seriousness of the situation. "Is something wrong? Are you all right?" he anxiously asked.

Receiving no answer to his questions but a frantically mimed response indicating that she was choking, he immediately rose from the table, rushed around behind her, seized her in a bear hug, and applied the Heimlich maneuver.

"Aahhgh!" replied Mandy, as she dislodged the French fry, propelling it halfway across the Riviera's dining room where the airborne fry ricocheted off a water cooler and landed in the uppermost branches of a potted plant.

"I beg your pardon, Amanda. Are you okay?"

"Yes. No. Oh it can't be him!"

" 'Him'? You know that man? Who in the world is he?"

"Oh, Mike. It's Dr. Sibescu, the chairman of my department. I can't believe it. I just can't." And Amanda West couldn't believe it. Was his presence there in Mamaia, in the dining room of the Hotel Riviera, an accident? Or had he been deliberately following them, watching and recording their every move?

"Well, if you're sure that's him, then you'd better believe it. That is, unless he's got a twin brother. Perhaps, I ought to go over and introduce myself and invite him to join us for an after-dinner drink. Or perhaps, judging from the way he looked at me, I ought to go over to see if he's chosen his second yet, and if it's to be pistols at twenty paces or else close-quarters combat with swords or knives or fists. What do you think, Mandy? You know the man."

"Oh God, Mike. Don't invite him over. He's a strange one. A nice enough man but—"

Mandy never finished her sentence, for, at that very moment, Dr. Sibescu arose from his table as if to leave the restaurant. However, acting as though he had just taken account of the presence of Mandy and her friend, he waved a friendly greeting to Amanda and approached her table.

"Why, what a pleasant surprise, Miss West! Meeting you here. I presume you have been out for a walk on the beach, enjoying Mamaia's acclaimed weather?" Dr. Sibescu's remarks were directed solely at Mandy. It was as if the man refused to even acknowledge Michael's existence.

"Yes, yes we have, Dr. Sibescu," Mandy replied, flustered by his presence at her table. "Dr. Sibescu, I'd like to introduce you to a friend of mine from America, from Hawaii. He's an engineer, and he's here giving technical advice to the people running the canal project. Dr. Sibescu, this is Michael Kukiliko. Michael, this is the chairman of my department, Dr. Nikoli Sibescu."

Dr. Sibescu politely, but coldly, offered Michael his hand and firmly clasped it, as if trying to prove he had the better grip of the two. Shaking Michael's hand, Dr. Sibescu asked, in letter-perfect English, "I am sorry. I did not catch the name? Was it 'Kololikeo?' "

Michael, sensing the note of sarcasm in the man's voice, riposted in fluent Romanian, "My name's Michael Kukiliko, Dr. Sabetascu; it's a difficult name even for most Americans. Just call me 'Mike.' "

Dr. Sibescu, in English, responded, "No, not a difficult name at all, Mr. Kukiliko. Incidentally, the proper pronunciation of my name is 'Siby-es-cue.' I do hope that you enjoy your stay here in our beautiful country, Mr. Kukiliko—and that your sojourn in Constanta proves profitable. A pleasure to meet you," he said, his voice teeming with obvious disdain and insincerity.

"Perhaps we shall see each other again soon. I certainly hope so. Miss West, so good to see you again. Mr. Kukiliko, good evening." And with that valediction, Dr. Sibescu bowed to the couple and left the dining room.

"Boy, he's an odd one now, isn't he? The way he was attempting to strangle my hand, I thought that I might have to challenge him to a bout of arm wrestling and use our table as the battleground for a classic confrontation between East and West. Is he always that strange?"

"Not usually. In fact, he's usually the kindest and most genteel of men. I don't know what's gotten into him lately. I wonder what it is that could possibly be bothering him so?"

That question was rhetorical, purely for Michael's benefit, for Mandy knew full well what was troubling Sibescu. She knew Sibescu was worried about her safety, about her compromising her access to the Ovid papers at the university and the Ovidian memorabilia at the museum, and about the danger she faced being seen in public with a notorious CIA operative.

Michael, not realizing Mandy's question was rhetorical, answered it. "Who knows what could be bothering him? Who cares? We've all got problems. Our only problem right now is to finish this bottle of Pinot Noir and return to Constanta without getting arrested for drunk driving. The hour's late, and I've got to get you home so you can get a good night's sleep. We've got a big day in store for us tomorrow, and I want you to be well rested for it. You've got to be up early on the morrow at the break of dawn, bright and chipper."

"We've got a big day in store for us tomorrow?"

"Sounds like an echo in here. Yes, Ma'am, we certainly do. If you've not made other plans, that is. I thought we could get an early start and take the coast road down to Mangalia, get us 'A Jug of Wine, a Loaf of Bread—and Thou Beside me singing in the Wilderness—' and have ourselves a picnic."

"Oh, Mike, I just love *The Rubáiyát of Omar Khayyám*! Oh, a picnic does sound like great fun. I'd love to."

"Then it's settled. We'll get up bright and early and head out before there's too much traffic on the road. I understand there are some interesting Greek and Roman ruins along the way, and perhaps we can stop and explore them—if that suits you. Let me settle up with the waiter. Leave him a pack of Kents or Marlboros, if you will. I think we'll come back here often, and I intend to be well treated!"

Mandy did as Michael had requested, and they left the Riviera and Mamaia, driving back to Constanta via the *Bulevardul Mamaia* until it circled *Lake Tabacariei* and became the familiar *Bulevardul V.I. Lenin*, the street on which was located the university and Amanda's office. The journey from Mamaia to Mandy's apartment lasted no more than ten to fifteen minutes.

And all the while, as Michael steered his tiny Dacia with one huge hand, his other massive hand rested ever-so-lightly on Mandy's knee, gently massaging it. Until that moment, she had never before experienced such unalloyed pleasure in anyone's company. She placed her tiny hand on top of her escort's. Amanda West was sublimely content.

After pulling the Dacia up to the curb in front of the entryway to Mandy's apartment and parking it there, Michael got out and walked around to Mandy's side of the car. He opened the door and offered her his hand which she readily accepted. As she pulled herself up and out of the car, Michael pulled her into him and wrapped his free arm around her waist, gently nuzzling her forehead with his lips. She loved it!

Suddenly, without warning, a car turned the corner, slowed as it caught and framed the embracing couple in its headlight beams, and, as suddenly as it had appeared, sped up and rushed past them, disappearing into the night. Although it was quite dark, Mandy felt certain she had recognized the driver of the car: none other than Dr. Nikoli Sibescu! She shuddered with apprehension.

"Are you cold?" Michael queried, thinking it was the dampness of the night sea air that had caused her to shiver.

"Yes. Let's go inside, Michael. It's turned rather chilly all of a sudden, and I'm not dressed for it."

"Sure, Miss Mandy. As I've said before, your wish is my command. My aim is to serve and please. After you." He opened the door for Mandy and, after ascending one flight of stairs, escorted her down the darkened hallway to her apartment.

"Would you like to come in for a drink, Mike? I mean we could mix up some *Borsec* and syrup and have a late-night phosphate."

"I'd love to, Mandy. But we've both got to get us some shuteye if we're gonna be in tiptop shape for tomorrow's outing. Let me have a rain check on that offer and take you up on it sometime when we've got nothing scheduled first thing the next morning. What say you?"

"Oh, that's fine," Mandy replied, although it was just the opposite of fine. It was horrible. She so desperately wanted to hold him—and be held by him. Her body ached for his, but she couldn't forcibly drag him into her apartment against his will. "You're right,

Mike. We'd better get a good night's sleep, or we'll both be out of sorts for tomorrow. Good night."

"Good night, Mandy. I had a great time tonight."

Standing on the doormat in front of Mandy's apartment, Michael suddenly took Amanda West in his arms and kissed her as she had never been kissed before. His probing tongue gently pried her sensuous lips apart and then, like that of a serpent's, dashed in and out, in and out, in and out, and all around her opened mouth. This was ecstasy!

She pulled him close to her; she felt her warm and throbbing bosom rub against his massive chest. She dug her fingers deeply into his shoulder blades, but, if her passionate clawing caused him any pain, he, stoically, did not acknowledge it.

Standing storklike on one foot, she gently rubbed her other foot up and down, up and down, and up and down against his shank, unconsciously synchronizing the motion of her foot against his calf with the penetrating stroke of his tongue as it massaged her sensuous lips and mouth. Her tennis shoe, the one she was rubbing up and down, up and down, and up and down suddenly fell off—the upward and downward movement of her foot against his leg must have abraded the knot and loosened the lace. The sensation of her soft white footie against his hard brown calf sent waves of carnal energy coursing throughout her body. She sighed twice!

What power does this man possess over me? she thought to herself. *Never before has a man's touch affected me this way.* It never occurred to her that someone could exercise such control over her body. Her will as well was at his disposal. She was spellbound.

It was finally Michael who reluctantly retracted his lips from hers and, fumbling for the right words, said, "Oh, Mandy. Mandy. Mandy. I've—I think—I've never—I'm so fond of—I've got to go. Really, I must. I'll pick you up shortly after 7:00 a.m. Tonight was so enjoyable. Good night and sweet dreams, Lovely Lady."

Then he kissed her one more time, gently, on her tremulously sensuous lips and left.

41-RUBA

Mandy sighed deeply several times, went inside her apartment, shut and locked the door, and collapsed on the couch, utterly sapped of her strength. *What is happening to me?* she wondered.

But this was also merely a rhetorical question, for she knew—call it woman's intuition!—what had happened. She had fallen in love. The bewildering question that urgently demanded answering was: but with whom had she fallen in love?

February 23, 1983
2801 Hoosier Rd.
Centreville, IN 45480
U.S.A.

Ms. June Featherstone
Harlequin House
Silhouette Lane
Fensucked-on-Strand
Ely, Cambridgeshire
England

My dearest, distraught June,

Your letter of 11 February concerning Nanny's sorry state arrived in last week's mail and nearly devastated me. I felt so helpless, for there was nothing in the world I could do to help. I was so worried that for two days I couldn't sleep a wink or hold down a thing—I lost four pounds and developed the most horrid bags under my eyes. P.P. gave me a rather harsh lecture concerning my duties to him and the children, and his exacting words worked wonders and brought me back to my senses. I've since regained the weight I'd lost, and I look as if I'm in the pink of health.

Please, by return mail, tell me what is the latest news about this unfortunate soul! Will the Queen actually press charges? Is it a capital offense to assault the Monarch? Is it England or France that does away with its deviates by lopping off their heads with a guillotine? (Not that—horrors forbid!—I think Hortense Crimpet is a deviate; she is just a confused old woman, and she should be treated accordingly.) I know "guillotine" must be a French word, but I have a recurrent dream of some bewigged king—looking very much like George III—angrily shouting, "Off with their heads; off with their heads!" And he's always shouting this in English, for I shouldn't understand a word of what he had said were he speaking French.

Oh, the thought of that poor woman and the trauma she—and you—has suffered sickens me. You are both in my prayers.

The story of Nanny Crimpet is simply too sad a subject to dwell overmuch on. Let me, therefore, move on to a lighter topic: the latest chapter, Chapter V, of *Tempestuous Summer—The Hottest Season*. As you read it, you'll easily discover that I've once again followed your advice. On practically every page Michael's magnificent presence may be felt by the reader. Just as you suggested, I've given both him and Mandy a free reign. I'm simply following them around Constanta, recording their actions. I'll let you in on a little secret, June, just between the two of us: when Michael came across Mandy in Ovidu Square, I had no earthly idea that he was going to invite her to Mamaia, or that they would dine at the Hotel Riviera, or that they would encounter the sinister presence of Dr. Sibescu who is, as far as I'm concerned, evil incarnate.

I simply don't like the man. Personally, he gives me the willies! I haven't yet quite figured out what his part is in this drama, but I think his inclusion in the cast of characters is a real boon to the story. One thing's for certain: he doesn't like Michael, and I'm afraid he might even do harm to Amanda. I intend to have Michael around to keep a watchful eye on Sibescu.

Isn't it amazing how you create your characters, breathe life into them, nurse them along until they suddenly find their own identity, and then they disown you? All of a sudden—Who knows what triggers it?—they wean themselves from you and take off on their own. They just begin to "do their own thing" and act totally independent of you. I just can't get over it; it's so strange.

Let me cite an example to show you what I mean. The conversation between Mandy and Michael concerning the purchase of the Kents in the dollar shop came about purely by chance. I did not originally intend to give either of them the opportunity to do any shopping prior to their trip to the beach. What purpose would such an incident have served? Indeed, at first blush, the inclusion of such a scene would seem to retard the plot development and divert the reader's attention from the main story.

Yet apparently the incident was of sufficient importance—perhaps it is illustrative of their relationship: i.e., Mandy as teacher of Romanian mores and manners and Michael as eager student—for, before I knew it, she had finished browsing around the dollar shop, had purchased the cigarettes, and had begun her discourse about her purchase functioning as an alternate form of currency. I had never intended to write such a scene. Yet, before I could stay my hand and rest my pen, Michael and Amanda had authored it, enacted it, and were out the door and on their way to Mamaia.

Odd as the inclusion of this episode seems, the stimulus which subconsciously prompted me to write it is, by far, much stranger. Two days before I began working on this particular segment of Chapter V, my cousin—the source for all of my Romanian background information—was telling me how Kents and Marlboros functioned as a second form of currency in Romania. However, at that particular point in time, I had neither the intention nor the desire to interject this bit of "local color" into my story. I simply had no use for it.

Then, lo and behold, when Mandy and Michael went to his hotel, the information somehow seeped out of my pen and onto the paper—without my conscious knowledge. Isn't that downright weird, June? Do things like this ever happen to you? Do you think this means I've got some talent? I think the whole scene developed quite nicely and gave the reader a "sense" of what it must be like to live behind the Iron Curtain.

And I'll tell you something else while we're on the subject of one's characters getting out of hand and wrestling control of their destinies away from their creator. I was terrified while writing about the dinner at the hotel restaurant. You know, when Michael first spots Sibescu menacingly staring at him. I didn't know if Michael and Dr. Sibescu would act like gentlemen and part as friends or if their meeting would degenerate into a shouting and/or shoving match, and they would come to blows. In fact, I was so involved with the action, and so tense while writing that particular part of the chapter, that I completely forgot about preparing dinner that evening. Well,

191

take it from me, June, P.P. was momentarily peeved. But it's not, thank God, in the Pilgrim nature to hold grudges, and the dear, sweet man called the neighborhood pizza parlor and ordered a large sausage-and-mushroom pizza to be immediately delivered.

Incidentally, if you have any idea what it is that Dr. Sibescu is up to or what he knows about Michael's past actions, present plans, and future intentions, please let me in on it. As I wrote in a much earlier letter, I pretty well had the story outlined as I envisioned it and had the characters drawn as I saw them. But once I actually gave birth to them and set them down on paper, they tore up my script, ripped the pen from my hand, and wrote their own lines. Thus, I presently have no idea what it is that Sibescu has in mind, so I should really appreciate any advice I might receive from you to help me bring this recalcitrant character back into (the story) line. I feel so foolish asking you if you know what one of *my* characters is intent upon doing.

Honestly now, June, how did you like the love scene at the end of the chapter? P.P. thought it bordered on the erotic. Do you think I was too frank about the physiological changes taking place within Mandy's body as Michael kissed her goodnight? Peter Paul said the entire description could have been transcribed verbatim from a John Updike novel, but I didn't think it was salacious or all that louche. Did you?

Well, I've certainly said a mouthful in this letter, and I must shortly bring it to a close. The next chapter will—obviously—begin to answer the question that ended Chapter V: "She had fallen in love. The bewildering question that urgently demanded answering was: but with whom had she fallen in love?"

However, I shan't write a word till I hear from you. I don't want to appear sacrilegious (because I really *do* worship your writings, June), but if, as he said in Chapter IV, page 46, Sibescu worshipped at the altar of Ovid (Now there's a strange phrase—talking of worshipping and altars—for a godless Communist to utter. Nevertheless, he said it; I didn't.), then I think I can safely say that I pray for guidance, kneeling at the feet of Featherstone. Goodness, I thought the preceding sentence would run on forever! I must go.

Fondest regards,

Fiona

Fiona Pilgrim

P.S. I cannot help but end this letter by voicing again the same grievous concern which began it. I remain intensely worried about the fate of Nanny Crimpet. Please give her my regards, and tell her she is in our prayers. You have asked me several times if I could send along a picture of P.P., the children, and me. You particularly stressed that Nanny was not comfortable with children but that she loved to surround herself with pictures of the little cherubs. Well, I came across the enclosed family portrait we had taken last year, and I'm sending it along to you and, especially, to Nanny. Perhaps she can pin it up in her cell and look at it when she gets depressed. I hope it perks up her spirits. Tell her we all love her, and we're pulling for her. Love, F.P.

encl.: Family photo of the Pilgrims; Chapter V of *Tempestuous Summer—The Hottest Season*

April 1, 1983
2801 Hoosier Rd.
Centreville, IN 45480

Professor Gordon K. Douglas
Department of English Language and Literature
Warren House
Harvard University
Cambridge, MA 02138

Dear Gordon, you (April) fool,

Fiona has sent June Chapter V along with the enclosed letter
dated February 23. Pay particular attention to its postscript. What
an absolute stroke of genius! The other day, I was airing the apartment and doing spring housecleaning when I came across an album
of family portraits. Ruffling through seven years of marriage, con-
densed in one musty volume of fading glossies and half-forgotten
memories, I suddenly found myself staring at a picture—taken over
two years ago—of the happy Leonard family: Mom; Dad; the Twins;
and Sis, photographed and bonded together forever in color by
Extachrome. With great care, I peeled the photo from the page it
had been mounted on and mailed the snapshot off to June.

Little will June or Nanny ever know that the woman who smiles
at them from the print, and who they think is Fiona Pilgrim, is, in
fact, none other than Betty Leonard, that vindictive nemesis of mine
whose constant threat to have me jailed if I don't continue to make
my monthly child-support payments drives me to sell insurance.

They'd probably both suffer coronaries if they discovered that
the darkly handsome gentleman surveying this scene of happy fa-
milial unity, his hand resting protectively on his wife's shoulder, is
not Peter Paul Pilgrim, perfect partner to the precious F. Pilgrim,
but is, in fact, Joe Leonard, failed and frustrated writer who sometimes—much against his will—assumes the guise of Fiona Pilgrim,
struggling writer of romance fiction. Well, no harm done in sending

along the photograph. It'll give them something to relate to and may even take the old lady's mind—at least the small portion of it that remains in proper working order—off her troubles. God save the Queen and protect her from Hortense Crimpet!

Really, though, I shouldn't jest about it. June's been uncommonly kind to Fiona, and I can tell how upset she is about Nanny and the troubles she's caused the Queen. God love 'em all: June, Nanny, and the Queen.

I wish I could be in Harlequin House's study when June reads the letter and looks at the photo. I wonder what her initial reaction will be? What will she think of the woman whom she thinks is Fiona Pilgrim? Better yet, what sort of impression will the man whom she thinks of as Peter Paul make? In all likelihood, she'd stop corresponding if she ever found out that Fiona, in reality, was Peter who, in actuality, was I. I bet she'd shit on the spot or have some sort of apoplectic seizure. Nanny, considering her current condition, would shit on the spot for sure.

These questions, however, will forever remain unanswered, for she's a million miles away. She'll never pay us a visit; that's for certain. And I certainly can't envision myself ever dropping by Harlequin House for a spot of tea. Why, with the sorry state of my empty pockets, I'd have trouble paying taxi fare across town let alone coming up with the funds for a transatlantic flight. Just think what it would cost for airfare to London.

Even if I were somehow able to finagle a flight, I'd have to go as Fiona and dress the part. I'd have to filch some of Betty's clothes and get some stuffing to round out the contours. And, with my bad luck, agents of the INS or the border patrol or customs agents would strip search me as I was going through customs and expose me for what I was: just your ordinary, run-of-the-mill, transvestite writer of romance fiction paying homage to the doyenne of the genre.

Well, all of this nonsense is nothing but idle speculation—flights of fancy that sputter to a halt halfway down the runway of my mind. However, there's one thing that's bound to come to pass:

within a fortnight or two—or three or four—I'll receive, along with directions for improving Chapter V and perhaps some suggestions for writing Chapter VI, a lengthy narrative detailing both June's and Nanny's responses to the photo. I know for sure she'll think the kids are darling. One can't—in good taste—very well tell a mother that her offspring are ugly. In the meantime, I might just as well pass the time by reading fifty or sixty of June's novels.

Yours,

Joe

Joe Leonard

P.S. Should you ever get disillusioned with academe, don't give it up for a career hustling insurance.

encl.: Letter from Fiona Pilgrim to June Featherstone dated February 23

15th April 1983
Harlequin House
Silhouette Lane
Fensucked-on-Strand
Ely, Cambridgeshire
England

Mrs. Fiona Pilgrim
2801 Hoosier Rd.
Centreville, IN 45480
U.S.A.

Dearest Fiona,

My dear distant friend, I have some good
news and some bad news to report. The good
news is that I received the snapshot you
sent us of Peter Paul (I almost feel as
though I am being entirely too formal in
referring to him by his Christian name rather
than P.P.), the children, and yourself. I am
absolutely delighted to finally see your
happy little family on film. The children
are darlings, especially Priscilla; she appears to be such a fetching little lass, a
bit on the heavy side, but, when she has her
growth spurt, everything is sure to reappor-
tion itself. Nanny was as thrilled as was I,
and, for a moment at least, it took her mind
off her troubles—of which she has more than
either of us can handle.

And that, Fiona, is the bad news. As though
she has stumbled across the antithesis of
the philosopher's stone, Nanny has an aura
about her that seems to immediately cause

anything she touches to transmute to lead rather than to gold. Why, I even had to go through the most frightful amount of red tape in order to obtain special permission to take the snap to Nanny so she could see it, for she has been transferred from Scotland Yard.

Steel yourself for what follows, Fiona; it is almost beyond imagination that a civilised government could treat one of its loyal, albeit senile, subjects in such a barbaric manner. Nanny is now lodged in the Tower of London!

Yes, the Tower! The authorities have closed the Tower to tourist traffic; once again—as in the days of yore—it is to be utilised not only as a repository for the safekeeping of the crown jewels but also as an impregnable fortress to imprison those anarchists, saboteurs, and assorted subversives and rabble-rousers who would overthrow the government by violent force. Hard though it is to conceive of, the government actually believes that Nanny Crimpet is a source of endangerment both to the House of Windsor *and* the Church of England!

She is jailed there in solitary confinement, I am told, because she made the most menacing threats against the life of our most respected prelate, the Archbishop of Canterbury; she vowed to assassinate him! It seems the authorities at Scotland Yard gave her some reading matter to pass the time in her cell. And while paging through one of the glossies she had been given, she came across a picture of His Grace with Her Majesty. Recognising the Queen, not as our reigning Monarch but as the surly youngish woman who had been so rude to her, Nanny assumed that the Archbishop was somehow in collusion with the Queen and that he was the instigator of Her Majesty's churlish display of ill manners. There is very little logic remaining in the old dear's powers of reasoning, yet—and I find this hard to believe—the authorities took her at her word and felt that the Archbishop would be much safer if Nanny were locked up in the Tower.

And, Fiona, once there—you know there must be a lot of truth in the old saying: "Things go from bad to worse"—things went from bad to worse. It seems that Her Royal Highness, Diana Princess of Wales, had decided to come and visit the Tower in order to allow baby Prince William Arthur Philip Louis the opportunity to play with the crown jewels and familiarise himself with some of the family heirlooms in the royal legacy. The Beefeaters who guard the crown jewels had closed the Tower grounds to the general public so that the Princess and Prince William would be afforded some privacy. After viewing the jewels, Princess Diana decided to take a stroll around the grounds.

She was in the process of pushing William in his pram when Nanny, high aloft in the Tower, first spotted them. You know how, from a distance, she just adores children! She thrust her hand through the bars of the window, yoo-hooing at the top of her voice and waving wildly with her handkerchief at mother and baby, trying futilely to catch either's attention. She commenced to make all sorts of clucking, chirruping, and cooing noises in order to attract the notice of either royal visitor, but all of her efforts went for naught. Neither Princess Diana nor Prince William took any note of Nanny.

Nanny, of course, took their failure to acknowledge her efforts to befriend them as a personal slight, dropped her handkerchief, and—oh, Fiona, this is so out of character. All her life, she's been such a perfect lady—never even the slightest breach of etiquette. A paragon of matronly virtue she has been. I swear her behaviour can only be attributable to the medication she's been taking.

She made the rudest gesture—expressive of the most contemptuous anti-Monarchist sentiment—in the direction of the Princess and the pram. I speak here of "the fig" or "the figo" as our own revered Bard of Avon termed it or the *digitus impudicus* (rude finger) as Amanda's beloved Ovid referred to the gesticulation. (Or was it Martial who labeled it thus? I forget which; it has been such a long time. Oh, my goodness, Fiona, how readily that sentence I just penned could be misconstrued. I meant that it has been many years since I read any of Ovid's poetry or Martial's epigrams; of course, it has indeed been a long time, two millennia, since one or the other of these two luminaries designated the gesture as such.)

While Diana saw nothing of all this disrespectful conduct, Nanny's falling handkerchief spooked some of the resident ravens, thus attracting the attention of several Beefeaters who noted this disgusting display of digital vulgarity. They promptly reported it to their superiors, and now Nanny is monitored on closed-circuit TV twenty-four hours a day!

You, Fiona, being so frightfully American and so unfamiliar with the British temperament, may not realise the seriousness of this nasty show of disrespect for Crown and Crosier. But to attack both the Royal Family and the Church of England—Oh, Fiona, my Nanny in gaol!

Why, I could simply go into a decline when I think that my most dear and trusted friend, convicted of treason, might have to spend the few moments she has left of her life withering away in a dank and dreary dungeon. But I must be strong, for I know I am her only hope. I pray that some sort of miracle might happen and untangle this horrid mess Nanny has got herself into.

In addition to praying for some sort of divine intervention, I do what little I can. My staff at Harlequin House bottled some fruits and put up some preserves this past summer, so I weekly take homemade jams, lemon curd, and chutney to the Tower since Nanny declares she cannot stomach the prison fare. I am, truthfully Fiona, quite worn thin with it all. But enough about my problems.

As I said in one of the earlier paragraphs, Nanny loved the snap—particularly she mentioned how adorable your daughter was—and insists on keeping it in her purse. I did take a searching look at your likeness, Fiona, and, though it doesn't at all match up with my preconceived image of you, you do seem quite pretty. It's interesting, isn't it, that writers—whom you think you get to know through their prose or poetry—very seldom look like you think they ought to look once you finally see them in person? You look like anything but a writer. A mother, yes—and a most attractive one at that.

And you would be attractive, wouldn't you, to be paired with such a partner as P.P.? I have studied his likeness (perhaps at too great a length, for he is exceptionally handsome), and I am left with the most persistent feeling that he might be a kindred spirit—for me as well as for you. Has he ever written anything? He has that aura about him—that nimbus of creativity—which characterises the imaginative soul. Simply put, Fiona, he looks like a writer ought to look. You must encourage him if he exhibits any leanings in this direction.

The children are just simply adorable. How I wish I myself had—well, I didn't choose to marry and parent, and so I must be about my business of writing and without any regrets. My books are my children, and I have certainly raised a large family, have I not? Nonetheless, when I look at you and Peter Paul—Fiona, I can candidly admit to you that

I'm jealous of the happiness which you two have found together.

Forgive me. I have rambled and maundered. But understand, my dear, I am racked with worry, and, with no time to proofread and edit it, my letter will have to stand as it is. As a matter of fact—

Fiona, the progress of this letter was just now interrupted by Hopkins—dear dependable Hopkins, my faithful major-domo—who brought me the latest medical bulletin from the Tower. (How could I, in the absence of Nanny, have ever managed Harlequin House without his aid?) My hands trembled as I perused it. The doctors have looked in on Nanny and have done all they can, but, poor soul, she languishes. In retrospect, I think it would have been far better for all parties involved in this wretched affair if I had implemented the "Buffy solution". Your Mother, Fiona, certainly had the right idea. I am numb from the anguish of it all. I am not thinking clearly.

17th April 1983

Well, Fiona, two days have now passed since I commenced writing this letter. Nanny's condition is unchanged, and her prognosis seems to be a State secret, for the doctors won't tell me a thing about it. The fact that her condition remains unchanged I interpret as an improvement; at least, the situation has not worsened. I myself have been abed—the doctor diagnosed it as nervous exhaustion—and have had, finally, a chance to read and critique the last pages you sent: Chapter Five of *Tempestuous Summer*.

I almost felt, again, as if I myself were actually there in Romania alongside Michael and Amanda, as charming a couple as were ever drawn on the pages of twentieth-century romance fiction. I could see myself standing by Ovid's statue in Ovidu Square, the wind whipping my kerchief about my ears. I could hear the washing of the waves and the screeching of the gulls. I could smell the salty sea air blown landward from the Black Sea as Mandy and Michael walked along the beach. Oh, Fiona, you have perfectly captured the ambience of it all, my dear.

And Dr. Sibescu certainly introduces an air of intrigue to the romance, does he not? He and his intentions are certainly mysterious. Why does he so wish to malign Michael? I have a suspicion, but first let me suggest that you should try to make him a bit more sinister.

Now, why does he find Michael so menacing? My guess is that he views him as a rival for the hand of Amanda. That may be hard for you to accept, but I'm left with the feeling that he might secretly be in love with Amanda and that he might feel threatened by Michael's presence. At any rate, he comes across to me as if he either loves her or, at the very least, desires her.

But I don't yet have the delicious feeling of menace that would add such a thrill to the story. If he were more sinister, this would make Amanda's position much more precarious. Perhaps Sibescu could have a bestial past that would terrify Mandy when she learned of it. On the other hand, maybe he does have Mandy's interest at heart; perhaps Michael is in the employ of the CIA. Who's to know? We'll just have to wait and see what develops.

I do love the last line of the chapter. It's what we in the trade call a "cliffhanger" sentence: "She had fallen in love . . . . but with whom had she fallen in love?"

I also very much like the French-fried-potato-choking scene in the restaurant. Such a perfectly natural thing to have happened. Such realism. I remember an occasion in Brighton, not all that far from The Royal Pavilion, at the most exquisite seaside restaurant where I was eating fish and chips. A rather longish chip became wedged in my windpipe, and—oh, well, suffice it to say, such things certainly do happen, and it's quite embarrassing when they do.

While there was much in this chapter I just simply adored, there also some material included which I found mildly objectionable. I simply cannot let pass without observation your comments concerning Michael's complexion. In one sentence (Chapter Five, p. 52), you describe him as being "tawny"—i.e., light brown to brownish orange. Then, in the very next sentence, you

207

use the word "mahogany"—i.e., moderate reddish brown.

Fiona, allow me to be exceptionally forthright here: make up your mind, and stop this vacillating! Establish a colour you can live with, and then settle on this one hue, once and for all. This is a cavil, but, nonetheless, it is a cavil worth mentioning, for you are dealing with a human being not some sort of Hawaiian chameleon. To be sure, this is a trifling objection over which I shan't make an issue.

There is, however, one other objection which I must voice and which is by no means minor. I feel very strongly about this matter, and, in all fairness to you and your audience, I must bring it to your attention no matter that the thought of having to discuss this subject with you makes my stomach queasy. I have avoided the mention of it until the close of my letter, for I needed the benefit of time to properly and charitably appraise my astonished disgust and word my response in a dispassionate manner. I was initially so disturbed by its tasteless inclusion in *Tempestuous Summer* that I put Chapter Five aside for a day and a half.

I am directing the foregoing remarks at the love scene—the one which describes Mandy and Michael's embrace at her front door after their dinner in Mamaia—which you, shame on you, Fiona, so obviously adored.

Fiona, your characters were not embracing one another. You were not describing a goodnight kiss. My dear, that description no more resembled a kiss than a meal of fish and chips purchased from a roadside vendor resembles Chateaubriand for two at Simpson's-in-the-Strand. Fiona, if you will pardon the directness of my remark, the goodnight kiss was—I shudder at the thought of it—a description of rape, pure and simple. I realise full well that both parties were fully clothed, and I know what effect you were attempting to elicit with the scene. (In fact, the effect educed was illicit.) But, Fiona, how could you have so forgot, so completely ignored, so blatantly violated, one of the basic tenets of romance fiction?

Why, the filthy language—all this "in-and-out, in-and-out" business—is obscene, and the mental picture I draw from your description is, pure and simple, pornographic. When reading this passage, I felt like a voyeur, and the furthest thing from our purpose is to pervert the reader's principles! It is quite obvious that the poor child's body is adrift in an emotional sea, no longer firmly anchored to the shores of morality by the chains of moral constraint, and that a wave of passion has engulfed her—her—her erogenous zones. (Forgive me!) A carnal surge has swept through Amanda's body and taken it "over the edge"—as one might say—and one never, never ever, becomes that descriptive. Lean more toward the fantasised romance, never the detailed, blow-by-blow description.

No, Fiona, you will have to either delete or rewrite this scene. Let Amanda fall in love. But under no circumstances can you allow her to be aroused beyond rapid breathing, or a blush, or a sigh, or a fleeting thought of what might transpire on her wedding night *after* her nuptials have been sanctified by the Church and licensed by the State and *after* she has become Mrs. Michael Kukiliko.

Now let me in no uncertain words set the record perfectly straight, so that you don't misunderstand what I have said and misinterpret what I have meant. I am—that is, the writer in me is—terribly offended by the explicitness of this scene. You have done a disservice to the genre and to your audience. We are writers of romance fiction not, as you Americans so indelicately put it, writers of "bodice rippers". And we are, my dearest Fiona, talking genre here.

However, the woman in me—I can say this, since we have become such bosom friends by post over these last months—the woman in me is excited, yet embarrassed, by the description. A good rule of thumb: don't let your readers know what tongues are doing; lips are quite adequate. Have I made myself perfectly clear? Fiona, I must say I'm shocked that you allowed P.P. to read it.

Except for the objections raised in the preceding three or four paragraphs, I should say that, on the whole, your novel is progressing extremely well. I have nothing further to say on the subject but write, write, write.

Fondly, but frantic over the fate of Nanny,
I remain, your friend,

June

June Featherstone

P.S. Oh, dear me, Fiona, I forgot to answer one of the central questions posed in
the letter attached to your latest installment. Of course it is acceptable for
your characters to wander about on their
own, free from your intrusive control. It
is at this point—when the characters break
the lead which has constrained them and,
free from your authorial dominion, run loose
hither, thither, and yon—that the book comes
alive for you. Why, after this happens,
writing the remainder of the novel becomes
no more difficult than boiling water. Just
follow Amanda, Michael, and Dr. Sibescu
about Romania. Watch their every move, and
then record their activities faithfully.
However, I must give you one bit of cau-
tionary advice: keep Michael on a tight
lead. Mandy is pure and *must* remain so.
Love. J.F.

April 25, 1983
2801 Hoosier Rd.
Centreville, IN 45480

Professor Gordon K. Douglas
Department of English Language and Literature
Warren House
Harvard University
Cambridge, MA 02138

Dear Gordy,

Here's the latest from June. (See letter dated on the IRS's happiest day.) She and Nanny both liked the snapshot. Great! I wonder how much they'd like it if they knew the truth: that Peter Paul was I and that the person whom they presumed to be Fiona was, in fact, the ogress Betty? Odd that June thinks I look like a writer—and a handsome one at that. Too bad she's not thirty years younger. If that were the case, I'd catch the next Concorde to London and wine, dine, and bed her before she could gasp, "God Save the Queen"—and with Nanny around, the Queen, God help her, needs all the support she can muster from any quarter. However, broke as I am, I couldn't even afford to take a Greyhound bus to Chicago's O'Hare to catch a connecting flight to New York's Kennedy. Ah, well, dream on, Young Man, dream on.

Gosh, I didn't think the love scene between Michael and Amanda was all that bad. Shit, nothing happened. They didn't make it to bed. Hell, he never even made it into the living room; in fact, he never got beyond the threshold for that matter. If anything, I thought the scene was too bland. It needed a little raw sex to spice it up.

But I'd better not forget whom I'm writing this book for. I'm trying to appeal to the taste of June and her readers, not my own, so I'd better tone it down somewhat. Can't ever forget your audience, or you're doomed and destined to fail. Henceforth, I'll really have to watch it closely.

Goddammit but she really gets carried away with her objections, doesn't she? That one sentence which began with Amanda's body being adrift on an emotional sea and which ended with its soggy remains being engulfed by waves of passion—whew! I thought poor June might actually drown in the soggy prose of her own extended metaphor and might never surface long enough to end her sentence with a period. She does get involved.

Nonetheless, her criticisms are all valid and germane if I want my writing to appeal to the type of readers who compose her vast audience. And her audience will be mine, or this whole nutty exercise is in vain. I've got to remember my audience. Would that Mandy and Mike could keep the reading public in mind and act with proper decorum, then I wouldn't have any problems.

Speaking of problems, what about June's? She must really be at her wit's end if she's entertaining the feasibility of the "Buffy solution" as a possible alternative therapy. Good Lord, I know how much Hortense Crimpet means to June, so the situation must indeed be drastically desperate.

But why in the hell haven't I read one thing about it in the newspapers or heard one word about it mentioned on radio? Why haven't I seen a special telecast, live from London, covering this bizarre event? I watch the evening news religiously, and neither NBC, nor CBS, nor ABC has yet to air the first word about it. Yet when a Cambridge homosexual in the employ of the British Intelligence Service is uncovered as a Moscow mole or when some high ranking minister in her Majesty's cabinet has an affair with a prostitute, the event's reported for days.

One would sure as shit think there might be more dramatic events to report that might make for better reading and more sensational headlines; for example, an attack upon the Queen in her private quarters; or a threat on the life of the Archbishop of Canterbury; or crude gestures directed at the photogenic Princess of Wales and the future king. Any one of these events is noteworthy and worthy of being noted by the press, yet not a word has yet been reported. Why are they trying to hush it up, and what powers wield such influence that they can keep these things under wraps?

It remains a mystery to me. I'd best stop worrying about June and Nanny. But I wish there was something I could do for them. I've actually grown quite fond of both of them: June with her generous advice and Nanny with her crazy antics. It's hard to believe that a year's almost passed by since I first wrote to them.

Time flies when you're having fun, right? Now it's time to turn my attention to Michael and Amanda and Dr. Sibescu. I wonder what sort of trouble those three are hatching up in Constanta?

It goes without saying—I know; I know. So why say it?—that I appreciate all the observations and remembrances you've been sending me about your stay in Romania. Thanks, and please keep them coming, no matter how trivial they might appear to you. One never knows what use Fiona will make of them.

Regards,

Joe

Joe Leonard

P.S. Should you ever get disillusioned with academe, don't give it up for a career hustling insurance.

encl.: Letter from June Featherstone to Fiona Pilgrim dated 15 April

June 6, 1983
2801 Hoosier Rd.
Centreville, IN 45480
U.S.A.

Ms. June Featherstone
Harlequin House
Silhouette Lane
Fensucked-on-Strand
Ely, Cambridgeshire
England

Dearest June,

Enclosed with this letter you will find Chapter VI of *Tempestuous Summer*. Let me share the following with you, my good friend: this chapter has been heart-rending to write. You shall find out why when you read it, but let me forewarn you: Amanda has been sorely mistreated by Michael, the unconscionable knave! I wish the whole sordid incident had never taken place, but it was all beyond my control. Michael just took off on his own accord, leaving poor Mandy stranded in Constanta. The philanderer trysted in Bucharest with a mysterious Miss Andrews, a woman who unexpectedly appeared from who knows where, who caught me completely off my guard, and whom I know absolutely nothing about. How she got into the story, I have no idea.

I, for one, was shocked when he did it, but I should have anticipated it: you know how men are and what absolute brutes they can be; you just can't trust them out of your sight. (Let me interject that I do, however, have absolute confidence in Peter Paul. In all the years we have been married, P.P. has never once given me cause to suspect that he might have broken, or let lapse, our conjugal vows.) I am anxious to hear your reaction to this latest turn of events. What do you suppose is Michael's real reason for being in Romania? How should Mandy respond to his cheating heart? Please

217

rush a reply, for I won't be able to begin Chapter VII till I hear from you.

Your last letter—dated April 15 and continued April 17—saddened me to the point of tears with its description of Nanny's deteriorated state. You can't blame the authorities, though, for reacting as they did what with everybody and his brother trying to assassinate a President here or taking a pot shot at a Pope there. What has the world come to? I do sincerely hope that, in the nearly two months which have lapsed since your most recent letter, Nanny has gotten a better grip on reality and that those in charge of the investigation have determined that it was all just a dreadful misunderstanding. (Do you realize, June, we've been corresponding now for over a year?) I pray for the old dear daily.

I'm just thrilled that both of you enjoyed the photo of the family. Perhaps you might reciprocate and send me a picture of you and Nanny together under a pleached arbor in the gardens at Harlequin House? Please do!

Your comments about me not looking the part of a writer disturbed me in the worst way. Do you think it possible that, as I mature and age, I'll begin to look more like a writer ought to look? Hemingway certainly looked more like a writer as he aged. (Why, both Mark Twain and Walt Whitman were the perfect pictures of what famous writers should look like. But who's ever seen a picture of a youthful Twain or Whitman? [Not that I'm equating my talents as a writer with theirs; I'm just making a general comment on the aging process.]) That's what I so liked about Hemingway. I thought his stories were so dreadfully boring and his characters' diction so unusually commonplace. Yet he had that writer's countenance, that noble visage that shouted out, "*I am an artist! Read me!*" He looked so much as he should have looked that I absolutely adored everything he wrote even though it was so uniformly awful.

You were way wide of the mark in your remarks about P.P. Why, he has difficulty writing out a grocery list, and he detests letter writing. He would struggle for hours over a two-line RSVP. Were it not for me and my letters, we would have lost touch long ago with all of our old friends who have moved away from the neighborhood. Why, I can't even get him to undersign the family Christmas card. Nonetheless, I'm so glad you found him attractive.

We also think the children are adorable. But what else could we think about the products of our union? However, it's so nice when others confirm our own opinions. We are very proud of our little clan.

You were right—yet once again!—when you registered your complaint about my description of Michael as being some sort of ". . . Hawaiian chameleon." Henceforth, I shall be careful to keep his color constant.

As regards to your other (major) objection—about what you termed the "rape" scene—I am mortified to think that I could have penned such a blatantly smutty episode. Of course, I had no idea at the time I was composing it that the scene was so smutty—so—so—well, it almost borders on the pornographic! Forgive me, June. Though its inclusion was thoroughly distasteful, I can assure you that I was totally innocent of willfully writing such obscene material.

In the foregoing paragraph, I referred to the scene in the past tense ". . . its inclusion *was* . . . ." because, once I realized what it was that I had written, I expurgated that entire section of the chapter immediately. I should not want my children to grow up and think that their mother wrote such filth or thought such thoughts. Not to mention how my association with writing so blatantly prurient in nature might affect my position as president of the PTA; I'd probably be recalled or impeached if it were ever to become part of the public record that I wrote such trash. Thanks so much for pointing this out to me and for saving me much embarrassment.

And speaking of embarrassment, I was—as were you—both embarrassed and excited when I reread the scene after you pointed out its meaning. I did discuss with P.P. both your letter and the episode which you found so offensive. He reddened when I told him how all this "in-and-out, in-and-out" business was interpreted by a writer of your stature. He was shocked—as was I that I could have written such material, material which he termed, ". . . suggestive and depraved . . . ." In fact, he was so repulsed by that which I had, *unbeknownst to me*, penned that we slept in separate beds for two weeks following your revelation. Since excising the scene from my manuscript, however, he has returned to sharing our double bed with me.

Let me close this letter by thanking you once again for all your past help. Your input into the process of writing my novel has been a godsend. I am eternally grateful, and I apologize, once more, for that horrible scene. *Mea culpa est*!

Ashamedly yours,

Fiona

Fiona Pilgrim

P.S. Please send us a picture of you and Nanny.

encl.: Chapter VI of *Tempestuous Summer—The Hottest Season*

Following the plans they had made the previous evening, Mandy and Michael met early the next morning and drove down the coast road to Mangalia. She felt so secure in his presence, so safe when he encircled her shoulder with his arm and drew her next to his hard body, so protected when he held her by the hand. She was, she was quite certain, in love. Yet she was also frightened, for she knew so little about the man whom she so deeply desired. And always there remained, like some soiled spot on a perfectly good blouse—a stain which stubbornly refused to be bleached away—the nagging doubts generated by Sibescu's admonition: Michael was not at all what he had initially appeared to be. If so, what then, or who then, was he? She didn't know.

And, as fate would have it, she knew no more about his background after their picnic outing that afternoon in Mangalia than she had known after their dinner at the Hotel Riviera the night before. There simply was neither a discreet means nor an appropriate manner by which she could broach this extremely sensitive subject. Nonetheless, while they were together, she enjoyed Michael's company immensely, and she got along famously with him.

In fact, they hit it off so well that, as the summer passed, they grew inseparable. She saw him every day without fail. During the working hours, Michael spent his time at the canal, trouble-shooting and problem-solving—at least that was what Mandy presumed he had been doing when he was absent from her; for all she actually

221

knew, Michael might just as well have been clandestinely meeting
with dissident Western sympathizers, plotting the overthrow of the
regime or the assassination of Ceausescu himself. Mandy, despite
Michael's presence in her life, did not change her work habits at all.
She carried on as usual, putting in eight to ten hours each day at
either the university or the Museum of History, compiling data and
cataloging facts relevant to her research subject. She was fast becoming ambivalent about her work, for she much preferred to occupy her time relaxing with Michael rather than researching Ovid.

They took all their evening meals together: he would either
take her out to dine or else she would prepare a light supper for him
at her home. Having discovered an outstanding restaurant—the
Casa cu lei (the House with the Lions), so named because the
cornice of its mansard roof was supported by four fluted columns
each of whose marble capitals was impressively sculpted in the
form of a lion—they went there so often that, by the end of the
summer, the maitre d' had assigned them their own special table at
which they were always seated. The couple's inexhaustible supply
of Marlboros and Kents had made them the restaurant's most welcome guests. The cuisine served within the *Casa cu lei* was as
noteworthy as the architectural excellence of the building's façade.
They loved eating there.

And it was so convenient, being located within a half a block of
both the Museum of History and the Roman mosaic and baths,
antiquities from the days of the Caesars. Mandy, the incurable romantic that she was, often dreamed that when Ovid first arrived
here in exile, his initial steps on foreign soil might very well have
been on these very marble chips which formed the figures and
background of the mosaic, for it had been—before the Black Sea
receded centuries after his arrival—the quay.

After dinner, Mandy and Michael would either walk along the
Black Sea coastline and the harbor jetties or visit the pleasant park
surrounding the White House, Constanta's city hall. The city hall
was a white, modernistic marble structure, and the citizenry jokingly referred to it as "the White House," after Washington, D.C.'s

most famous residence. Here at the park, finding an unoccupied bench and being surrounded by magnificent Greek and Roman artifacts, the two lovers would sit holding hands and soaking up culture. Amanda, contemplating the objects all about her, felt as though she had been sucked down into the vortex of time, and classical history was swirling about her on all sides in a dizzying cyclorama of that period's *objets d'art* (objects of artistic importance): before her were weathered friezes from the Periclean period; behind her were huge earthenware urns, twice as big as a man, in which the Romans had stored their oil; on both sides of her were toppled pillars in the Corinthian order, their acanthus-covered capitals severed as they fell and scattered some distance away from where the pillars themselves had come to rest. The park was steeped in history, and Mandy, happily sitting beside Michael and lost in thought, felt at times that she was but an inch away from communing with Ovid.

On other occasions, they went to a neighborhood café where they would drink wine, people-watch, and talk in nebulous terms about their futures. Some evenings, Amanda and Michael would simply remain at home, sitting on her balcony, drinking *Borsec* phosphates, and eavesdropping on the Romanian sailors who, on the street below, bartered and negotiated with the local women of easy virtue. As the night wore on, Amanda West and Michael Kukiliko would invariably find themselves standing on her balcony—her back against his massive chest, his arms around her tiny waist—looking seaward at the twinkling lights of the ships bobbing on the distant horizon as the vessels lined up to enter the harbor. It was a romantic summer!

Over the weekends, they would often leave Constanta—Michael at the wheel of his Dacia—and visit the scenic spots which Romania offered the tourist. Twice, they drove to Bucharest, a city so lushly full of lime and chestnut trees that Mandy—in the diary she kept detailing where she and Michael had gone and what they had seen there—couldn't make up her mind how to describe Bucharest.

Was it a city within a forest or a forest within a city? Whichever, it was a charming cityscape to be sure.

But Mandy was much more taken by the journey itself than by the end of the journey. The trunks of the trees which lined the highway between Constanta and the capital city had been painted white to a height of about five feet above ground level. (This had been done as a safety measure to aid drivers trying to negotiate the road at night.) Amanda—inveterate dreamer that she was—imagined that she was being escorted down a great reception hall, guarded on both sides by giant white-booted footmen, spaced at intervals of thirty to forty feet. She had seen nothing like this back home in Wisconsin.

One weekend, Michael drove far to the north to Iasi, the ancient capital of Moldavia. There they toured the seventeenth-century Church of the Three Hierarchs, a building justly famous throughout Romania for its elaborately carved gargoyles and statuary. That particular trip seemed to be one devoted to church going, for, from Iasi, they visited six or seven of the beautifully painted monasteries surrounding Sucevita.

However, the most memorable moment of that weekend was much more secular in nature. Michael had been driving down a poorly maintained secondary highway—for what seemed like hours to Mandy who was fast becoming nauseated as the Dacia swerved and pitched from one side of the road to the other, trying to avoid the craterous potholes which pitted its surface—when he suddenly announced that he was lost. Michael asked his navigator to check the next roadside marker they came upon for the name of the nearest village, and the number of kilometers to it. He needed the information, he told her, in order to locate the place name on his map and fix their position. The car rounded a sharp curve, narrowly averted plunging into a chuckhole that looked to Mandy as if it might be only a few feet shallower than the Mindanao Deep, and practically ran into a signpost bearing a very familiar name. They were about to enter the village of Borsec!

Michael hadn't been lost but had wished to surprise Mandy

with a visit to the springs from which bubbled forth their favorite mineral water, *Borsec*. What a wonderful time they had there!

Mandy's favorite trip by far that summer was the one to Brasov and the mountain resort of Poiana Brasov. Here the two wayfarers walked the flower-bordered paths and hiked the mountain trails. The Transylvanian Alps were all abloom and as beautiful as Amanda had imagined them to be. The happy couple picnicked in a mountain meadow colorfully filled with alternating patches of buttercups and bluebells.

On Sunday, rather than return to Constanta the way they had come, Michael decided to take a detour and travel to the town of Bran, site of Dracula's castle. The tour of the restored castle, with Michael at her side, was a mysteriously romantic adventure for Amanda West.

Oh, it was a marvelous time that summer. And the highly sensitive subject of them sharing the same room when they would overnight away from Constanta—the only issue which could have spoiled Amanda's pleasure in being Michael's traveling companion—never came up. Michael never so much as once placed her in a compromising position where she might feel uneasy, for he always gentlemanly reserved—in advance!—two single rooms.

The summer passed, and they grew to love Romania and each other, although neither of them had the courage yet to voice the depth of affection each had for the other. He never once attempted to be too forward, and she never once brought up his troubling past.

But Mandy's doubts about Michael remained and were reinforced every time she had any dealings with Dr. Sibescu. She saw him nearly daily at the university, and he was always most cordial, although in a coolly official sort of way. Yet on five separate occasions during that summer, he had come, from out of nowhere it seemed, upon Mandy and Michael together, and he positively glowered at them. They had run into him three times on the beach in Mamaia, once in Cluj-Napoca where they had journeyed to attend a folk-dance festival sponsored by the Performing Arts Department of the University at Cluj, and once in Bucharest. The meetings on the beach might possibly have been accidental, Mamaia being only four kilometers distant from Constanta. But the other two? Could they have been chance encounters at such a considerable distance from Constanta? Or had he been deliberately following them?

Amanda West had no alternative but to speculate about the possibility that Dr. Sibescu was shadowing her; if she gave voice to her suspicions and raised the question about how it had come to pass that he had so often come upon Michael and her, she risked alienating him. And she sorely needed his connections and patronage to carry on her research. Thus, for the duration of the summer, she wondered about Dr. Sibescu's motivation, but he gave her no further warnings about Michael and Michael's hostile intentions. He limited his conversations with her to discussions about the progress she was making with her research and with the monograph on Ovid she had begun to write.

Then, one weekend in early September, something singularly strange and untoward happened. Something happened that nearly broke her heart. Mandy had spent the most pleasant Friday evening with Michael, dancing at the Hotel Riviera and listening to the music of a jazz band, an anomaly behind the Iron Curtain where jazz was considered to be a sure sign of the decadence of Western society. On the way back to Constanta, they talked of nothing but their plans to get up early the next morning and drive to Tulcea where they would visit the Danube Delta, site of Europe's largest bird sanctuary. Michael had talked much over the summer about such an ornithological outing, but they had heretofore never been able to work it into their schedules. However, some of his associates at the canal project had told him that this particular Saturday would be an ideal time to visit the sanctuary because so many of the migratory birds would be using it as a roosting stopover.

Passionately embracing Mandy at her door, Michael excitedly declared, "Mandy, I just can't wait till tomorrow. You've no idea how much I'm looking forward to it. Ever since I first learned how to read, I've been nuts about birds. I don't know why. While all my playmates were reading *Winnie the Pooh* or *Uncle Remus*, I was fascinated by Peterson's *Field Guide to the Birds of North America.* Tomorrow's gonna be a great day, Miss Mandy: the chance for an unusually large number of sightings with you at my side— doing something I immensely enjoy with someone I enjoy immensely."

Mandy blushed and gushed, "It's amazing, Mike, but I too have—for the longest time now—been interested in birds. I hope the weather holds, and we register some unusual sightings."

Mandy heard herself saying these words, but she could scarcely believe she had, with a straight face, uttered them. If the truth were known to Michael, he would have been shocked. She had been allergic to birds since she was a small child. On the occasion of her fifth birthday, her older brother had saved up his allowance and had bought her a parakeet. Within a quarter of an hour of the bird's introduction to the household, Mandy broke out in hives, and the gift was returned posthaste to the pet shop whence it had come.

On another occasion, Amanda's parents had purchased a goose-down pillow for her canopied bed, and, from the very first moment she rested her tiny head upon it, she broke out in the most gruesome rash and came down with sneezing fits so violent that she bloodied her nose and ruined her bedspread. Consequently, she hated birds.

So while it was quite true that she could hardly wait for the advent of the morrow, her avian interest was no more than three or four hours old. Mandy had developed a fondness for birds about the same time that she found out that Michael had at last finalized his long-talked-about sightseeing, bird-watching expedition to the Danube Delta.

"Great! Me, too. I wouldn't miss it for the world. Goodnight, Miss Mandy. I fond you."

"You what?" Mandy questioned, thinking she had misheard him. Had Michael just said, "I found you"? Just what or who had been missing, and why hadn't she noticed its or his or her absence?

What or who is it that you have lost, she wondered "Did you just say, 'I found you'?" Mandy asked, perplexed.

"I said, 'I fond you.' Like saying I'm fond of you. But, come to think of it, I'm also very glad I found you and became so fond of you."

"Me, too, Mike. I fond you, too. Goodnight and sweet dreams."

Michael drew Amanda West into him and kissed her passionately on her lips and neck until she could hardly catch a breath, panting so heavily was she.

"Goodnight, Mike," she managed to moan.

"Goodnight, Mandy. Till tomorrow then." And, against her unvoiced wish, he left.

Amanda locked the door to her apartment, washed her face, undressed, slipped on her chiffon negligee, and retired for the evening, hoping to get a good night's sleep so she would be fresh for Saturday's trip.

Little more than an hour had passed when she was jarred from her sound sleep by the incessant jangle of the telephone.

"Hello? Who's there? Who is it? What time is it? Who is this?"

"Mandy. Hey, it's me, Mike. Look, I'm sorry to disturb you at such an ungodly late hour, but something's come up. I've just received an urgent call from Bucharest. I've got to meet—I've got to pick up—I've got to meet some people at 9:00 sharp tomorrow morning for an important meeting at the Intercontinental. I tried to postpone it but couldn't get out of it, couldn't reschedule it. I've no alternative but to cancel out on tomorrow's Danube trip. Forgive me, and give me a rain check on it. Okay?"

"Oh, sure, Mike. Okay. But I was really looking forward to it."

"As was I. Look, I'll make it up to you soon. I promise. I'll be back sometime Sunday evening. Let's make a date for a late dinner. Around 10:00 at the *Casa cu lei*. How's that sound?"

"Oh, okay. Sounds fine to me."

"Good. Mandy, I'm really sorry to have awakened you, but I've gotta be outta here soon and on the road if I'm to make that meeting in Bucharest by 9:00."

"Yeah. Sure. *Drum bun* [Have a safe trip]," Mandy said, lapsing momentarily into Romanian and using that tongue's expression to wish one a safe journey. She quickly caught her error, "I mean drive carefully. I'll miss you, Mike."

"I'll miss you too. And I'll be thinking of you all the while. Bye for now."

Then he hung up, and Mandy was alone with her thoughts and doubts. Why had he canceled their outing? If she had meant anything to him, could he not just as easily have canceled this meeting and have rescheduled it for sometime next week? After all, he had been waiting all summer to visit the Danube Delta. Why, scarcely a day had passed that he hadn't mentioned it.

And even if this meeting were as urgent as he had made it out to be, there wasn't any reason why he could not have asked her to accompany him to Bucharest. Was there? While he was attending his meeting at the Intercontinental, she could have visited the embassy, only a short block away. Even if it were Saturday and the embassy were closed, the Marine guards would be on duty. And a visit to the embassy would afford her the opportunity to chitchat with some other Americans, a rarity for her since no Americans, save Michael, lived in Constanta.

Or else she could have gone to the reading room of the American Library, only a block away from the Intercontinental in the opposite direction. She could have caught up on what had been happening between the covers of *Time* and *Newsweek*. Or she could simply have window-shopped to pass the time while the man she loved—Yes! She loved him, and she knew it!—attended his meeting.

But Michael had never so much as dropped even the slightest hint in this direction. Thus, he drove through the night—alone to Bucharest—while Amanda West fitfully tossed and turned, trying to figure out why, if he cared for her at all, he hadn't even had the common courtesy to invite her along.

The next day, Saturday, passed without incident. Although extremely tired and agitated from a night of lost sleep, she diverted herself from wondering and worrying about Michael by thinking about her other love, Ovid. She spent the entire day, and a good share of the early evening, at the university, reading old manuscripts and rewording some pivotal passages in the monograph she was writing. She returned to her apartment as dusk was darkening all Constanta. More than half expecting some word from Bucharest, she remained fixed to her phone till almost midnight so that she wouldn't miss his call. But the call never came.

Thoroughly exhausted from the previous night's lack of sleep and the research she had carried out that day, Mandy despairingly gave up hope of hearing from Michael and went to bed. She slept soundly, dreaming that she was snugly wrapped in her lover's encircling arms. He was kissing her passionately on her nape and massaging her shoulders with his massive hands when she was awakened from her dreams by a loud knock at her front door.

She squinted at the clock on the nightstand and vaguely perceived that it was 6:45 in the morning. The sun was already out and brightly shining. Michael, she knew, had returned to her, and it was the start of a new day in their relationship. She hastily threw on a terry-cloth bathrobe over her sheer, and quite revealing, negligee, knotted the sash, and rushed to the door. Without taking the usual precaution of peering through the Judas hole to ascertain who was calling, she unlocked the door and opened it.

"Oh, Mike. I've been so—" she ebulliently announced before realizing it wasn't Michael Kukiliko whom she was addressing. Rather, in his stead stood—impassive in a dull tan trench coat, looking every inch the part of the spy Mandy thought him to be—the sternly forbidding presence of Dr. Nikoli Sibescu.

Mandy gasped! She could not believe her eyes. Clutching the lapels of her robe tightly together so that the *décolletage* (plunging neckline) of her negligee would not be exposed to Dr. Sibescu's prying eyes, she fired a staccato barrage of questions at her visitor: "Good Lord, Dr. Sibescu! What in the world are you doing here at this hour of the morning? Has something happened to my mom or my dad? Is something wrong? Has there been an accident? Are my folks okay?"

"Miss West, forgive the intrusion. I apologize for disturbing your sleep. But I come on a matter of utmost importance which I have no desire to broadcast to everyone within earshot. Rather than share it with all of your neighbors on this floor, I suggest that you invite me in, so we can discuss it privately just between ourselves."

Mandy hesitated momentarily for she suspected how alluring she might appear, and she did not want to compromise herself or put to the test the stern moral code under which she had been raised. Yet, at the same time, she knew that Sibescu was a devoted scholar, and she suspected that all those years of reading, studying, and researching had dulled, to the point of atrophy, his carnal appetite. Thus she judged him to be no threat to either her virginity or her general well-being. "Forgive me. How rude of me. Come in. Please. Please forgive my appearance. I was expecting some— that is, I wasn't expecting you."

"To be sure. That is self-evident. You are disappointed to see me, no? Yet you would have been unreservedly happy had someone else been at the door rather than me. You make a mockery of the advice I have given you. You are constantly in the company of that individual who goes by the name of—"

"Just a darn minute!" Mandy vehemently interrupted her guest. She herself was shocked by her own spunkiness. "You're not my father, and I'm not a Romanian citizen. I don't have to seek your permission or obtain your approval when it comes to picking my friends—as long as they're not Romanian. I'll choose my own friends, and you have no right to butt in on my life! I'm an American, and so is Michael, and what we do is our own business—not yours. I don't have to have your okay to see another American." After venting her wrath in such an inhospitable manner, Mandy felt momentarily lightheaded. She paused, and Sibescu, not to be deterred in his mission, took immediate advantage of this caesura.

"Quite so. Quite so," he acknowledged. "I see I tread on extremely delicate ground here, on thin ice. But—how shall I phrase

231

this so you do not become offended—Miss West, I am concerned about you and your future in our beloved country. It seems that every time I see you, you are in this man's company." And as Dr. Sibescu uttered the words "this man's," he scowled ferociously.

Ignoring his scowl and feeling foolhardy and a little lightheaded, for she had not yet had either breakfast or coffee, she countered, "So what? Who cares? He's a wonderful man. I don't know what you've got against him."

"I? I have nothing personally against him. Just so long as he does nothing to jeopardize your position here and hinder the research you are doing. Incidentally, Miss West, just where is this 'wonderful man' of yours right now?" Sibescu sarcastically queried, as if to prove a point.

"In Bucharest," Mandy matter-of-factly answered.

"Ah. 'In Bucharest,' you say. And for what purpose, may I ask?"

"Yes, he's in Bucharest. He had an urgent meeting he had to attend. Why all these questions? Has something happened to him?" she frightfully asked, her brow now knit with anxious worry.

"No. Not to my knowledge. My questions are phrased in such a manner only to ascertain what information Mr. Kukiliko passed on to you about this alleged 'urgent meeting' of his. And the answers you have given certainly prove a point."

At this juncture in their conversation, Sibescu menacingly reached into the inside pocket of his raincoat, as if about to draw a concealed handgun he carried in his shoulder holster, and withdrew a somewhat bulky envelope. He continued, "You say this Kukiliko fellow had an urgent meeting to attend in Bucharest. I should say it must have been very urgent indeed—" And here he paused dramatically and eyed Amanda intensely, "if these are any proof of what prompted him to abandon you and rush off to Bucharest. I should very much like to read the minutes of this intimate meeting, Miss West."

And with a flourish worthy of a Shakespearean actor, he flung down upon the coffee table which separated him from Amanda the envelope he had taken from his coat pocket. Upon hitting the table, the contents of the envelope fanned out like a deck of dropped cards. Mandy could see at once that the envelope had been stuffed with photographs. In utter disbelief, she shuffled through them and, to her horror and disgust, discovered that each one was of the same two subjects in many different poses; yet all of the various poses had one feature in common: the people pictured in the photos were obviously very much in love. One member of the couple was unfamiliar to her: a beautifully photogenic young woman, strikingly Eurasian in looks. The woman's companion she recognized immediately: it was none other than Michael! Something caught in her throat, and she was unable to speak.

Sensing he had scored a victory, Sibescu broke the silence which had reigned since he had presented the incriminating evidence to Mandy. "My dear unfortunate Miss West, I warned you about this man and his unconscionable skullduggery. These disgusting pictures were taken yesterday at the airport and at the Intercontinental. You can see Mr. Kukiliko here, for example." And Dr. Sibescu pointed an accusatory finger at Michael. Mandy's vision was impaired by her tears, so she couldn't clearly see Michael's figure as pointed out by Sibescu. But she didn't need to see it, for she had seen far too much already. "Look how he is hugging and kissing this woman. And look here, in this one, they are dining together. So cozy and chummy they are. And, if you will excuse my impertinence, they shared the same room last night at the Intercontinental." And as a cruel afterthought, he added, "It was booked in her name."

As if stabbed in the heart, Mandy cried out, "Oh, no!" as she painfully studied his heartbreaking pictures. "It can't be. Are you sure? How did you get these pictures?" she sobbingly asked. Had she had her wits about her she would never have asked him such a blunt question, for she already knew the answer.

Sibescu, however, was not at all offended by her interrogation and forthrightly replied, "You know full well, Miss West, that, because of our history fending off the Ottoman Turks and Hapsburg

Teutons and because of our being a Latin island in the midst of a Slavic sea, we are a suspicious people. Our past has taught us to be wary of foreigners. So we keep a close watch on all visitors to Romania—be they Communists or Capitalists. And this friend of Mr. Kukiliko's is no exception. Her movements, like every other foreigner's, are kept track of. And because I am, as you already know from our previous conversations, in charge of security for the university, I have access to such information concerning the whereabouts of visitors to our region. And since Mr. Kukiliko unfortunately resides in the territory over which my office exercises jurisdiction, I had little difficulty obtaining these photographs. Does that answer your questions?"

"Yes. Yes," Amanda sniffled. "But who is she?"

"The woman in the picture registered at the Intercontinental as a Miss P. Andrews. She flew into Bucharest from Zurich late Friday evening and called—you needn't pretend you don't know how I know she called. Your phones are tapped, as you suspect, and we monitor every conversation. She called Mr. Kukiliko early Saturday morning to arrange for their, their—may I be indelicate and use the dirty word 'assignation'?"

The word made Mandy's heart skip several beats, she blinked twice, and two tears splashed onto the photographs dispersed about the coffee table. She bit her sensuous lower lip, hoping the pain might restore her equilibrium.

Dr. Sibescu continued, "And he ran to her the moment she snapped her fingers as if, please excuse the vulgarity of the metaphor, she were a bitch in heat, and he, a stud dog."

"Oh, no! It can't be! It can't be!" Amanda sobbed convulsively.

Dr. Sibescu rose from his chair opposite Amanda and sat down on the couch with her. "There, there, Miss West. You must be strong. Just be thankful that you have eluded this villain's grasp and found him out for what manner of man he is before it was too late. One cannot imagine for what evil ends he might have used—or abused—you."

Mandy, feeling betrayed by Michael, asked Sibescu, "Who is this girl? I mean, why is this P. Andrews woman in Bucharest? What brings her to Romania?"

"We do not yet know. I expect she is here on some covert mission. I would not be at all surprised if we discover that she is with your CIA. Perhaps she has just come to give Kukiliko—or whatever his real name is—his latest set of orders. She is probably just a messenger. I suspect this is the case, for she is not staying. In fact," and he looked at his watch as he said, "they are most probably breakfasting together at this very moment. They have to check out of the Intercontinental quite shortly, for she has reserved a seat on Swiss Air's 10:00 flight back to Zurich. So you can expect your friend—or may I take the liberty of referring to Kukiliko as your former friend—back here later this afternoon unless—" and Sibescu's voice grew heavy with sarcasm as he repeated, "—unless he has another urgent meeting."

With that remark ringing in her ears, she watched Dr. Sibescu rise from the couch and make ready to depart. "I am sorry, truly sorry, that I had to be the bearer of such bad tidings, Miss West, but—as the English aphorism goes—'forewarned is forearmed.' You are dealing with a devious character. Do not allow this man to take you in and make you out to be the fool."

Amanda, still sobbing, assured him that she wouldn't. "I won't. I won't. I won't. Oh, I've never been so miserable. Please leave me, Dr. Sibescu. I need to be alone to sort all this out," she said as she vacantly thumbed through the photos, all of which showed Michael in a happy state, kissing or embracing the beautiful Miss P. Andrews.

"Of course. Don't bother to escort me to the door. I shall let myself out. Good day, Miss West. I shall be in touch. And if you need anything, call me at home—I am listed in the book—or at the university. Good day."

"Good-bye, Dr. Sibescu," Amanda sobbed.

"How could Michael have so deceived me?" she muttered, as if in a daze. After spending the entire summer together, she felt that he had become her most faithful, her best, friend. But, Sibescu had just shown her irrefutable proof that Michael Kukiliko was a perfect stranger who couldn't be trusted out of her sight.

"Oh, I'll never, as long as I live, trust another man," she brokenheartedly proclaimed to the four walls of her living room as she desperately wrenched her sensuous lips and uttered a long and mournful sob.

By the time the sun was setting over the Black Sea that evening and dusk was rolling in with the waves, Amanda had sufficiently composed herself. Or so she thought. She had resolved to sever her relationship with Michael the minute he appeared, if the cad had the nerve to show his face again. *I must forget this dreadful man,* she brooded. *How could I have been so gullible? How could I have been so taken in by him? How could I have been so blind? To think of the amount of time I wasted this summer trying to build a meaningful relationship with him, and, all the while, he was waiting for his hussy to arrive with a new set of orders.*

Yet he treated me so well, and I enjoyed his company so much. How could he be so evil? Why didn't I detect something? I would never have suspected him of two-timing me. But pictures don't lie. Dr. Sibescu had him pegged right from the very first.

Her musing was interrupted by a sharp knock on the door, followed instantaneously by the ringing of her doorbell. Her heart jumped to her throat. Should she let him in and settle it all now, once and forever? Or should she sit there, waiting in silence and pretending she wasn't at home? She wanted to avoid a confrontation, but she knew that—sooner or later—she would have to have it out with him.

Reluctantly and with a shaky step, she approached the door and looked through the peephole. Although his figure was quite shrunken in stature, Amanda West immediately recognized the foreshortened stub of a man who stood in the middle of her peephole as the cause of all her anguish.

Gosh, he is a handsome devil though, she thought to herself.

She opened the door, and, as she did, he thrust at her a huge bouquet of fragrant cut-flowers, saying as he did, "Hey, Miss Mandy! Boy, did I ever miss you! Here's a small token of my affection for you."

And before she could reject his flowers or tell him to get out of her house and out of her life, she found herself once again encircled by his massive arms. However, this time she did not respond to his advances. Her guard was up! This time she was repulsed by his embrace and recoiled from his nearness, knowing that, less than twelve hours prior, those same arms had been hugging the attractive Miss P. Andrews. Within Michael's embrace, Amanda West now felt dirty and contagious, like a disease.

Michael sensed immediately that she was not as receptive to him as she had previously been. Amanda pushed him from her and coldly asked with an icy glare, "And how did your *meeting* in Bucharest go? I presume it wasn't too taxing. You look rested and well."

"My meeting—was—how shall I put it—my meeting was—" Michael fumbled, searching for the correct words, "—it was extremely productive. I shall tell you all about it in due course. But may I ask, Miss Mandy, why so sullen all of a sudden? I was hoping you would at least have been happy to see me. You've no idea how much I missed you."

Amanda, fully aware of how—and with whom—he had just passed the weekend in Bucharest, was angered by the brazenness of his words and stung by their manifest insincerity. She sharply retorted, "I've got a damn good idea just how much you missed me." And to herself she added, *You cheating lech, you.*

"Mandy, what's troubling you? Is something the matter?"

"Michael, *everything's* the matter. Please get out of here; leave me be."

"What ever is wrong, Mandy?"

"I don't want to discuss it, Michael," she sobbed. "Please, just leave me alone and let me be!" she shouted angrily through her tears.

"But can't we sit down like two rational human beings and discuss whatever it is that's bothering you so? There's got to be a logical explanation, I'm sure, for whatever it is that's got you so riled and so upset. Please confide in me, and perhaps I can help."

"Help? Help?" she gasped. "Oh, Michael, please leave this instant and take these with you. Give them to—give them to—give them to someone else." And on that angry note, she picked up the bouquet and threw it at him.

"Get out! Immediately! I never want to see you again!"

Michael was stunned speechless by this unexpected turn of events. He had no idea what could have caused Mandy to act in such a hostile manner. Trying to regain his composure and stumbling for the right combination of words that might bring some sort of understanding to that which he could only perceive to be an incomprehensible situation, he falteringly addressed her. "I— these—apparently—I see that you have no desire to be with me tonight. I have no earthly idea, Mandy, why you're acting so strangely all of a sudden; however, I have no recourse but to honor your wishes. If you change your mind and come to your senses, you know where to reach me. At the Victoria. Goodnight, Mandy. I'm sorry you find my company so offensive."

And with these words ringing in her ears like a death knell tolling the end of their relationship, Amanda West watched Michael Kukiliko turn away and depart her apartment. Left alone in silence, save for her heavy sobbing and labored breathing, Mandy began to ponder her future with or—more likely, it appeared—without him.

June 30, 1983
2801 Hoosier Rd.
Centreville, IN 45480

Professor Gordon K. Douglas
Department of English Language and Literature
Warren House
Harvard University
Cambridge, MA 02138

Dear Gordy,

Before I get to the heart of my letter, let me congratulate you heartily on your advancement from associate to full professor. Wonderful news! Who would have ever thunk it possible? I view your ascension to the uppermost rank of the professoriate at America's premier university as incontrovertible evidence of the deteriorating state of higher education in our country. Who have you been sleeping with on the promotions committee?

Seriously, Gordo, I couldn't be happier for you. Bravo! Now that I have sufficiently stroked your ego, let's focus on June and Fiona. Okay?

Well, here's Chapter VI. Another chapter finished and shipped off to June and Nanny. Wait till they get their hands on this latest installment. They should be intrigued by Michael's mysterious behavior. What a strange turn of events. From one page to the next, I have no idea what's going to happen to whom. I wonder who this mysterious Miss P. Andrews is, where she comes from, and how she fits into Michael's life?

Maybe Sibescu was right. Maybe Michael—the dirty no-good two-timing son of a bitch—is a spy and has, from their first meeting, deluded Amanda. Well, time will tell. At least the introduction of the beautiful P. Andrews supplies the story with the "other woman" whose inclusion June had, in her first letter to Fiona, so strongly insisted upon. Sibescu may not be so bad a person after all

239

and not nearly so far off the mark about Michael's deceitful character and questionable intentions as Mandy had at first thought.

It seems as though he was right about Michael. Shit, that surprises me no end. I thought Kukiliko was an okay sort of guy, and now he's apparently on the payroll of the CIA and messing around with this Andrews chick. No matter what Michael does hereafter, one thing's for certain: the rotten bastard has broken Amanda West's heart. I'd like to meet him in a dark alley some night and kick the living shit out of him. That would be fair payback for the way he has deceived Mandy, don't you think?

And all this has come about entirely by accident rather than by any conscious design on my part. What has happened thus far is exactly what should, according to June's plan, have happened: boy has met girl; girl has met boy; boy has fallen in love with girl; girl has fallen in love with boy; girl has suddenly, and for no apparent reason, been dumped by boy. Now all I've got to do is come up with some credible scenes so that the plot can progress, and the story can be finished according to the accepted formula; the two estranged lovers have to be reunited in such a manner that the girl sees it has all been a terrible misunderstanding. She has to discover that she has not been betrayed and that the boy has not been unfaithful to her. Their rapprochement can only lead to one thing: their union must be sanctioned by the State and sanctified by the Church so they can live happily ever after. Easier said than done. Got any ideas how I can pull this off, Gordy?

I'll bet June will have some good advice as to how Fiona should bring this all about. She seems to know far more about what my characters' next moves are going to be than do I. I'll just set aside the novel for several weeks—put it on the back burner and let it simmer for a while—until I hear some hot news from June.

Yours,

Joe Leonard

P.S. Should you ever get disillusioned with academe, don't give it up for a career hustling insurance.

encl.: Chapter VI of *Tempestuous Summer—The Hottest Season*

1st July 1983
Harlequin House
Silhouette Lane
Fensucked-on-Strand
Ely, Cambridgeshire
England

Mrs. Fiona Pilgrim
2801 Hoosier Rd.
Centreville, IN 45480
U.S.A.

My dearest Fiona,

I'll wager you're quite surprised to hear from me so shortly after having just sent off a packet. I received only yesterday the latest installment of *Tempestuous Summer* (Chapter Six) along with your letter of the sixth of June. I read both of them posthaste and felt—because of how close we have grown and because I am so concerned with your success—duty bound to respond immediately. I have, Fiona, much to say, some of which is, unfortunately, not of a pleasant nature.

Concerning the developments in *Tempestuous Summer*, I am—in a word—appalled. I am absolutely furious with Michael and these rakish shenanigans of his. Disgusting! How could he treat Amanda in such a debauched fashion? Why, the nerve of him to carry on in such a manner! How dare he do this to her when—on the surface, at least—he loved her so much? Is he completely bereft of moral fibre? The reprobate! I suspected, of course, that something was amiss when he so rashly cancelled the bird walk—deceitful scoundrel!—and flew off to Bucharest. But that he could be so—so—so debauched as to spend the night with that young woman, indeed that he could go straight from Amanda's arms to hers—well, Fiona, my first impulse was to throw the manuscript across the room, so angry was I!

I was, in fact, in such a pique that Hopkins had to personally attend to me. He brought me a cup of warm milk and honey so that I could rest. When I was a child, Nanny calmed me by dissolving a large dollop of honey in tepid milk.

I don't know what came over me. Perhaps it was the shock of it all: to think that a man I trusted could have been party to such a dastardly plot. I nearly burst into tears. This was most uncharacteristic of me, for I am, if I do say so myself, generally the very model of equanimity.

Of late though, my emotions have been in such a surge that the slightest provocation upsets me. I have noticed that, as I grow older, I have periods of deep melancholy. Perhaps the fact that I was in such a particularly deep funk might explain why Michael's treachery hit me with such force, the villain. I must cease this discussion at once, for I am again becoming overly agitated, and I might break out in a rash. Suffice it to say, I have registered my objection.

You have, at my urging, asked me all along

to aid you with the writing of *Tempestuous Summer*. And I have, as best I could, very willingly complied. To this point in time, it has been a joy for me to render you whatever help I could. However, in answer to your latest entreaty, I must reply with a resounding "*NO!*" No, Fiona, I cannot help you unravel this bizarre twist of plot. I am too incensed with Michael at the moment to offer you any sound, dispassionate guidance.

And this—objective counsel—is precisely what you need. The story has taken a turn for the worse, and you must either start afresh and find yourself a new hero, or you must somehow rectify Michael's unconscionable behaviour—and that may be well nigh impossible!

My sympathies are one-hundred percent with poor Amanda, whose broken sobs echo in my own chambers. If Michael is somehow to correct his wretched betrayal of this poor innocent and once again find himself in the good graces of Amanda, it's up to you, Fiona, to show him the way. (Such a redemption will be nothing short of miraculous!) I'll have nothing to do with him and his kind. Most probably, it will turn out that he has fooled us all: you; me; Nanny, who was quite taken with him prior to his liaison with this Miss P. Andrews, a strumpet (forgive me my intemperate use of language) who obviously suffers from a loose moral upbringing; Mandy; and even this benighted Miss P. Andrews creature who is apparently the latest to fall victim to his insincere line. I am convinced that he is one of those men one reads about who are so morally insolvent and ethically bankrupt that they are beyond saving and rehabilitation. I want nothing more to do with him.

As for Dr. Sibescu, why can't this love-lorn, jealous pip-squeak act the part of a real man and come out with it and declare that he wants Amanda? Short of employing a hit man to get rid of Michael, he's done all he can—the sneak—to break the two of them up, so it's obvious to the reader that Sibescu, too, loves her. In my present mood, I might almost wish her to accept him! It would serve Michael right and teach him a lesson he'd never forget, the lecher.

Excuse the impassioned diction in the foregoing several paragraphs, Fiona, but I am very angry. You can see, from my intemperate comments, my dear, how involved I have become in your story. If I knew Michael—if I should meet him now—I could barely be civil. In fact, I shouldn't be civil. I should give him such a tongue lashing that he would think twice the next time he decided to break a poor girl's heart. I demand complete honesty from those near and dear to me and will not tolerate a lie. If Michael has done what it seems he has done—how could it be otherwise? We have pictorial proof!—he should suffer horribly and prove himself worthy before Mandy can forgive him. If, indeed, she can ever find it in her broken heart to forgive him after what he has put her through.

I should have known—from the passion with which he kissed our pure Amanda and then left her, panting, at her door—that he was not what he at first appeared to be.

Enough of this talk of Michael and his duplicity! Let us have some happier tidings, a sea-change transition from bad news to good news. Brace yourself, Fiona! A miracle has happened! Our prayers have been answered. Our Nanny is free! How this came about would be the stuff of which a novel is made, but allow me to abridge it for you in this short letter.

You'll find what immediately follows almost beyond belief, but it has turned out that Nanny and the Archbishop of Canterbury—of all people!—the Most Reverend Thomas Cranmer, the very same personage she so viciously maligned and threatened to do away with, were romantically involved during the War! Yes, though hard to believe, it is true. He was a pilot in the RAF (that's the acronym for the Royal Air Force, Fiona), and she, a Wren (that's the acronym for Women's Royal Naval Service). They were, for over two years, assigned to the Supreme Headquarters Allied Expeditionary Force (SHAEF) staff in London and developed the deepest affinity for each other. However, after D-Day they were both reassigned to different duty stations.

Apparently, he was shot down and severely injured, suffering a brain concussion which resulted in a case of temporary amnesia. Recuperating in the hospital, he forgot all about his affection for, and commitment to, our dear Nanny, and he fell madly in love with the nurse who was attending him; they were married before his memory was fully restored.

While skimming the wedding announcements in *The Times*, Nanny found out about this *affaire de coeur* (a love affair) and was crushed. She resolved, then and there, never to open her heart to another man for fear of being left alone at the altar on her wedding day. (You can easily imagine how she feels about Michael and the duplicitous way he has beguiled Amanda!) Shortly after the war was over, she joined the staff at Harlequin House, and we have been her family ever since.

Well, Reverend Cranmer was widowed three years ago this coming September, and, from what I can piece together from disjointed conversations with Nanny—who remains at a great remove from her normal, coherent self— the warmth he once felt for Nanny had not entirely guttered out over the years. Upon hearing that a Hortense Crimpet was imprisoned, he investigated the matter, and a certain emotion was rekindled. He was shocked to find that she had been gaoled in the Tower, and he forced her immediate release— even scotched the news stories about her fracas with Her Majesty. Incredible, is it not?

He had his own physician see her, and she is fast becoming her old self once again—a delight to be around. It seems that she was allergic to the medication they had pre-

scribed for her, and now, but for an occasional lapse of memory which the Archbishop
finds charming, she is in fine health.

Fiona, the scene in the Tower when he
first came to see her would have brought
tears to your eyes. I dampened two handker-
chiefs myself. "Cranny!" she greeted him
warmly, recognising him immediately the moment he set foot in her cell. "Crimpey!" he
shouted in delight as he grinned and held
out his arms, dropping—in the process—his
crosier on the bare stones of her cell. It
made a frightful, clanging noise as it fell,
but, fortunately, it suffered no damage.

Very affecting it was. A lump forms in my
throat now as I write of it. He is to visit
Harlequin House next week, and Nanny is bul-
lying the cook and the gardeners (Michener
and Strickland, they of the green thumb) to
have all in order for his visit. One would
think the Queen of England herself were coming for a visit—a most unsettling contemplation considering the horrid consequences of
Her Majesty's last tête-à-tête with Nanny—
what with all of the lavish preparations
underway. We had to drive down to London
last week to visit Harrods. Nanny purchased
a new frock for the occasion.

I asked you earlier in this letter to
brace yourself for the good news about Nanny
and His Grace. I have even more good news,
so remain braced. Are you ready, my dear?
I'm coming to America! Are you shocked? It's
to do with the American rights, or something
of that nature, to one of my works. I leave

all these monetary and legal matters in the hands of my agent and my solicitor respectively. One of your American networks wants to film a miniseries—I believe that's what it is called—to be shown on the telly.

I know you're familiar with the novel they've selected. It's one of my favourites; it's the one in which the heroine, an heiress who has culinary ambitions, assumes the guise of a scullery maid and finds employment in the kitchen of a great manor house. After but a week amongst the pots and pans, she falls madly in love with the pastry chef. Her parents discover what has happened; they immediately threaten to disown her and to entail the manor house and entire estate to a distant relative in Australia if she continues to carry on any further with a man so beneath her station.

Her situation appears to be desperate, and her heart seems ready to be broken, for she is terribly in love. Just as it appears to her that their relationship is doomed, he reveals that he is actually a Lord in disguise who, much like her, also has culinary ambitions. The last chapter—the one in which they make from scratch, bake, and decorate their own wedding cake—always brings me to tears. Surely, you must remember it? *Love Among the Scones*.

A certain American writer from the South— my goodness, Fiona, but you do have such a plentiful crop of Southern writers, don't you? Why, they seem to spring up everywhere like mushrooms on a summer's day after a good warm rain. Is anyone outside the borders of the Confederacy literate? A certain American writer of questionable talent stole my title, changed the wording a bit, and, without so much as a word of acknowledgement or gratitude, appended it to—believe it or not—his erotic novel about (of all things!) eschatology!

Can you imagine the depraved mind that could—or, even worse, would want to—write a novel whose major themes are sexual desire and the end of the world? I'm sure you're probably saying to yourself, "That June; she's such a prude". Let me set the record straight. I'm not. I write for my audience, and he writes for his. All well and good. And I do so enjoy an occasional read in foreign territory *provided* the trip is worth the trouble.

Hence, I don't object to his story because it's so salacious; I find it so displeasing because the attempt to integrate the two disparate topics he's chosen to write about is quite clumsily handled, and the end result is, frankly, downright silly. Thank goodness he didn't give me any credit in his foreword. I should have been utterly abashed.

Although *Love Among the Scones* was panned by some critics—*The New York Times Book Review* had the nerve to refer to it as a "potboiler"—I never felt any of their half-baked criticisms were justified. I just loved the book and think it will make a smashingly good watch.

I shall be in New York on the third of

next month, and, if you will send me your telephone number (I insist upon it!), I'll ring you up. I shan't fly three thousand miles and miss the chance to talk with you, P.P., and the children. It shall be such fun, finally hearing your voice. I so look forward to it.

You will find, wrapped inside the square of tissue which I've enclosed with my letter, a likeness of myself in the rose garden with my dogs, Harlequin House's brace of Old English mastiffs. Our family has raised them since the fourteenth century. That's Alcuin to my right and Aethelred on my left. And yes, Fiona, that's I between them. I can easily anticipate your stunned reaction as you stare, mouth agape, at the photo: you are astounded, am I not correct? Yes, that is truly my likeness. You didn't expect it, did you? Allow me to explain what seems to you to be an impossibility.

You see, Fiona, when I penned *Sultry Heart*, my very first novel, I was but fifteenish and looked much too much the part of an ingénue to be producing a work of such mature nature. My publisher felt that my picture on the dust jacket would impede sales and would prove to be a disservice to my career. We had to have an older woman of serious visage whom the reader could take seriously. Thus, the paradox is resolved: the woman in the snap accompanying this letter is I, June Featherstone; the woman whom you see gracing the dust covers of all my novels is actually dear Hortense Crimpet, my

Nanny, standing in for me as she has always done since *Sultry Heart* was first published.

I suppose, once I came of age so to speak, I could have set the record straight. But I have always been so uneasy about publicity and so forth—while Nanny seemed to thrive on it—that we decided to do nothing about the impersonation. Over the passing years, I conducted every interview concerning my writing over the phone, and, on those rare occasions when my publisher begged me for a "photo-opportunity" session with the press, I've sent Nanny in my stead with the understanding that she is not to breathe a word about the nature of my art. A rather successful ruse Nanny and I have perpetrated over these many years, don't you agree, Fiona?

Now, perhaps, you can more readily understand why I was so distraught, so thoroughly beside myself, when she was not herself. I was sure that, if anything harmful had befallen her, I most certainly would have been unmasked—not to mention that I would have been utterly devastated without my dear old friend's companionship and our daily converse. I am unreservedly relieved that, in the battle for my stand-in's wits, a battle which pitted senility against sensibility, the latter has won a major victory with, if I might risk being irreverent, the divine intervention of the Archbishop of Canterbury.

I must close. Everyone is all abustle at Harlequin House, getting ready for the arrival of our distinguished guest.

Please send me your telephone number, or I shall be terribly disappointed when I arrive in your country. I wonder what you think of my likeness? We shall see.

As for Michael, that conniving miscreant, deal with him sternly, and don't tolerate any nonsense from him.

Fondly,

June

June Featherstone

encl.: Photo of Alcuin, Aethelred, and me

July 10, 1983
2801 Hoosier Rd.
Centreville, IN 45480

Professor Gordon K. Douglas
Department of English Language and Literature
Warren House
Harvard University
Cambridge, MA 02138

Dear Gordy,

Holy Shit! Never in a million years (and that's no exaggeration) would I have expected what has happened to have happened. Read June's letter of the first of July, and check out the picture she sent me. Can you believe it? Jesus Keerist! This June Featherstone is a real knockout. What a gorgeous woman: fantastic figure, covergirl face; a head of auburn hair so richly abundant that it might rival Rapunzel's. Looks to be about my age. What a catch she would be: beauty; brains; money; connections; a member of the landed gentry.

A catch for someone other than me, however. When she discovers how I've misled her, the shit is going to hit the proverbial fan. All of us—Fiona, Peter Paul, the twins and their sister, Michael, Amanda, Dr. Sibescu, and especially me—are going to become *personae non gratae*. We're all going to be vying for first place on her shitlist, no doubt about it.

Study that photo. Goddamn it, Gordy, but would this horny bastard like to bed her. Now. Today. Forget about the third of next month.

Shit, what a predicament I'm in. I've got no choice but to talk to her and come clean. And the minute I open my mouth, the masquerade will be all over. Once she establishes that she's been taken in and duped, she'll make certain that my chances of ever seeing *Tempestuous Summer* in print are nil. Null. Zero. Zip. Why, with the influence she commands, she'll have me blacklisted with every publishing house in the world. Shit, I probably couldn't even pay a vanity press to publish me now. My game is over; my goose, cooked. I'm ruined. Hear that flushing noise? That's the sound of my career going down the toilet.

Unless—unless one of two things happens. Fiona could develop a horrible case of laryngitis and be unable to speak to June. Peter Paul, functioning as her proxy, would then have to act the part of Fiona's spokesman for the duration of June's stay. I might just be able to pull it off, far-fetched though it sounds.

Or else I might simply spill the beans, apologize profusely for my dissimulation, and beg her to be compassionate and take pity on me. After all, I didn't devise this scheme to cheat or defraud her. All I was trying to do was to get her to use some of her connections to help me get something published.

I never meant her any bodily harm. Who would ever want to harm a body like that anyway? God, what a beauty she's turned out to be. Certainly a far cry from the grandmotherly Nanny Crimpet whom the world takes to be June. What a shock this has been. I'm nearly at a loss for words.

June, though, always seems to have an abundant supply of words at her disposal, doesn't she? And she certainly didn't exercise any restraint in using any of them when it came to her critique of Percy's *Love Among the Ruins*. This woman never ceases to amaze me. She's full of contradictions. From one moment to the next, I don't know what to expect. How can someone literate enough to be familiar with a (justifiably) obscure writer like Percy write pulp that's no more edifying than a Dell comic book? Let me rephrase that question: how can someone with my values sell insurance? I'd better pass on answering that last question lest this short missive, largely about June, becomes a lengthy tirade, solely about life— whole life, term life, and my life.

I've got to bring this letter to an abrupt close and start on Chapter VII. Time's running out on me; the clock is ticking, every second bringing me closer to my doom; the sand is sluicing through the neck of the hourglass. If I can finish one more chapter, then I can send it along with my next letter—probably my last letter—and try to squeeze one or two last bits of advice from her before this charade is over. Trouble is, she didn't give me too much advice about how to handle this weird state of affairs that seems to be developing in Constanta. She said, "No, Fiona . . . I'll have nothing to do with it . . . . As for Michael, that no-good miscreant, deal with him sternly, and don't tolerate any nonsense from him." Now that advice sure as shit wouldn't qualify as one whole hell of a lot of help in anybody's guide-to-writing-romance-novels instructional manual.

Perhaps this is the point in the story where the characters come "alive," and I'm supposed to sit back, take it easy, and record the actions of my characters as they work out their difficulties among themselves. No harm in trying. I don't even have the beginnings of a small notion as to how Michael and Amanda are going to patch this thing up and iron out their problems. So, I'll just stay out of their way and watch what develops. Gosh, I feel like a voyeur.

Yours,

Joe

Joe Leonard

P.S. Please return June's picture. I bought a cheap easel-back frame, and I'm going to insert the photo in it, put it on my writing desk, and let June be my muse.

P.P.S. Should you ever get disillusioned with academe, don't give it up for a career hustling insurance.

encl.: Picture of June and canine companions. Look at the size of those hounds. Each one appears to be about as big as a Clydesdale; letter from June Featherstone to Fiona Pilgrim dated July 1

July 21, 1983
2801 Hoosier Rd.
Centreville, IN 45480
U.S.A.

Ms. June Featherstone
Harlequin House
Silhouette Lane
Fensucked-on-Strand
Ely, Cambridgeshire
England

Dear June,

I am in receipt of your wonderful letter dated July 1. Thanks ever so much for the picture, June. I am thrilled that dear Nanny has recovered and is once again her old self. What wonderful news! I'll have much more to say about this shortly, but first I want to say a few words about the enclosed chapter (Chapter VII).

It's simply the strangest thing, June. For the longest time, not knowing what to do or where to begin, I stewed and stewed over Chapter VII and Michael's dastardly behavior. The only thought that kept recurring was your advice to deal sternly with Michael. Well, I just couldn't seem to get started; nothing seemed to click. I simply couldn't figure out how to reconcile Michael's disgusting behavior in Bucharest with the noble (feigned?) front he had presented to Mandy in Constanta. The only word that I could think of to describe his actions was "schizophrenic." It seemed to me to be an irresolvable mystery.

Then one day, without a forethought of what was about to happen, I sat down, determined to write something—no matter how badly it turned out. I started to write, and the result is Chapter VII.

It couldn't, even if I had planned it, have turned out any better. At least, I don't think it could have. You won't believe what happened. Of course, you'll find out soon enough when you read it, but

I'll let you in beforehand on a wonderful secret: the mysterious Miss P. Andrews is Michael's daughter! Yes, it's true! Michael is a widower, and he never was unfaithful to Mandy. I'm so happy for both of them.

I have no idea how Dr. Sibescu is going to react when he finds out that Michael and Amanda have, despite all his efforts to the contrary, been reunited. I hope he doesn't overreact and cause them any harm or make a nasty scene. I guess I'll have to wait until Chapter VIII to find out.

June, I'm simply mad about Chapter VII, and I wouldn't want to change a thing—unless, of course, you find something which you think needs changing. Come to think of it though, perhaps there is one thing I might change, and I'd like to hear your thoughts on the subject.

I'm not crazy about the manner by which Josie Kukiliko, Michael's first wife, has decided to exit the story. It sounds so silly a way to die even though—as I once told you, a similar incident actually occurred here in Indiana. My first thought was to have her buried beneath an avalanche at Zermatt or St. Moritz. But before I could do away with her in a fashion that I deemed plausible, Michael—the big blabbermouth—had to go and tell Amanda his own version of Josie's death. His loose tongue has undone all my plans, and now I'm stuck with Mrs. Kukiliko being submerged by some killer swan. It just sounds downright stupid to me. But if Michael and Amanda are comfortable with it, who am I to complain?

Please let me know what you think about all this. I gave them a free hand—just as you suggested—and, all in all, things seem to have sorted themselves out quite nicely, don't you think? Golly, but I hadn't intended to stray so far for so long from the subject with which I began my letter. Now, let me return to the good news about that wonderful friend of ours, Nanny.

I am touched beyond words that she has been reunited with her soul mate after so very many years apart. Who would have ever thought such a rapprochement possible? Would it be indiscreet of me to ask if I don't hear wedding bells ringing in the not-too-distant future? What a joy that they should find each other again after such a lengthy separation. It brings tears to my eyes; I'm so happy for both of them. And happy for you too, June, that, at long last, Nanny is, once again, Nanny.

Your description of their reunion in the Tower, after being apart for forty years, is equal to some of your most memorable prose. Perhaps you might some day write a story about "Cranny" and "Crimpey." (Aren't their pet names for each other just precious?) At their advanced ages, it would certainly be a story about "Love Among the Ruins."

Forgive me for being so flip; I thought I might try my hand at word play. And if the pun fails, it at least serves a useful end: it brings to mind your wonderful news about *Love Among the Scones*. You asked if I remember reading it. Would a practicing Catholic forget the name of the reigning Pope? Would a loyal subject of the Crown fail to recall the name of the ruling Monarch? Would a resident of the City of Seven Hills be unfamiliar with the lupine history of Romulus and Remus? Could anyone as familiar with your work as I am ever forget *Love Among the Scones*? The love scene amongst the pots and pans in the scullery is a classic. In my opinion, *Love Among the Scones* has always ranked as one of your best novels.

And to think that they are going to film it. Great! There is so much trash on our TV screens today that it's about time they honored you by showing your work as well. I can't wait till it's aired. I'll bet the Nielsen ratings will be at an all-time high for the time slot occupied by *Love Among the Scones*. I'm sure you're wondering what these Nielsen ratings are. A select group of people are polled to see what shows they have watched, and, from these figures, statisticians project how many TV sets in America are tuned in to a certain show: these projections are referred to as the Nielsen ratings. Golly, am I ever excited about the prospect of watching *Love Among the Scones*.

And I'm equally thrilled by the thought of us conversing with one another in less than three weeks. In fact, I'm literally dumbstruck by the prospect—a word or two of explanation will very shortly clarify the foregoing remark. You were absolutely correct about the effect your picture had on me. I could scarcely believe my eyes. What a prank you and Nanny have played on your public all these many years, you two tricksters.

I shared your picture with P.P.—we have no secrets between us—and, upon viewing your likeness, he remarked, "Boy, is she some knockout!" (That's an American expression which means he thinks you're extremely attractive.) And, indeed, you are exceptionally lovely. Time has been kind. Oh, June, I'm so excited. I can barely wait to hear from you.

You do realize, of course, with all the responsibilities of motherhood—the lunches to be made for the children; the laundry to be washed; the shirts to be ironed; the groceries to be purchased for the week's menus; et cetera—that it would be next to impossible for me to meet you personally in New York (although I can't think of anything that would please me more). I simply can't abandon P.P. and the children and dash off. Indiana is much more than an-afternoon-jaunt-in-the-auto from New York.

So, unless you can come to visit us—and I know that you could never work such a stopover to far-off Indiana into your busy schedule (Need I state the obvious? Undoubtedly, you know that you require no formal invitation to visit us, and you'll always find a warm welcome and a friendly smile at the Pilgrim home.)—we'll have to be satisfied with meeting one another over the phone rather than face-to-face.

And therein lies the problem, June. I stated above that, "I'm literally dumbstruck by the prospect" of conversing with you. I promised you then that I should soon clarify that remark, and now I shall. I have never before mentioned this to you—simply because I never before could envision that a situation could ever arise in our pen-pal relationship where the problem would present itself—but I suffer from a terrible affliction. I can write, as you well know, pages and pages of letters, but, when it comes to talking with someone over the phone, I'm like a recluse. Whenever I'm called upon to answer the phone, or to speak to someone on the phone, I become so extremely nervous that I develop the stutters to the point that I become unintelligible. And I know—as well as I know my own name—that, the minute I hear your voice, I'll be so nervous that I won't even be able to articulate the first syllable of the first word I want to say to you. (This is so embarrassing for me to tell you all of this.) So it may be that my darling Peter Paul will have to act, for want of a better word, or words, as our "intermediary" and "interpreter."

Despite my awful dread of speaking with you, I look forward to hearing from you very shortly. It is only because of your constructive suggestions and encouraging words, June, that I have been able to persevere and author *Tempestuous Summer*. I shall be eternally in your debt.

Fondly,

Fiona

Fiona Pilgrim

P.S. My phone number is 482-0304, and the area code is 765. My love to Nanny and the Reverend Cranmer. I'm crossing my fingers and praying for their future happiness.

P.P.S. I nearly forgot to remind you: if you would be so kind, please comment on Chapter VII before your departure for the States, and let me know how you think things are going with Amanda, Michael, and Sibescu. Except for Josie Kukiliko's unfortunate encounter with that pernicious bird, I'm just delighted with the way the story has unfolded. I'm so anxious to hear your reaction. Till the third, or thereabouts. F.P.

encl.: Chapter VII of *Tempestuous Summer—The Hottest Season*

The week following Michael's return to Constanta passed painfully slow, and Amanda West dreaded the start of each new day as much as she had hated the end of the previous one. During patches of fitful, hallucinatory sleep, she dreamed that it had all been a horrible mistake, that there was a logical explanation to account for Michael's inexcusable behavior, and that he was—in fact—an honorable man worthy of her love and devotion. In her sleep, she and Michael were just at that point in the marriage ceremony where the minister queries the congregation if anyone present knows why this couple should not be joined in Holy Matrimony. Without fail, just as she and Mike were about to become man and wife, Sibescu would come running down the aisle, waving a sheaf of photographs showing Michael and the mysterious Miss P. Andrews together in Bucharest.

Every startled eye in the church turned away from the altar and focused on the frenzied man who dashed down the aisle all the while repeatedly shouting, "This Kukiliko fellow is not what he seems to be!" It was always at this moment, like clockwork, that she woke up with a start every night, sobbing uncontrollably. And this same performance was repeated at least three to four times during the course of each night. The dream was like a badly edited 8-mm home movie of her wedding: every time she ran the detestable reel through her unconscious, the film broke on the same frame. She was fast becoming, she was convinced, an insomniac. Poor Amanda looked wan and dejected.

Her only escape during the waking hours was Ovid, and she plunged headlong into her research on him. The Monday which began the second full week of her life without Michael started out with a pleasant surprise: she made a major discovery which, she thought, might very well turn her short monograph into a lengthy book. This happy turn of events enlivened her spirits and—though melancholy and wistful—she once again began to sleep through the night without being awakened by Sibescu, sprinting down the aisle, littering pews, aisles, and the altar with his hated collection of photos, and shouting at the top of his voice, "This Kukiliko fellow is not what he seems to be!"

Yet, despite the fact that she was able to rid her dreams of him and sleep soundly now, she could not so easily dismiss Michael from her waking thoughts. She missed him terribly. Her heart ached for him, and her arms longed to hold him, and, in turn, she craved to be held by him. Twice, Mandy deliberately walked by the Victoria, secretly hoping that, by conscious design, she might accidentally meet him; but their paths never crossed. On one occasion, she thought she had spotted him driving by her office at the university, but she wasn't certain it was actually he. Michael had gone from her life but remained in her every thought—he was forever out of sight but never out of mind.

Quite the opposite, however, was the case with Dr. Sibescu. She thought not a thing about him except when the dream would recur, and he would interrupt her wedding—and her sleep. Yet he was there at the university every day, amiable and concerned. He spoke with her daily, never once bringing up the subject of Michael.

And the more she distanced herself—in space and in time— from Michael, the less frightening Sibescu appeared. He was, after all, a distinguished scholar of international renown, the head of her department, a major figure in the Communist Party, and an extremely attractive man, apparently of honorable intentions. She was not romantically drawn to him but—outside of Michael and her acquaintances at the American Embassy in Bucharest—he was the only friend, male or female, she had made in Romania. Their relationship was professional and platonic, and she no longer felt ill at ease when he would stop by her office to chat or when he would ask her to share his table in the faculty lounge for coffee or lunch. Perhaps, she began to think, she had misjudged Sibescu's intentions in the same manner that she had misinterpreted Michael's actions. *I have wronged Dr. Sibescu,* she reflected, and she resolved to be kinder to him.

Three weeks had passed since that fateful day when Michael was unmasked, and his true character was revealed to her. The pain was becoming bearable. One morning, while in her office, Mandy was interrupted by a knock. Looking up from her desk, she was somewhat surprised to discover Dr. Sibescu who, pushing the door ajar, politely inquired, "Good morning, Miss West. I hope I am not disturbing you. May I come in? I thought I would drop by and pay you a short courtesy call. I hope I have not interrupted you in the middle of anything important."

"No. No, not at all. Do come in. Please. I'm glad to see a friendly face. I was just collecting my thoughts. What can I do for you?"

"Miss West, do you recall last year—about this same time it was—when the rector dismissed all those students attending the university and cancelled all classes for a fortnight so that the students would be free to join the farmers in the fields to help harvest the grapes?"

Mandy nodded her assent that she did.

"Well, the rector has dismissed the students next week to help gather this year's vintage. And since there will be no classes next week, and the teaching faculty have no obligations which must be met, we have rented a bus, and we shall all—as a group; all of your colleagues in the department, myself included—travel to Bran in Transylvania and visit the castle of Vlad Tepes."

At the mention of the place, Bran, and the name, Vlad Tepes, Mandy's heart skipped a beat. Prince Vlad, or Vlad the Impaler, was Romania's greatest folk hero, having impaled over 15,000 of the hated occupiers, the Ottoman Turks. The Romanians referred to him as Vlad Tepes, but in the West he was known as Dracula. And it was in Transylvania, at Castle Dracula, that she had spent, less than two months ago, a most happy time with her Michael. Her eyes watered and several tears trickled down her cheeks, but she displayed little other evidence of the stinging hurt the memory gave her.

She listened impassively as Sibescu continued, "Although we— I mean we, the Department of Romance Languages—have never before extended invitations to any of the visiting professors or researchers from the West to join one of our faculty outings, we feel that you have brought so much honor and recognition to the department and to the university with the work you have already done on Ovid that it would be our privilege to have you join our excursion. Everyone is going. May we count you in, Miss West?"

Mandy's immediate reaction to Sibescu's proposal was entirely negative. She was sickened at the suggestion of returning to a place which was so closely associated with the memory of her happy times with Michael. Personally, she abhorred the prospect of going back to Castle Dracula, but there were other considerations—professional ones—that had to be measured before she rejected Sibescu's offer out of hand. Everyone on the faculty had been, officially, so helpful to her since she had come to Constanta; yet, socially, they had shunned her as if she were some sort of Capitalist pariah. Now, for the first time in over a year, she had been asked to join one of the department's social activities. To decline the invitation would be a slap in the face, not only to Sibescu but also to every other member of the faculty as well.

"Yes," she haltingly replied. "Yes, Dr. Sibescu. I'd be more than happy to join you. I'd be delighted to come. I think it should be loads of fun."

"Good. Then it is settled. We leave punctually from the university, Friday, October the second, at 5:00 a.m. An early start, to be sure, but it is a long trip to Transylvania. The kitchen staff is preparing box lunches, so you need not bring anything but your camera and film—and, oh yes, a sweater or jacket, for the mountain air can be very brisk this time of year."

"Okay. Thanks, Dr. Sibescu. I need a break. It'll be good to get away for a while. Forget about Ovid and Constanta and things. It might be just what the doctor ordered."

The time intervening between the day Sibescu extended his invitation and the date of departure passed without incident: although she walked by the Hotel Victoria seven times, she never once saw his car or bumped into him.

Soon October the second was upon her, and she arrived at the university, not knowing how she would be treated by her associates. However, it mattered little how they acted toward her, for she had come to view this trip as a matter of will and strength, something to be gotten through rather than enjoyed—an obligation met. She realized she could not allow the course of her life to be dictated by her past or by "what-might-have-been" had not Michael been such a cheat and a libertine.

Any reservations she had about the faculty not accepting her into their number were dispelled immediately upon entering the bus. She was warmly received by everyone, like a dear friend or favorite relative welcomed after a long absence. She was delighted by how amiable and friendly they all were. Throughout the length of the trip, they laughed, sang Romanian folk songs, told humorous stories, played practical jokes, and gossiped about faculty members in other departments.

She was enjoying herself so fully that she nearly forgot about Michael until the bus came to a halt in the parking lot at the base of a steep hill, atop of which perched the sprawling wings of Castle Bran. The sight of the building—the aging granite walls of the fortification, growing against all laws of gravity from the sheer cliffs, and the turreted battlement and keep, distinctively roofed in red clay tiles—jarred her memory, triggering recollections of her visit here with Michael in a happier time when the prospect of a shared future with the man of her dreams seemed imminent. She suddenly became quite dispirited as she mulled over the last time she had visited here.

No one, however, noticed her change in mood, for everyone was busy making ready to leave the bus and tour the castle. Sibescu, ever the administrator and chairman of the Department, was herding people off the bus and pointing them in the direction of the main entrance. He ushered Amanda to the door, thus interrupting her melancholy musing.

"Miss West. We are here. Is it not glorious: the setting, the woodlands, the meadows, the mountains, the weather? Could it be more beautiful? I must attend to some minor details: matters concerning admittance to the castle and tariffs. Please join one of the guided tours or wander about on your own. Whatever suits you."

"Thanks, Dr. Sibescu. I think I'll just walk around and take a self-guided tour. Earlier this summer, a friend—I—what I mean is that, earlier this summer, in Constanta, my friend bought me a book which has a map and illustrations and all kinds of interesting information about the castle. I'll just wander about on my own and see what I can discover."

"Fine, Miss West. As you wish. We shall certainly bump into each other eventually. If not, I shall see you around lunch. We are all meeting back at the bus around 2:00 for a bite to eat. Enjoy yourself."

Amanda thanked him and proceeded to take a self-guided tour of the castle, a tour she had taken less than two months previous. However, at that happier time in her life, it had been an escorted tour, and her guide had been a most handsome fellow.

She was standing alongside a parapet, minding her own business, just daydreaming and looking out across the wooded slopes of the Transylvanian foothills. As was often the case, Mandy was thinking of Michael when her reverie was suddenly shattered by an infectious laugh and an English—perhaps even American—voice. Surprised to hear her native tongue spoken in this remote corner of Romania, she quickly turned around to see just what sort of tourists would be visiting such an out-of-the-way spot as Castle Dracula.

Amanda West could not have been more stunned had it been

Count Dracula himself who had found a visit to Castle Bran so hilarious. In fact, the sight that greeted her eyes so shocked her that she almost lost her balance and nearly fell over the parapet to a certain death hundreds of feet below on the jagged crags of a rocky gorge. The laughing young woman who found life so amusing was holding on to the arm of her escort, someone Amanda West knew far too well! It was Michael Kukiliko himself. In the flesh!

Mandy's first impulse was to run and hide. Her second was to rush up behind Michael and his date before they had discovered her presence and push both of them over the guard rail into the bailey far below. *Oh, this is too cruel of him, the beast*, she thought to herself.

How could he bring this girl, to this place, when, only two months ago, he and I had spent such a wonderful time here together? Perhaps he has a certain itinerary he follows, and he takes every woman he plans to seduce to each place on his route.

She hated him; she loved him. She wanted to push Miss P. Whateverhernamewas over the parapet. She wished she had never come.

Upon turning the corner of the wooden rampart, Michael had spotted Amanda immediately. With the woman clinging to his arm, he eagerly approached Amanda. He smiled engagingly and addressed her warmly, "Why, Amanda. Amanda West. What a small world! What a coincidence! Of all people, you're the last person in the world I expected to meet here."

Amanda silently replied, *I bet I am, you womanizing Lothario. Perhaps if we overnight here for several days we might run into some of the other women you've dragged up here under false pretenses, you philandering creep. Gee, all we need is one more of your former lovers, and we'd have enough for a bridge foursome: you, me, P. Andrews, and whomever else it is that you've misled.*

Michael effusively continued, "Mandy, I'm so very happy to see you again. You're looking just as beautiful as ever."

Amanda could not believe he could be so brazen: to pay her a compliment such as that while his latest conquest was standing there, hanging on his arm and on his every word, looking up at him adoringly and smiling benignly as if everything were pure innocence, and they were all just one big, happy family.

"Amanda, how are you? God, but I've missed you so! How have you been?" Michael inquired as though he genuinely cared for her.

"Just great, Michael. Just simply great," she glared, throwing daggers at him with her eyes. "Aren't you going to introduce me to your friend?" And she barked out the words, "your friend," as she gave both of them a dirty look.

Michael, suddenly discomfited, reddened and stammered, "Ah—ahem—we—um—yes—of course—how rude of me. Ah—well, it's a long story, Mandy—but—but—yes, where to begin?"

He paused as he put his arm around the beautiful woman whom he was escorting and drew her close to him, kissing her on the forehead as he did. The audacious nerve of the man! Amanda could not believe his insensitivity. As likely as not, he knew very well how much she had once cared for him. And now, right in front of her, he was embracing the woman who had supplanted her in his affections. She wanted to push both of them over the parapet. She could not believe that any man could be so brazenly immoral, so inhumanly unkind, to act in such a manner. She curled and bit her sensuous underlip to steady her emotions.

Michael, stammering and hugging his companion, continued awkwardly searching for the correct words, "Ah—yes—well, what should I say? How to phrase it? I wanted to tell you about this under entirely different circumstances, but the opportunity just never presented itself. And then you became so angry with me that—that—that—well, Mandy, enough of this hemming and hawing. I'd like you to meet my daughter, Pam Andrews."

"Your what?" Amanda blurted out in stunned disbelief.

"My daughter." Michael laughed at the bewildered expression

on Mandy's face and hugged Pam, again giving her a fatherly kiss on her forehead.

"Pammy, this is Mandy West. I think I might have mentioned her name once or twice."

" 'Once or twice'? " Pam laughingly replied as, in the European manner, she offered Amanda her hand.

"Mandy, Dad's done nothing but talk about you and sing your praises since I saw him in Bucharest a month ago and since I came back yesterday. On the way up here, I told him, 'Dad, for God's sake, change the subject, will you please? I'm getting sick and tired of hearing nothing but Mandy this and Mandy that.'

"But seriously, Mandy," Pam smiled, "I'm really happy to meet you." And with that Pam stopped shaking Amanda's hand and warmly embraced her father's dumbfounded friend.

Amanda West knew not what to say. She wanted to explain then and there to Michael what had transpired in her mind and what she had thought he had done behind her back, but she couldn't find the right words. She felt horribly bad that she had not given him the opportunity to explain just what had been going on in Sibescu's ostensibly incriminating photos. She stood there silently for several seconds, which seemed like several minutes, and then managed to return Pam's warm greeting.

"Oh, Pam. I'm just delighted to meet you," Amanda said.

"Amanda," Michael interjected, "There's a logical explanation for all this. Believe me, there is. There's a logical explanation for everything: the fact that I have a daughter; the fact that I never told you anything about her; the fact that I hid her existence from you; the fact that I never even mentioned to you that I had been previously married. But here, obviously, is not the place to discuss it. Why don't the three of us go down into Bran to the *Café Stefan cel Mare* for lunch? I'll try, as best I can, to clarify everything for you. I hear they serve excellent *sarmale* there."

And at the mention of *"sarmale,"* Michael turned to his daughter and addressed her. "That's something you're going to really love, Pammy. It's a Romanian specialty: delicately seasoned ground meat cooked and then wrapped in vine leaves and served with a gravy made from *smantana*, the best sour cream in all the world. Absolutely delicious. Guaranteed to please even the most discriminating of palates. It's on me, girls. What say we adjourn to the *Café Stefan cel Mare* for lunch?"

And with Pam on one arm and Mandy, nearly exploding with happiness, on the other, Michael led them down the graveled footpath to the restaurant. After they had finished a superb meal of *sarmale*, accompanied by an excellent Pinot Murfatlar, Michael made amends to Amanda and made sense out of what she had considered to be his inexplicable, caddish behavior.

"Mandy," he began, "for the longest time—from the first moment I set eyes on you—I've wanted to bring up the subject of Pam and my other children, but the opportunity never—"

Amanda, unable to contain her shock, interrupted him. " 'Other children'? You have other children?" she gasped.

"Yes. Quite. I've a son, Joey, who's now fifteen, and a baby boy, Alexander—well, he's not so much of a baby any more, but he's the youngest in the family. Alex just turned seven last month. As a matter of fact, I was home for the last two weeks helping him celebrate his birthday. Both the boys are enrolled at the American School in Lugano, Switzerland. All this will make much more sense to you as I relate the story in its entirety.

"Where was I? Oh, yes. I've wanted to tell you, for the longest time, all about my past because I intend—at least I intended before you became so angered with me several weeks ago—I intended for you to share my future, so you had to be made aware of my past." And, with these words he reached across the table, took her hand in his, and gently squeezed it.

"Mandy, I have been evasive about my past for only one reason: a terrible tragedy occurred in my life. And, quite naturally, it generated much sorrow, sympathy, pity—you understand what I am saying, no? Well, every time it was brought up, people—friends or strangers—began to feel sorry for me. I did not want to become the object of everyone's pity. I wanted people to value my friendship and either like me or dislike me on the basis of my worth as a human being and not base their feelings toward me on the fact that something terrible had happened. I didn't need people's sympathy; I needed their friendship based on my ability to be a friend and to satisfy a certain person's needs or wants. Do you understand the point I am trying to make?"

"Yeah. Sort of," Mandy replied, simply exuberant to be once again in his presence.

"Well, if my past experience served me as a dependable gauge to forecast how you would most probably have reacted when you found out about what had happened, I knew that you would only feel sympathy towards me. And this was certainly not the emotion I wished to engender when I was intent upon building a lasting relationship. At least, that's my opinion. So I wanted you to like me for me and for no other reason."

"Oh, I do, Mike. I really do."

"Well, you can't imagine how happy it makes me to hear that, Mandy. So all the truth is now out. That's why I didn't tell you previously about Pam and her brothers."

"But where—" Mandy hesitated for a moment, searching for a discreet way to word her question. "—where is their mother? I assume she—she's—no longer with them?"

"That's quite true. Tragically, their mother passed away over four years ago, and time has, finally, healed the wounds although the children—and, of course, I too—miss her horribly much.

"As you already know, my family has, among many other interests and investments, several hotels on Waikiki Beach. Josie, my wife, and I had gone to Europe on a buying trip for the hotels. Additionally, we were redoing the family chateau in St. Moritz, and she had gone on alone to the town of Bruges in Belgium—it's famous for the quality of its handcrafted lace—to order from the nuns in the convent there some lace curtains and a matching tablecloth for the chateau's dining-room table. I had finished my business in Brussels, and we had agreed to rendezvous in Ghent which is about halfway between Bruges and Brussels.

"It was here in Ghent that I received the bad news. Apparently, she had finished her business with the nuns and had decided to rent a rowboat to pass the time of day until my arrival. She had purchased several loaves of bread and was rowing about the canals, feeding the ducks and the swans. I am told she inadvertently rowed between a pen minding her cygnets and the cob. Suddenly separated from his family, the cob—ill-natured things they are even without provocation—attacked her boat. She lost her balance, fell overboard, and, with the nasty beast flogging her with his huge wings and pecking at her with his large beak, she drowned. Even under the best of circumstances, she had never been a strong swimmer. She always hated the surf."

Amanda squeezed his hand, and a tear rolled down her cheek as she said, "Oh, you poor dear man. What you must have gone through. What pain you've endured. And the children, motherless."

"Yes. Well it was hard on us all. But children are resilient, and one does have his memories to sustain him in hard times. In any event, after her death, I simply closed up the houses in Hawaii and in the States and moved into the chateau to be near the children. I've got a very trustworthy friend who runs the hotels and plantations and other investments for me, so I rarely go back to Hawaii.

"But, I could see that I was fast becoming a prisoner of the chateau and that it was most unhealthy for me to lead such a solitary life. So I decided last May that, if I were ever to mend, I could not remain inactive. I decided to stop brooding, and I contacted the firm I had been employed by before I inherited the family businesses. They rehired me and sent me here to help design the canal project. And it's the best thing that ever happened to me, Amanda West, for I met you."

Amanda smiled at him, squeezed his hand once again, and replied, "Thanks, Mike. I feel the same about you. Gosh, this is all so—so—well, I guess it all makes a sad sort of sense. But what about Pam?"

"What about Pam?" Michael asked.

"Yeah, what about me?" Pam echoed.

"Well, Mike, I know the boys are enrolled in a boarding school. But what about—" and Amanda turned and directed her question at Michael's lovely daughter who had been silent throughout Michael's recounting of her mother's death, "—you? How did you get down here, and how come your name's not Kukiliko?"

Pam answered immediately. "Oh. Well, that's easy to explain. I'm enrolled at the American Fashion College of Switzerland in Lucerne. I'm gonna be a high-fashion model someday—at least I hope I am. I go to school Monday through Thursday; then, if I luck out, I'm able to line up some modeling jobs on Fridays and the weekends. When I was down here last month visiting Dad, I was on assignment for *Vogue*. They're doing a photo shoot, a huge spread on European folk dress, and I got the chance to model some lovely handmade Romanian blouses—and a chance to see my dad.

"As far as my name's concerned—well, that's also easy to explain. You can see by looking at me that I'm half Hawaiian-half Caucasian. Mom's maiden name was Andrews. She came from an old family in England. I don't know if you've been to England, Mandy, but Mom's family is well-known in Bedfordshire and Lincolnshire. Anyway, I thought 'Andrews' sounded a lot more dignified than 'Kukiliko.' "

At this point in her conversation with Mandy, Pam turned to her father and winked at him, saying "No offense, Dad."

"None taken, Honey."

She then redirected her remarks to Amanda. "So I took my mother's maiden name, hoping that if it didn't help my career, it certainly wouldn't hinder it like 'Kukiliko' might have. Don't you honestly think, Mandy, that 'Andrews' sounds a lot more sophisticated—more professional—than 'Kukiliko?' "

"I suppose so. Although I don't think there's a thing wrong with the name 'Kukiliko,' " Mandy said, as she thought of herself as Mrs. Amanda Kukiliko. "I kind of like the sound of it."

"Well I told you I'd attempt to explain everything to your satisfaction," said Michael. "Have I succeeded?"

Mandy hesitated momentarily but realized a better opportunity

277

would probably never again present itself. "You've answered all my questions, Michael, except one."

"And what might that be, Miss Mandy?" Michael responded.

"Michael," Mandy said, as she looked at him adoringly, "you've told me why you acted the way you did. Now I'll tell you why I was so angry with you—although I can see now that I had no right to be angry—when you canceled our visit to the Danube Bird Sanctuary. On that Sunday morning, while you were taking Pam from the Intercontinental to the airport, Dr. Sibescu visited me. He showed me pictures of you and Pam, pictures taken when you greeted her at the airport that Saturday and then other shots taken later in the day at the Intercontinental. Of course, at the time I had no idea who this mysterious Miss P. Andrews was, and I was crushed that—from the evidence Sibescu laid before me—you had rejected me in favor of another wo—"

Michael heatedly interrupted Mandy to voice an objection. "Whoa! Mandy! Wait! Stop! There's no other woman. There's never been any other woman. And there never will be any other woman."

"Oh, Mike. I know that. Now. I feel just terrible about the way I acted, not giving you even half a chance to explain yourself. I know how you feel, and, with all my heart, I believe you. But I didn't know it then. And not knowing that Pam was your daughter, I think my reaction was quite normal. So when Sibescu showed me picture after picture of you with your arm wrapped around this very attractive woman, I was devastated.

"But, you see, Mike, that wasn't the first time Dr. Sibescu had spoken to me about you. When you first arrived in Constanta, he took me aside and took me into his confidence. He warned me about seeing you. He told me you weren't what you appeared to be. In fact, he came right out and told me you were with the CIA. I must know the truth, Mike."

Amanda, hoping Michael would respond to this information with a vehement denial, paused briefly. But he said nothing. There was nothing left for Amanda to do but put into words the one question which had caused her so much consternation since Sibescu admonished her about Michael's cloak-and-dagger past. "I must know the truth, Mike. Are you, or are you not, with the CIA?"

Michael laughed at the suggestion and shook his head from side to side. "No, of course not, Mandy. How ridiculous. Of course, even if I were connected with the CIA, I'd be duty bound to deny any association with them. But I swear to you that I'm not with them, have never so much as been approached by them, and don't think I'm of any use to them."

"Oh, Mike. I'm so relieved—and so pleased. And so happy."

"Me, too," Michael said.

Pam interrupted their discussion and questioned, "Why do you suppose this Sibescu fellow fed Mandy all this phony information about you, Dad? Something's rather strange here, I'd say."

"Beats me," Mandy answered. "But you're right about one thing, Pam. It's all awfully strange."

"I don't know," Michael said, determinedly. "But I'll tell you one thing, Miss Mandy. I'm not one to sit around and stew about things. Let's track this guy down, confront him, and find out what's troubling him."

"Oh, Mike, I don't want to cause a scene. I don't wanna—I can't afford to—offend him. He's crucial to the success of my research. You've got to handle him with kid gloves lest he become upset and take out his anger on me. Without his patronage, I wouldn't be able to have access to half of the documents I need to carry out my research."

"Believe me, Mandy, I'll act with restraint. But we've got to get to the bottom of this, once and for all. I just wanna find out why he's got his heart set on turning you against me. Leave a pack of Kents on the table, if you would, please—small token of thanks for excellent service and fine food. Let's find Sibescu."

And on those words Michael paid for the lunch, Mandy left a pack of Kents on the table, and they all left the *Café Stefan cel Mare,* searching for Sibescu and the answer to the question which evaded them all: Why did Nikoli Sibescu so hate Michael Kukiliko?

25th July 1983
Harlequin House
Silhouette Lane
Fensucked-on-Strand
Ely, Cambridgeshire
England

Mrs. Fiona Pilgrim
2801 Hoosier Rd.
Centreville, IN 45480
U.S.A.

My dear good friend,

I have just received in this morning's post your note of 21 July, accompanied by Chapter Seven of *Tempestuous Summer*. I'm afraid that, if I don't sit down and respond immediately, both letter and novel might get set aside and lost in all the commotion, for turmoil reigns supreme at Harlequin House! I'm in such an absolute muddle, preparing for the trip. Believe you me, things are all topsy-turvy here.

Fiona, I am on pins and needles waiting for the time to pass. I can scarcely believe that, in scant more than a week, I shall be in the Colonies. My dear, I want you to know that I am as excited about meeting you as I am about the filming of *Love Among the Scones*. And when I write—as I have written in the preceding sentence—"meeting you", I mean precisely what I have written. My use of that particular construction is quite deliber-

ate. I have decided—perhaps impetuously—to
fly to Indiana.

Yes, it's true! After reading about your
problem vis-à-vis phone conversations, I
promptly determined that, after the negotiations were completed, and after I had
approved the script, I should fly directly
from New York to Indiana and meet you face
to face. I should be done with my business
in New York by 6th August at the latest, and
I shall visit with you thereabouts—assuming
of course that my decision meets with your
approval.

Since you will have no time to respond,
one way or the other, to my proposal, I
shall call you—or rather, I shall call and
speak with Peter Paul—when I arrive in New
York. I feel quite confident that you are as
eagerly looking forward to meeting me as I
am to meeting you, but I should never have
been so ill-mannered and presumptuous as to
force myself on another person and arrive at
her door, unannounced and uninvited as it
were. However, in your letter of 21st July,
you so graciously wrote, ". . . you know
that you require no formal invitation to
visit us, and you'll always find a warm
welcome and a friendly smile at the Pilgrim
home".

Well, the sincerity of those words trig-
gered in me the most intense desire to actually look you directly in the eye and see
for myself the friendly smiles of the Pilgrim family and experience firsthand your
proffered "warm welcome". Prior to the re-

ceipt of your offer, I should never have considered paying someone a visit sans a formal invitation. But, once I received your lovely letter, I felt as though I were a prodigal sister returning home to her family after a lengthy absence. So, Fiona, I am taking you up on your most generous offer, and I do so much look forward to setting eyes upon you, Peter Paul, Priscilla, and the twins.

There. That's over and done with. Now to your letter and Chapter Seven of that delightfully good read, *Tempestuous Summer—The Hottest Season*. I am not at all sure I trust Michael's "logical explanation". It may all seem quite logical to a schemer like him, but, as far as I'm concerned, it requires a giant leap of faith for me to believe the man. His story is too facile—too tidy. All the pieces of this bizarre puzzle fall into place a bit too easily for my liking.

That woman, whom he *claims* to be his daughter, seems far too attractive and fawningly devoted. If this situation were occurring in the real world rather than in the fictive world of romance fiction, I should immediately demand a blood-typing test and DNA sequencing to establish consanguinity in order to validate his claim!

And do you really think a quintessentially capitalistic magazine like *Vogue* would run a story about Communist folk dress? How could Pam, or whatever her name is, be on assignment for *Vogue* when she hadn't yet graduated from the American Fashion College of Switzerland—if there even exists such an institution? In fact, don't fashion colleges teach the basics of *haute couture* (high fashion or fashionable attire for women) rather than modelling? I am of the opinion that Michael followed Amanda to the castle to get back in her good graces and, with wily cunning, invented his family for her.

That his wife's boat should be swamped by some overprotective, territorial swan and that Mrs. Kukiliko should submissively sink to the bottom of some lake or canal—these seem to me to be bold-faced lies designed to gain the jilted Mandy's sympathy. I simply can't accept these sorts of villainous fabrications! Just how gullible does he take Mandy to be? Didn't anyone hear Josie's cries and come to her aid? Was not the boat equipped with life jackets? Why didn't she repulse the creature and bash him about his head with an oar? You tell me Michael feels "comfortable" with his wife's unlikely demise. Well, I don't. It sounds downright idiotic to me—and dirty, too, for it immediately brings to mind that sodomite, Leda—and I can tell you unequivocally that I should be absolutely humiliated to ever pass away in such a ridiculous manner.

Because of the reservations just voiced, I'm not as prone as are you to so readily accept Michael's "logical explanation" and to so easily forgive his behaviour. Of course, it is your book, and he is your character, so it's up to you, finally, to present him to the reader as hero or villain.

And, at least in the first draft of *Tempestuous Summer,* you've obviously decided to make him out to be a hero. Well, I disagree. I'm in agreement with Sibescu. I think Michael Kukiliko is a CIA operative and is, with typical American self-righteousness, involved in some secret mission bent on overthrowing the Communist regime. (Forgive the reproachful nature of the foregoing remark, Fiona, but the whole world is quite familiar with your country's penchant for meddling and mischief-making.) But when he's not plotting some sort of *coup d'état* (the overthrow of a government in power by a cabal of erstwhile governing officials), he devotes his spare time to "playing around" with poor Amanda's heart.

I'm sorry, Fiona. I love the plot, the setting, your writing in general, and your depiction of Amanda West in particular. But Michael Kukiliko is not the man we first thought him to be, and I can't believe Amanda doesn't see through him.

Of course, I could be wrong. You and Amanda could be right. Michael could actually be everything he presented himself to be in Chapter Seven. We shall have to wait until Chapter Eight, and the final confrontation with Dr. Sibescu, to find out which of us is right.

Before moving on to another subject, allow me to raise one other objection concerning Chapter Seven. While I adored the scene

at the parapet, I thought it was a bit too
abbreviated. Thus far in *Tempestuous Summer*
(An excellent first draft, by the bye; what
a good story we shall have when we revise
it!) you've not had—as far as I can recall—
a *FLEEING*-and-*FAINTING* scene, a staple of
the genre.

Perhaps in your next rewrite, you could
arrange it so that Amanda could come across
Michael so suddenly and so unexpectedly that
his presence would send a shiver of terror
throughout her entire body. She, startled,
could gasp; he could approach her, perhaps
even menacingly; she could turn away in despair and disbelief and bolt (*FLEE*) down the
nearest steps, desperately trying to escape
his hated presence; he could pursue her; she
could then catch her heel on the stairs,
tripping just as he was about to grab her,
and strike her head on a handy ledge, falling into unconsciousness (*FAINT*); he, of
course, could blame himself for any injuries
she sustained and could be kissing her hair
and murmuring incoherently to her when she
awakens; she could moan lightly and flutter
her lashes.

This sort of treatment would punish the
philandering Kukiliko and cause him much
more anguish than he has presently suffered.
In short, Amanda should have the opportunity
to make the brute suffer *before* she forgives
him. Now this sort of episode would make for
a jolly good read. Think about it, Fiona.

Once you've finished the first draft and
rewritten it—incorporating in the revision,

I should hope, many of my suggestions—I'm quite sure I'll have very little difficulty placing *Tempestuous Summer* with a publisher, perhaps even my very own. We shall discuss this, and your next chapter, when we meet, perhaps over tea and biscuits. (Can one purchase McVitie's Digestive Biscuits in the States? Or should I bring along my own supply? Do you have a grocer in your part of Indiana that sells Twinings Earl Grey tea, the proper loose-leaf variety not the tea-bag variety that you Americans use?)

Do you, perchance, make rhubarb pies, Fiona? I have read of them and often wondered how one would put together a pastry such as that. (*Love Among the Scones*, you certainly must have guessed, reflects my culinary leanings.) Perhaps, if you are so inclined, we might share some favourite recipes. We shall see.

Regarding your reticence, I have but one comment: nonsense. You'll see that it will be fine. I do, of course, want to meet and talk with the children and P.P., but it is the heart of the writer (you, Fiona Pilgrim) that I have come to know and trust. I look forward to meeting you in the flesh as much as I have so thoroughly enjoyed meeting you through these correspondences of ours. I shall call and speak with Peter Paul once my travel plans are finally settled. I warn you, Fiona, I shan't be put off.

Now let me turn my attention to matters of a more personal nature. In regards to your question about the possibility of forthcoming nuptials between our Nanny and the Reverend Cranmer, let me say that the prospect of an exchange of vows appears remarkably favourable, indeed imminent. Thomas—His Grace insists we address him by his first name—has been our house guest here for over a week, and the two of them are inseparable. They stroll, arm in arm, through the gardens, cooing sweet nothings into each other's ears. (Actually, they are both stone deaf, so there is much more shouting and screaming than cooing going on during their perambulations.)

It's adorable to see them, acting as if they were two love-smitten teenagers with eyes for no one else in the world but each other. When they are not walking, they sit, hour upon hour, in one of the gazebos: he reading his missal; she doing her petit point. They are as charming a couple as I have ever seen. Nanny has never been happier. It seems life for her, as well as for all of us, is ever changing.

Well, dearest Fiona, this has probably been the shortest letter I've yet penned, but, since we'll be meeting one another within a fortnight, I don't feel as though I've slighted you. Besides, you've grown so much professionally since you first wrote to me that you barely need any help or direction from me at all. In any event, we shall very shortly have a very lengthy tête-à-tête. In the meantime, continue to write and, perhaps by the time we visit, you'll have brought *Tempestuous Summer* to a successful conclusion. Until the week of third through eleventh August?

Your dear friend,

June

June Featherstone

P.S. My dear Fiona, I have no wish to end this letter on a sour note, but I must voice a comment—call it a rather frivolous observation—concerning a sentence you penned in your letter of 21st July, a sentence about which Nanny was absolutely choleric. Truth to tell, I have not seen her so beside herself since she was incarcerated in the Tower. I calmed her down by telling her that you could not possibly have foreseen that the sentence could be read as she had interpreted it and that you certainly meant no ill intent. You wrote, "There is so much trash on our TV screens today that it's about time they honoured you by showing your work as well". You do see how this sentence lends itself to misinterpretation? Yours, J.F.

August l, 1983
2801 Hoosier Rd.
Centreville, IN 45480

Professor Gordon K. Douglas
Department of English Language and Literature
Warren House
Harvard University
Cambridge, MA 02138

Dear Gordy,

Read the enclosed letter dated July 25. It requires little comment except *she is coming here!* In person! To meet me! Or rather to meet Fiona Pilgrim. It's midnight, Gordy. The masquerade ball is over, and I'm about to be unmasked. The princess who June thinks has authored *Tempestuous Summer* will shortly be exposed for what she truly is: a pauper, a deceptive scribbler who pushes insurance for a living while misrepresenting himself as housewife and homebody, Fiona Pilgrim.

I wonder if there isn't some way I could do away with June's pen pal? Then June could meet the bereaved widower and console him in his hour of sorrow. Perhaps Fiona could be buried under tons of snow in an avalanche; I recall June was especially fond of the avalanche as a jet-set *coup de grace*. But I can't credibly rid myself of her in this manner since there are no mountains worth speaking of in Indiana and no snow in August.

Had I not already used the killer swan as a vehicle to carry off Michael's wife into the Great Unknown, I might have employed him to do away with Fiona. That at least makes some sort of perverted biological sense: employing a love-crazed swan to get rid of a pen pal. Ha! In case you were sleeping, Gordy, I just penned a fine pun, the "pen" being a "female swan." (This is no time for punning. My whole literary career is at stake. Got any ideas how to save it?) No, the swan's been used already. And once is enough.

Indeed, once may even have been far, far too much. The swans are out.

There must be some way to kill Fiona that's socially acceptable and that will credibly remove her from the scene. Isn't there? With Fiona's death, Peter Paul would be free to fall in love with June, marry her, return to England and become Peter Paul I, Duke of Harlequin House, and live happily ever after. I'd be palatially ensconced in Harlequin House, but, sooner or later, June would notice that I'd forgotten to bring the children with me. How should I account for the fact, except for a horrible lapse of memory, that I'd left Fiona's babies back in Indiana, apparently orphaned by the death of their mother and abandoned by the departure of their father?

But I'd miss them and feel guilty as hell about abandoning them to pursue my own selfish ends. Not to mention that, the first month I missed sending the child-support payment, Betty would have Harlequin House surrounded. We'd be besieged by hoards of child-welfare authorities. The minute my deadbeat ass emerged from my castle, and I showed my face, they'd throw me in jail—or "gaol," as June would write—before I could say, "The support check's in the mail!"

I had better stop this damn daydreaming and get back to *Tempestuous Summer*. I've got to resolve the conflict between Michael and Sibescu and bring the story to a happy ending. And I've got to find some way to placate what will soon be an extremely angry June Featherstone. That'll take a miracle.

A miracle? Hey, perhaps I could pray to St. Jude, patron saint of lost causes. And if ever a cause were lost, Gordy, that would be mine; I could ask him to intercede with whoever's doling out miracles and ask that individual to send one my way. Only through some sort of heavenly intercession will June ever be able to forgive me for deceiving her so. Maybe she'll still help me find a publisher (one lives in hope). I'd best bust my ass and have something to show her just in case such a miracle does happen. Pray for me.

Yours,

[signature: Joe]

Joe Leonard

P.S. What do you make of the "we's" in the following sentence? "An excellent first draft, by the bye; what a good story *we* shall have when *we* revise it!"? Do you think they're friendly, collaborative "we's"? Or do you think June is about to appropriate my novel and publish it under her own name? God, am I to be screwed once again by a woman? First Betty; now June?

P.P.S. Should you ever get disillusioned with academe, don't give it up for a career hustling insurance.

encl.: Letter from June Featherstone to Fiona Pilgrim dated July 25

August 5, 1983
2801 Hoosier Rd.
Centreville, IN 45480

Professor Gordon K. Douglas
Department of English Language and Literature
Warren House
Harvard University
Cambridge, MA 02138

Dear Gordy,

Well, I've finished *Tempestuous Summer* (enclosed, find the final chapter). *Gloria in excelsis! Ete missares.* The ending is so saccharine and syrupy that the FDA might force the publisher to affix a warning label on the dust jacket forbidding diabetics to read it. Certainly Weight Watchers will put it at the top of its list of most-fattening books for the calorie-conscious reader. It's that sweet.

Nonetheless, I had to end it in this manner for to do otherwise would have been inconsistent with the dictates of the genre. I've followed June's advice to the letter to the very end of this ridiculous exercise.

Speaking of June, she was right about one thing: Sibescu. Come to think of it, she's been right about many things. Say what you will about her subject matter, you've got to give her credit: she's a very percep-tive person with a prescient gift. Turns out, just as June had suspected all along, Sibescu had the hots for Mandy and lusted after her but didn't have the guts to put his feelings into words—the age-old Miles Standish-courtship syndrome. He finally developed a guilty conscience and confessed everything to her. Michael never was with the CIA, and the whole story Sibescu told Mandy was a complete fabrication, made up by him to keep Mandy from falling in love with Michael.

And while I'm on the subject of fabrications, your favorite cor-respondent is about to be caught, shamefacedly, in the *BIG LIE.* June called last night from New York. She sounded awfully nice, and, much to my surprise, awfully sexy. We chatted for over half an hour.

Of course all this time she thought that I was P.P. speaking for the dumbstruck Fiona who had been rendered speechless by the call.

The negotiations have been completed, and she's already approved the scriptwriters' adaptation of *Love Among the Scones*. We talked much about this, and I promised to relay our conversation word for word to Fiona who, in June's mind, remains very much alive. I'm at my wit's end, trying to come up with a credible way to destroy my pseudonym before June arrives on the scene.

That's right, Gordo, she's coming. Here. To Nowheresville, Indiana. On the seventh. I told her we'd love to put her up, but graciously, thank the Lord, she declined, saying she'd rather stay at a motel. I've made reservations for her at the local Holiday Inn. Of course, in my heart of (lustful) hearts, I'd like nothing better than to have her stay with us so that I might have carnal knowledge of her. But she's going to be so pissed when she finds out how I've tricked her that—well, the imagination blenches at the thought of the vengeance she might wreak upon me and my manly appendage. Heaven has no rage like love to hatred turned, / Nor hell a fury like a woman hoodwinked into believing that she's been corresponding with Fiona Pilgrim rather than Joe Leonard.

I must close this letter and return to the business at hand: I've got to think of some plausible way to kill Fiona.

Homicidally yours,

Joe

Joe Leonard

P.S. Should you ever get disillusioned with academe, don't give it up for a career hustling insurance.

encl.: Chapter VIII of *Tempestuous Summer—The Hottest Season*

The question preoccupying Amanda West's mind as Michael escorted her and Pam back to Castle Bran was just how would Dr. Sibescu react when he discovered her in the company of Michael Kukiliko and Miss P. Andrews, a woman whom Dr. Sibescu had (mistakenly) believed to be Michael's mistress? Amanda knew that somehow she had to avoid a confrontation between the two men, for she needed both of them. She loved Michael very much, yet, in a much different manner, she also loved Ovid.

And it had only been through the intercession and good offices of the influential Dr. Nikoli Sibescu that she had obtained access to most of the documents and Ovidian memorabilia which had enabled her to make the remarkable progress she had thus far made with her research. He had intervened on her behalf: said a few words to the archivists who kept watch over the Ovidian Collection at the university and at the museum.

Thus, despite the fact that she was as anxious as was Michael to discover why Sibescu was so intent on breaking them up, she knew—come what may—that she had to serve as a mediator between Michael and Sibescu in order to preserve her professional relationship with the latter as she pursued her emotional relationship with the former.

They arrived at the large, asphalted car park at the foot of Castle Bran where the bus from the university had parked. Sibescu, his back partially turned away from them, was busily checking over the roster, marking off the names of those who had already boarded the bus. Absorbed in his task, he did not notice the presence of the three Americans until they were almost upon him.

He turned around and, obviously caught off guard, fragmentally stammered, "Ah—well—yes—indeed—"

Then he coughed nervously several times as if clearing his throat. "Ah, it seems, Miss West, that you have found some friends here at Castle Bran." And as he made these remarks and regained his composure, he sneered at them, gritting his teeth as if firmly setting them for some horrible confrontation of Armageddon proportions.

Amanda shuddered and winced. She felt a knot tightening in her stomach. An altercation had to be avoided! She feigned, as best she could, equanimity and acted as though there was nothing at all out of the ordinary. Very civilly she replied, "Yes. Quite a surprise, isn't it? You already know, Dr. Sibescu, my old friend, Michael Kukiliko," and she nodded in Michael's direction as she uttered these words.

"And this"—and at this point, Amanda West dramatically paused, made an introductory gesture in the direction of Pam, and ushered her into the conversation—"is Pam Andrews, Michael's daughter." Amanda paid special heed that she had carefully articulated, and had placed particularly heavy stress on the two syllables in, the word "daughter."

Sibescu's eyebrows raised, and his brow furrowed. "His what?" he gasped, genuinely shocked. The revelation had caught him quite by surprise, and he seemed as shocked by Pam's filial relationship to Michael as he had been by their presence in the car park at Castle Bran.

Amanda, feeling more confident now that Sibescu was momentarily discomposed, continued, "I said 'Michael's daughter,' Dr. Sibescu. Pam is Michael's daughter. I was as surprised as you apparently are. He's brought her up here to show her Castle Bran and, quite by accident, we bumped into each other."

"I see," Dr. Sibescu hissed, glaring at the three of them. "Well, as they say, it certainly is a small world, is it not? And what are your immediate plans, Miss West? Do you intend to return with your colleagues on the bus to Constanta, or have you already made other arrangements with your dear friend, Mr. Kukiliko?"

Amanda was about to reply that she had not yet given the first thought as to how she would return to Constanta when Michael stepped forward, wrapped his massive arm around her shoulder, drew her protectively near to him, and answered Dr. Sibescu's question for her. "She's coming with us."

Mandy, hoping that ill-feelings between the two men could be averted, halfheartedly added, "Of course, if this causes you any undue inconvenience, I suppose I could return by bus."

"No. No. Not at all," Sibescu negatively responded to Amanda's offer. "I understand. Very well, Miss West. As you wish. I do hope that you have enjoyed yourself here and that you have a pleasant trip back to Constanta. We shall miss your company."

Then, appearing as though he was thoroughly annoyed at having to speak to them, he turned toward Michael and Pam and aloofly announced, "I have many administrative duties to attend to. Will you excuse me?"

"To be sure," Michael icily replied. "Although I'd like to have a word or two with you in the very near future concerning Mandy and me. But now and Castle Bran are obviously neither the time nor the place for such a discussion. Would you mind if Mandy and I stopped by to see you sometime the first part of next week?"

"Since my secretary keeps my appointment book, for me to give you a definite answer now is impossible. However, I am quite sure I can work you into my schedule. Give me a call at the office Monday morning, and we shall set up an appointment." Dr. Sibescu delivered his address to Mandy, Michael, and Pam in a detached, palpably insincere manner. Dry and stilted, his words were drained of any warmth and delivered without any emotion.

Michael replied in a similarly impassive manner, "Fine. Monday then. Good day, Dr. Sibescu."

"*La revedere*; *drum bun*," Sibescu mechanically remarked as he turned his back on them and walked over to one of the nearby kiosks where sightseers could purchase the beautifully handcrafted Romanian blouses or the delicately carved wooden plates and plaques which bore the mustachioed face of Vlad Tepes.

After he was out of hearing range, Pam—who spoke not a word of Romanian—questioned, "What did that weirdo just say? What's eating him?"

Michael, translating for her, answered, "He said, 'Good bye and have a pleasant journey.' But he didn't seem all that sincere, did he? And I have no earthly idea what's bothering him, Honey."

"Well, maybe he said, 'Good bye and have a pleasant journey,' Dad. But it sure didn't seem to me like he meant one word of it. I think he'd be quite content if we crashed and all ended up in the hospital. If looks could kill, I bet we'd all be pushing up daisies right about now."

"True, Pammy," Michael concurred with his daughter's evaluation of Sibescu's demeanor. "He's certainly not overly fond of us, is he? At least not you and me."

"He's evidently very taken with you, though." He addressed this last remark to Mandy.

"Right now, I'm not so sure of that, Mike. Let's forget about him. What say we head back to Constanta? I'm anxious to get home."

"Fine with me. Let's hit the road, you two," Michael suggested as he led them to his Dacia which was parked nearby.

With happy hearts, they left Castle Bran and drove back to Constanta. During the trip, Pam had the opportunity to tell Amanda all about life in Hawaii, about her experiences at the American Fashion College of Switzerland, and about her boyfriend, the scion of an old and titled Lucerne banking family whose investments included much of the acreage comprising the canton in which Lucerne was located. Michael had met the boy, liked him, and felt Pam had made a good match.

When not talking about Pam and her past experiences, present situation, and future plans, they talked about Mandy's. Mandy told Pam about her life as a coed at the University of Wisconsin, about her experiences as a graduate student, about the results of her research in Constanta, and about how the monograph she was writing would advance her academic career. The two women discovered a mutual affinity that boded well for the development of a good friendship. Michael, elated that his daughter and the woman he intended to make his wife had hit it off so fabulously well, was in an unusually buoyant mood. The events of the day could not have unfolded better for him had he himself had a hand in planning them. It was a delightful trip for all concerned.

By the time they reached the outskirts of Constanta, the sun was just beginning to set on the Black Sea. Michael wanted to take them all out to eat at the *Casa cu lei*. But Mandy insisted that they stop by the pastry shop and purchase some *pateu cu carne* ("meat pies") and *pateu cu branza* ("cheese pies") so that Pam could dine at her apartment and experience what Romanians typically ate when they sat down for supper at their own tables.

Amanda's wishes prevailed, and the threesome ate at her home. Pam simply adored the flaky crusts and delicious flavors of the *pateu cu carne* and the *pateu cu branza*, edibles she had never seen on a menu in a Romanian restaurant. The meal, accompanied by *Borsec* and strawberry syrup, was followed by a delicious torte. The conversation was as delightful as the meal, and it would have been hard to say which of the three enjoyed the evening more.

It was Michael who finally, albeit reluctantly, brought the merrymaking to an end. "Mandy," he said, "I truly can't remember when I've had a more delightful evening. But the hour is very late." He glanced at his watch and announced, "My, how the time do fly when you're having fun. It's been great, being together with you once again. But it's well past midnight. I'm sure you must be totally exhausted, having risen at such an early hour this morning. I think Pammy and I had better head over to the Hotel Victoria and get us a little shuteye. You about ready to call it a day?" Michael asked his daughter.

"I'm beat, Dad. I could really use a good night's sleep. But, gosh, hasn't today been just grand? Seeing Dracula's castle and then finally meeting, after hearing so much about her, the mythical Mandy—who turned out to be everything you had made her out to be." Pam winked playfully at Mandy as she directed this comment at her, and Mandy blushed.

Pam continued, "It's been a fabulous day, but I'm ready to crash. Lead the way home, Dad. I can't wait to hit the sack."

"I'm tired, too," Mandy added. "But I've had a great time— needless to say. Oh, Mike, I'm so happy to see—to be with you again."

"Same here, Mandy. Let's not let something—or someone— ever again come between us and separate us. Well, we'd best be going."

"Could you both come by for breakfast tomorrow morning?"

"Hey, we'd love to," Michael answered for both of them. Then he directed a question at his daughter. "Wouldn't we, Honey?"

"Sure thing, Dad," Pam readily assented.

"Good. Then it's settled. I'll expect you both for breakfast. Is nine too early?"

"No, Mandy. That's fine with me. And Pammy's always been an early riser. She's a morning person. And when we meet tomorrow for breakfast," he added teasingly, almost as though it were an inconsequential afterthought rather than a proposal of great moment, "I'll want to ask you a very important question."

"Can you give me a hint as to what it relates to?" Mandy asked him.

"No. You'll just have to patiently bide your time till the morrow."

"Okay. Then I'll expect you both for breakfast. Goodnight, Pam. Goodnight, Mike. I've had a splendid time today."

"So too have I, Miss Mandy; so have I," Michael replied as he took her hand in his, raised it to his lips, kissed it gently, and said, "*Sarut mana.*" Then he drew her into him, enveloped her in his massive embrace, and passionately kissed her goodnight.

Mandy loved his warmth and nearness, but felt embarrassed because of Pam's proximate presence. Pam, although delighted to see her father obviously so happy, felt out of place. She coughed nervously, and said, "Ahem—ah—well maybe I should walk back to the hotel and leave you two lovebirds alone. It's only a few steps away."

Michael immediately released Mandy from his embrace and apologized to his daughter. "Not on your life. Certainly not at this late hour. I'm sorry, Pammy. I guess I just got a little carried away. I'm just so happy to be with Mandy again. We must be on our way. Till breakfast."

And without any further affectionate embraces or endearing words, Michael bade farewell, and he and Pam returned to the Hotel Victoria. Mandy, her head swimming as she recounted the events of that wonderful day, mindlessly began to clean up the dishes and put away the leftovers from the evening's meal. Her reverie was abruptly shattered by the unexpected ring of the doorbell. Thinking that either Michael or Pam had forgotten something—not more than five minutes could have elapsed since they had departed—she opened the door without taking the usual precaution of screening her callers by viewing them through the peephole.

She was so shocked by the sight which greeted her that she actually dropped the plateful of *pateu cu carne* and *pateu cu branza* she had been carrying to the refrigerator when the doorbell had interrupted her housecleaning.

The plate shattered, scattering food all about the doorway and skittering shards of china into the hallway. Dr. Sibescu immediately bent down and began to clean up the mess as he apologized in hushed tones to Amanda. Never once did he raise his eyes to look at her. Addressing the fragments of porcelain dispersed about the hallway and the remnants of the evening's meal rather than the hostess of that meal, Dr. Sibescu implored her to grant him an audience. "Miss West. Please, please forgive me for the intrusion at this late hour. But I had to talk with you. Alone. I had to wait until Mr. Kukiliko and his daughter left. Please allow me to come in."

"What!" Mandy gasped as she clutched at her throat in disbelief and fright. "You've been spying on me?"

He looked up at her and laughed. "Spying? I should hardly think my actions amounted to spying. I needed to talk with you, and I did not want to barge in on your company and cause an unpleasant scene. So I merely waited outside until they had departed.

"Now. This mess is cleaned up, and I apologize for frightening you so. May I come in and dump this clutter in the trash? I assure you, Miss West, I am a perfect gentleman, and you have nothing to fear from my presence. I mean you no harm. Besides I must talk to you now. Tonight. It is of the utmost importance. Please. I have something very important to tell you."

Mandy hesitated for a moment. Then, perhaps because his entreaty struck her as sincere, she gave in to his plea and invited him in. She shut the door and showed him where the garbage can was. After depositing the refuse he had cleaned up, Dr. Sibescu faced Amanda West and said, "May we talk? I know how late it is, but I have thought—all the way back, the entire length of the trip, from Castle Bran to Constanta—about you. About me. About Mr. Kukiliko. And I have something on my mind that is greatly troubling me. I have come to make a clean breast of things and clear my conscience."

Mandy was nearly as shocked by Sibescu's beseeching speech and deferential manner as she had been by his appearance at her door: this proud and powerful man had come to see her, repentant it appeared, to confess his sins and beg her forgiveness. He truly sounded contrite. She could hardly wait to hear what he had to say.

Mandy asked him to take a seat opposite her. Sibescu sat down and nervously began to wring his hands as he agonizingly searched for the words he needed to voice in order to apprise Mandy of what exactly it was that had occasioned his visit. After several seconds of silent indecision, he began, "Miss West, I know of no other way to begin except to start at the very beginning. So I shall. And so also shall I be brutally honest with you."

Mandy interrupted him. "I should expect nothing less from you, Dr. Sibescu."

"Ah, but there is the rub, Miss West; there is the rub. I fear I have not always been entirely straightforward with you. You see—well—how should I say—Miss West, from the very first moment you arrived in Constanta, from the very first time you entered my office, I have—um—um—I fell in love with you the minute I first laid eyes on you."

Amanda could scarcely believe what she had just heard. Incredulous, she gasped. Her sensuous lips opened wide in astonishment at this acknowledgement of his affectionate feelings for her. "*What?*"

"Yes, I said it; it is the unvarnished truth. Unfortunately, I could never bring myself to say it before, due to both personal considerations and professional concerns. You see, I am by nature a shy sort of man, not at all comfortable in the company of women. This was especially the case, I found out in your presence, when I became emotionally attracted to you.

"And of course, the politburo could only react to the news that I had fallen in love with someone from the West by stripping me summarily of my party membership and my various committee assignments. For these reasons then, Miss West, you can see that I could only admire you secretly, from afar—and dream that someday—in another time or place—you might—how shall I say—this is all so terribly difficult for me to voice—that someday you might find me equally attractive."

"Dr. Sibescu, I'm at a complete loss for words. I think you're a very attractive man, and I value your friendship, but I never for once even dreamed that you—"

Sibescu raised his hand, interrupting Mandy in mid sentence and said, "Please, Miss West. Allow me to finish what I have come here to say; this is exceedingly difficult for me. For that first year, when you were here alone, I loved you and felt that, someday, my love might be requited. And I patiently waited for some sort of sign from you. Sadly, none was ever forthcoming. In fact, except for the times when you needed some sort of assistance concerning your work with Ovid, you barely acknowledged my existence.

"But since you had formed no attachments with anyone else,

-RUBA

your disregard of me caused me no pain that I could not bear. I sat patiently by, and I waited, and I hoped that you would eventually discover a warm spot in your heart for me.

"Then Mr. Kukiliko unexpectedly appeared, and I felt that I would soon lose you—even though, truth be told, I never had you. But don't you see: his presence in Constanta threatened to destroy the fanciful relationship I had imagined I had established with you. I became insanely jealous and plotted to keep you from falling into his grasp."

Mandy, seeing the truth for the first time, but not being able to comprehend the reality of it, asked incredulously, "Do you mean, Dr. Sibescu, that all those horrible things you told me about Michael—about his background—about his motivations—about his intentions—that all that—"

"Yes, Miss West. They were all flagrant lies, I am ashamed to admit—lies meant to keep you from developing a friendship with him."

"But what caused such a change of heart? I mean, why are you telling me all of this now?"

"Perhaps the effects of a guilty conscience. I finally realized, after mulling over my unconscionable actions these past months, that I had been grossly unfair to both you and Mr. Kukiliko. My behavior was inexcusable. I apologize for the hurt I have caused you, Miss West. I never intended you any harm. Foolishly and selfishly, I just wanted you for myself. And on the bus trip back from Castle Bran, I resolved that now would be as good a time as any to correct the error of my thinking and redress the wrongs I have done you. I made up my mind that, as soon as we arrived back in Constanta, I would come by your house, confess everything I had done, ask your forgiveness, and—" As he struggled to form the words to complete the sentence, Sibescu's lips began to tremble and his voice broke, "and wish you and Mr. Kukiliko a most happy life together."

Amanda West didn't know what to say. She sat there, speechless, for several seconds and then reached across the table which distanced her from her caller. She warmly took his hand in hers, saying, "Thank you. Thank you so much for leveling with me. It took an awful lot of courage for you to confide in me as you have tonight and to admit what you have done. I think you are a wonderful—even though terribly misguided—man, Dr. Sibescu. And you've been an indispensable help with my research. But I've never cared for you—never could I have cared for you—in the same manner that you say you care for me. I hope you understand."

"I do, sadly. I do understand. Everything is now crystal clear to me. I do not know why it took so long for the realization to sink in. Perhaps I was blinded by love. But now I can see clearly, and I understand and accept your decision. The only excuse, which is really no excuse, I can offer is that a man in love is like a cornered animal: a crazed and desperate beast that, feeling threatened, will go to the extreme and do anything to save its life—or, in my case, his love. Forgive me.

"I shall not keep you awake any longer. You may relate to Mr. Kukiliko the details of our conversation. And if, after he has heard how shamefully I have acted, he still feels a need to speak with me, I shall be at his disposal. Goodnight, Miss West, and best of luck— oh, yes, you can expect my continued cooperation with your Ovidian research as long as you and Mr. Kukiliko reside in Romania. I shall continue to use my influence to open as many doors for you as I can."

Amanda thanked Dr. Sibescu for his offer and escorted him to the door. A lump formed in her throat as she bade him goodnight. *The poor, lonesome, lovesick man*, she thought to herself, *how sad he is.*

She finished tidying up the apartment, thinking all the while of what Sibescu had said and how it all—now that she had been made aware of what had been going on in Sibescu's crazed and jealous mind—made sense. Michael was, indeed he had always been, what she had first conceived him to be: an honorable man of noble intentions and good repute, a man with whom, she contemplated with much pleasure, she could happily live the rest of her life. With this pleasant thought occupying her mind, Amanda West went to bed and slept a very, very sound sleep.

Completely refreshed, she arose the following morning with the sun, and, after taking an invigorating shower—it chanced to be Sunday, and no hot water was to be had in any shower in the entirety of Constanta's city limits—she went shopping. After setting the table for breakfast, Amanda went out on the balcony, settled into the chaise longue, watched the pelicans and sea gulls plummet headlong into the Black Sea, and day-dreamed, turning over and over again in her mind the illuminating disclosures of the previous evening.

Shortly after 9:00, the doorbell rang. Mandy rushed to the door and squinted through the peephole to discover a Lilliputian Michael accompanied by his equally tiny daughter. Mandy happily opened the door, and, as she did, Michael, who had been concealing something behind his back, presented her with a magnificent bouquet of roses.

"Oh, good morning. Oh, Michael, you shouldn't have. How thoughtful. Thanks so much," she gushed as she accepted the bouquet.

"It's nothing. Just a tiny token of my affection for you."

"Well, thank you just the same. I love them. It's so considerate of you. Come on in, and sit down. The table's set, and breakfast's ready. And I've got some startling news that's bound to liven up the conversation."

"Hey, Mandy, we're all ears," Pam volunteered.

So, after Mandy had arranged her flowers in a vase and set it in the middle of the table, the three of them sat down and ate breakfast. And Mandy recounted for her guests all that had transpired after they had gone back to the Victoria the previous evening. After hearing the full story, Pam exclaimed, "Gosh! Who would have thought that's why he hated Dad so much? That explains everything. He was jealous of Dad, and that's the reason he never liked him."

"Apparently so, Honey. Perhaps now that he's come to his

senses and realizes that he never had even a ghost of a chance with you," and as Michael directed this remark to Mandy, he gently took hold of her hand in his and continued, " and that he and I were never in competition for your affections, that I never was—in any sort of manner—his rival, well perhaps we might be friends some day. At the very least, I should expect he'll be civil towards me now."

"Oh, I do hope so. He's absolutely instrumental for the success of my research; that is, if we—or I—stay in Romania."

"You were right the first time, Darling. You mean 'we.' I told you last night there was something important which I wanted to ask you. And there is. But first there's something I haven't said to you, something I foolishly vowed I'd never say again—in English or in any other language—after Josie's death. Mandy, *te iubesc*."

Pam, intently listening to the conversation and quite confident that she knew the direction it was headed, asked, "Aw, come on Dad. You know I don't speak a word of Romanian. What did you just say?"

Mandy, tightly clasping Michael's hand, answered Pam's question. "He said, 'I love you.' And I love him, Pam. Very much. *Te iubesc*, Mike."

Michael drew Mandy's hand to his lips, kissed it ever so gently, and said, "*Sarut mana*, Mandy. I can't think of a more opportune time to ask you this question, so—I want to spend the rest of my life with you. Will you marry me?"

Mandy's heart pounded. She thought it would explode, so full of happiness was it. In fact, she was so lost in reverie imagining what it would be like to be Mrs. Michael Kukiliko, how she would buy a Hawaiian cookbook and learn to make him his favorite dishes, what she would name their children, how wonderful it was to love and to be loved—all these delightful possibilities so filled her mind that, absentmindedly, she failed to answer her suitor's question. She simply looked at him adoringly as he waited for an answer.

Puzzled by Mandy's failure to respond to his request, Michael repeated his question: "Mandy, please. Will you marry me?"

"Oh! *Oh, yes. Yes. A thousand times yes!* Oh, Mike, you've made me the happiest woman in the entire world. I love you. I want to marry you and be your wife; and Pam can be my maid of honor." Amanda turned her attention to Pam, awaiting confirmation. "Would you, Pam?"

"Oh, Mandy, I'd be delighted. I never thought I'd ever see Dad truly happy again. But he is. Thanks to you. You're the answer to a prayer, Amanda West."

Mandy smiled at Pam and squeezed Michael's hand as she counted her own blessings. She had met the man of her dreams, and now she would soon marry him. Sibescu had accepted Michael and had resigned himself to being merely a professional collaborator in her Ovidian research. What more could she ask for? She had everything her own way. Everything had turned out just as she would have hoped. She truly was, she felt, the happiest woman in the entire world: she would marry the man of her dreams and live happily ever after.

THE END

August 10, 1983
2801 Hoosier Rd.
Centreville, IN 45480

Professor Gordon K. Douglas
Department of English Language and Literature
Warren House
Harvard University
Cambridge, MA 02138

Dear Gordy,

You won't believe what's happened! (You goddamned skeptic, why shouldn't you believe it? Think I'm lying to you, trying to pull the wool over your eyes?) I wish I could take credit for what took place and tell you that it was all deliberately choreographed and painstakingly carried out according to an elaborate plan. But the truth is that what happened was an unpremeditated occurrence— sheer chance—rather than the end product of some well-thought-out, deliberate design.

I was so concerned about what June's reaction to my deception would be that it totally slipped my mind that it was my weekend to look after the kids. And damned if Betty hadn't made irrevocable plans to be out of town, so we couldn't swap weekends. We've had such a fight over custody anyway that I don't think she would have agreed to switch weekends with me even if she didn't have a damn thing to do.

So here's the situation which faced me that Saturday morning: June was arriving at 10:00, and Peter Paul was supposed to meet her plane. But I was stuck with the kids. What could I do?

I had no alternative but to pile the kids into the car, and all of us drove to the airport. During the journey, I explained to them what a jam I was in and how crucial it was to the success of my novel that this lady they were about to meet believed that they were Priscilla, Paul, and Peter Pilgrim rather than Erica, Jason, and Justin Leonard.

They agreed to play along and looked upon the meeting as a big game. I promised them I'd double their allowances if we somehow managed to pull off the hoax, and, thus coaxed, the mercenary little bastards performed their roles with a professionalism worthy of a troupe of Broadway actors.

Her plane arrived right on schedule, and, the minute she stepped off the jetway, I knew I was in love. I shit you not, Gordy, she's about ten times more beautiful in person than in the snapshot she sent me, the one I subsequently forwarded to you.

She began to survey the crowd which had assembled at the gate to meet the plane, and, simultaneously, I began to lose my nerve. I was about to turn tail and run when her eyes fixed upon Erica who would stand out in any crowd, fat as she is the little porker. June waved wildly and shouted, "Hello, Priscilla. Priscilla Pilgrim. Hello, Dear. Yoo-hoo."

Were I to have coached Erica and rehearsed with her what to say, I don't think she could have hit her lines any better or performed any more professionally. Already counting the money she would earn if she could pull off this impersonation—she'll probably spend it all on hot-fudge sundaes and Twinkies, my porcine princess—she excitedly yelled, "Aunt June! Aunt June! Welcome to America!" (This kid is as deceitful as her father. Deception must run in the family. It's all in the genes.)

Well, Erica's "Aunt June! Aunt June!" greeting broke the ice and melted June's heart. She fussed over the children and went on at such great length about how darling they all were that I thought for a moment she might have forgotten about their absent mother, and I was home free. Just as I was breathing a huge sigh of relief, she suddenly turned to me and acknowledged my paternal role in the Pilgrim family's Welcome-to-Indiana reception. "And I take it you must be Mr. Pilgrim. How do you do? Mr. Pilgrim, where is my dear Fiona? Where's Mum, children?"

In answer to her query, I immediately responded before the kids had the opportunity to tell her that this was Mum's weekend off and that Dad had custody of them, "Call me Peter Paul. Mum's been called suddenly out of town. An emergency of sorts. Nothing life-threatening, though. Mum'll be back shortly."

That sounded plausible enough, and she bought it without questioning me any further as to Fiona's whereabouts. So we journeyed home, and, en route, she and the kids really hit it off. The woman has a hell of a sense of humor. She's down to earth with absolutely nothing pretentious or phony about her. She's not at all like you'd expect her to be from the books she's written.

She ate lunch with us, and then we all went for a walk in the park; in league with the kids, she swung on the swings (Where else but the swings would she swing?), played on the monkey bars, and teeter-tottered. Everyone had a great time—except for me who was living in constant fear that she would once again express a desire to see Mum. I could easily see she was enjoying herself immensely. The kids fell in love with her English accent, mimicking her unmercifully, but she turned out to be a good sport and didn't seem to be in the least bit offended.

The boys had a Little League game later that afternoon, and June insisted on going to it. I can think of only a few things in life more boring than watching a Little League game when your own children are not playing. Nevertheless, she yelled and cheered just as loudly and enthusiastically as any fan in the bleachers when Jason was up to bat or when Justin caught a fly ball to deep center. Surprisingly, she never commented that Paul and Peter had the unfamiliar names "Jason Leonard" and "Justin Leonard" prominently stenciled on the backs of their baseball jerseys. (For all I know, as unfamiliar with the dress code of American baseball as she is, she may very well have thought that the twins' team was sponsored by a firm named "Leonard.")

After the game, the kids insisted we take her out for a typical American meal. So we pigged out at McDonald's, and she survived that ordeal with narry a sign of botulism or acid indigestion. She said she enjoyed the meal, but I noted that much of her Big Mac remained uneaten and met the same fate as the rest of the waste on her tray.

I begged Erica not to throw a tantrum and do me a favor and baby-sit her brothers. She remonstrated not a bit. Conniving devil that I've become, I stilled beforehand any objections she might have voiced by stocking the freezer compartment of the fridge with a gallon of Breyer's ice cream. The promise of filling her pudgy tummy with her favorite dessert never fails but to put her in the most beholden of moods. So, around 9:00, June and I left the kids, and I drove her back to the motel.

Now here's where it gets interesting.

I knew the hour of reckoning was fast approaching, and I needed a couple of shots of something strong to steady my nerves, so I suggested we stop by the lounge for a couple of drinks. I downed two or three highballs in relatively quick order, and she drank several bloody marys. Well, the liquor worked its magic, bolstering my courage and loosening my tongue, and I poured forth everything from A to Z. Everything—all of it: the truth, the whole truth, and nothing but the truth, so help me, Fiona Pilgrim.

I talked, for over an hour, without interruption except for an occasional quaff, and she sat there, sipping her booze and dispassionately listening to how I had deceived her. Her behavior was either an impressive display of that vaunted British reserve we hear so much about or else she had become so drunk listening to me confess my sins that none of what I was saying sunk in and registered with her.

In any event, after I had so contritely bared my soul, June's only comment was, "I should like another bloody mary, Mr. Pilgrim. Or Peter Paul. Or whoever you are. What, in fact, is your real name, and are those darling children actually your progeny?"

I ordered her another drink, admitted that I had fathered that adorable little brood, and affirmed that I was Joe Leonard.

She finished her drink, and we chitchatted about this and that. Never once did she bring up *Tempestuous Summer* or Fiona.

Then she offered me her hand and said, "My, my, Mr. Joseph Leonard, this has all been such a shock. Whatever will Nanny say?

I must retire and sort all of it out. I should love to see the children again soon. Would that be at all possible? Tomorrow?"

I was shocked she was still speaking to me, and I happily invited her to have breakfast with us the next morning. She readily accepted. Maybe it was the stiff upper lip the British are so proud of keeping rather than the bloody marys dulling her wit, but if I were her, I should have never wanted to see me again.

To make a long story short and spare you all the mundane details, she stayed at the Holiday Inn for two more days, taking all of her meals with us. Every night, after putting the twins to bed and leaving Erica in charge, we drove over to the lounge for drinks and conversations about life, literature, and the pursuit of happiness. God, what a woman she is. Yes, Gordy, you've already said to yourself, "It sounds like that fool Leonard has fallen in love." Indeed he has: head over proverbial heels.

She flew back to England yesterday, and already I feel lost without her. I miss her terribly. Incidentally, she's taken the ms. of *Tempestuous Summer* with her, and she's going to show it to her publisher. It seems she doesn't begrudge me a bit for what I did.

There's tons more to say, Gordy, but I'm tiring. I just wanted you to know that all's well with me and the kids, and I'm in love.

Yours,

Joe

Joe Leonard

P.S. Should you ever get disillusioned with academe, don't give it up for a career hustling insurance.

10th September 1983
Harlequin House
Silhouette Lane
Fensucked-on-Strand
Ely, Cambridgeshire
England

Mr. Joseph E. Leonard
2801 Hoosier Rd.
Centreville, IN 45480
U.S.A.

Dearest Joe,

The fact that you haven't heard from me since I left you and the children—one month ago from today's date to be precise; please tell the little darlings that Aunt June sends hugs and kisses from England—does not mean that I've forgot about you or that you have not been in my thoughts. Indeed, quite the contrary is true. Of late, Nanny and I talk of little else but my experiences with one Joseph Leonard (formerly known as Fiona Pilgrim). And the result of our many conversations is this long, and long overdue, letter.

When I first told Nanny about your deception, she was quite miffed. She felt that I had been cruelly betrayed, and she likened your behaviour to that of Dr. Sibescu's: she considered him to be a man who could stoop so low that he could justify any sort of duplicity just so long as it advanced his own selfish cause. She was furious with you, Joe.

However, I came to your defence and explained that you had done what you did not to deceive me because of any depraved intent on your part but simply to get *Tempestuous Summer* published. (Incidentally, both she and the Archbishop loved the concluding chapter of *Tempestuous Summer*. I, however, did not: a word or two of explanation follows shortly.) I begged her to forgive you, and, after the initial shock of what you had done wore off, she became much more tolerant of your behaviour.

Indeed, she has gone so far as to include your name and the children's on the guest list of those who are to be invited to the wedding. Yes, it's true! It's really going to happen. She and Tom, as he now insists on being called, have decided to share their remaining years; they will marry before the year is out, sometime during Christmastide, and Nanny wants you and the children to attend.

I know already what your immediate response to Nanny's wish will be. You are saying that you can't afford such a trip. Am I not correct in my assumption, Joe?

Before you summarily reject Nanny's invitation, let me tell you what I have done to persuade you to visit us. I have spoken with my banker, and he has made all the arrangements with Pan American Airways. You merely have to call their free number and confirm the date and time of departure with the airline after you have made definite travel plans.

I realise full well that my offer is a bit forward, but Nanny and I have discussed—again and again these last several weeks—what sort of attitude I should adopt toward you. I could be coy, demurely hoping that you would seize hold of the initiative and take the first step in making an emotional commitment. But, as far as I am concerned, such a course of action, or rather inaction, would have been characteristic of Sibescu waiting for Mandy to show some sign of affection for him, and I never liked the man. Or else, I could be rather brazen and straightforward, outrightly declaring my feelings for you. As you will immediately discover, I opted for the latter approach; hence this letter.

You obviously are aware that I was much smitten by you. When you first related to me the Fiona Pilgrim pretense, I felt no anger whatsoever. In fact, I felt only compassion and empathy, for I had, early in my career, done much the same thing as you did. Indeed, I believe I would have killed to see my first words in print. I made a Mephistophelean bargain of sorts: I sold my talent—not to the daughters of Zeus and Mnemosyne and the literary canon but, rather, to the marketplace and to the highest bidder.

I write that which I write for one reason and for one reason only: it sells. I do not write romance fiction because I love the subject, because I relate to the characters,

319

or because I find the plots interesting. I write because, by doing so, I am able to retain title to Harlequin House, my ancestral home. Our beloved estate has been in the family since time immemorial; why, it is recorded in the *Doomsday Book*.

When I penned my first novel, I chose the romance genre not because it appealed to me but because I sensed there might be a market for such novels—and I was spectacularly correct. (In truth, Joe, the subject matter nearly puts me to sleep.) You see, my father passed away when I was but in my teens. I was his sole heir, and he left me land rich but cash poor. I had no money to pay the inheritance taxes on the great estate he had bequeathed me. The intent of the exorbitant inheritance taxes in this country is to make the landed gentry literally, figuratively, and quite quickly, dirt poor.

My solicitors informed me that, unless I could come up with a large sum of money very quickly to settle the encumbrances imposed on Harlequin House because of Father's death, I should be forced to put it up for sale on the property market. Faced with this horrid prospect, I wrote a most horrible book at a most opportune time, and the rest is, as they say, history.

The earnings from my pen have not only allowed me to keep Harlequin House in the family, but they have also allowed me to considerably increase the demesne and to live rather sumptuously. So you see, Joe, I write what I write only to maintain my standard of living. At least, you, as Fiona Pilgrim, have written that which you wrote to serve a nobler end: to earn a large enough sum of money to support you and your children in order that you could devote yourself to your more serious prose.

Now that I have told you all of this, perhaps you can imagine how I feel about the trash which circumstances have dictated I write. And can you not also easily imagine what a good laugh I had when I read your—that is, Fiona Pilgrim's—first letter to me? But in that letter, I recognised myself, years ago, begging for someone to help me get my own first novel published—no matter that it had little, if any, literary merit. That is why I consented to help you—not because I felt *Tempestuous Summer* had any more merit than any of the other pap penned by anyone else, including myself, writing romance fiction.

And this very same reason is why, as I stated earlier in my letter, I was not enraptured with the concluding chapter of *Tempestuous Summer*. You see, I found the entire novel—as I find my own supremely successful novels—silly. As silly as that rabid duck, or whatever sort of creature it was, that did away with Josie Kukiliko. Nonetheless, my evaluation counts for naught, for, if Nanny liked it (And she loved it!), then, rest assured, you have a bestseller on your hands. That woman is an infallible gauge of how well or how ill a book will be received by the reading public! Start counting your money now.

I think I've said everything I'd set out to say. I felt I owed you this explanation, for I could see you were completely non-plussed by my failure to become irritated with you when you confessed what you had done. I realised, as you spoke, that we were kindred spirits—"on the same wavelength", as you Yanks would say. At the same time, I also realised—allow me to be brazen once again—that I was not only intellectually attracted to you but also physically and emotionally as well. You ignited a fire within me, Joseph Leonard, that has not been quenched—indeed it has been fanned—by your absence from me. Do I make myself clear?

Lest you misinterpret my intentions in the foregoing remarks, perhaps I had better take the necessary precautions to make my-self even more clear. I just proofed the last paragraph, and it reads like a proposi-tion some hussy might make; I can assure you, what I propose is something entirely different.

I suggest that you, Erica, Jason, and Justin come to Nanny's wedding where we can get to know one another better under circum-stances entirely different than those when last we met. Perhaps, if my feelings for you are reciprocated, there might just be the foundation for building a sound, long-last-ing relationship. Before closing this let-ter, I want you to know that I have never before asked a gentleman to visit me at

Harlequin House and overnight here. But then I have never felt toward any other man as I feel towards you, Joe.

I must post this letter immediately before good sense returns, and reason forces me to tear it up. I expect that I shall hear something from you in the near future as to your reaction to my suggestion.

Most affectionately yours,

June

June Featherstone

P.S. A squeeze and a big hug to the children from "Aunt June".

September 20, 1983
2801 Hoosier Rd.
Centreville, IN 45480
U.S.A.

June Featherstone
Harlequin House
Silhouette Lane
Fensucked-on-Strand
Ely, Cambridgeshire
England

Dear June,

I have read and reread your letter of September 10 no fewer
than twenty times, and I can't believe its contents. I should have
written first and declared my feelings, but I truthfully had no idea
how you felt about me and how such a letter would be received.
Now that you have taken the first step and acted so "brazenly" and
set down your feelings, let me express how I feel towards you. In a
few words, I've fallen in love with you, June. Not a day goes by
that I don't think of you hundreds of times and of the all-too-few
days we spent together. From the very moment you set foot on the
ground and I laid eyes on you, I was in love.

Of course, I'm mature enough to know that the first flash of
physical attraction rapidly fades, and there has to be something else
to keep the fires burning. And in our case, I'm sure there is. So
often in the past, I've been attracted, like a moth to a flame, to
beautiful women who shine brightly but give off no heat. But you—
you're so different: so beautiful, yet so down-to-earth; so proper,
yet such a good sport with the kids; so literate, yet such an easy
conversationalist. June, you're a joy to be with. I'm in love. What
else can I say? What else needs to be said?

We accept your gracious offer to attend the wedding. We've
already filled out the requisite forms for our passports, had our

pictures taken, and mailed the required amount of money to the State Department. I've contacted Pan Am, and I'll book the flight within a fortnight. Betty has agreed to let me have the children over the Christmas break. Since they're out of school anyway, they won't miss any of their classes when we come for our visit.

Please forgive the shortness of this letter, but I wanted to RSVP as soon as I could, thank you for your most generous offer, and let you know that the children and their daddy will be there. I'll sit down tonight and write you a longer letter. I can hardly wait to see you again. I miss you more than I can ever put into words, so I shall herewith hush my pen with but two words:

Much love,

Joe

Joe Leonard

November 15, 1983
2801 Hoosier Rd.
Centreville, IN 45480

Professor Gordon K. Douglas
Department of English Language and Literature
Warren House
Harvard University
Cambridge, MA 02138

Dear Gordy,

Just a short note to tell you that I read your latest article in *The Chronicle of Higher Education* and found it enlightening and to let you in on my travel plans. I just received confirmation from Pan Am that our reservations are firm. We leave December the 15th and return on January the 4th. June and I have been writing daily and have grown very close. She calls me long distance at least twice a week.

I'll wager I'm the first to wish you a Merry Christmas and all the best for a happy and prosperous '84.

Leonard in love,

Joe Leonard

P.S. Should you ever get disillusioned with academe, don't give it up for a career hustling insurance.

January 3, 1984
Harlequin House
Silhouette Lane
Fensucked-on-Strand
Ely, Cambridgeshire
England

Professor Gordon K. Douglas
Department of English Language and Litera-
ture
Warren House
Harvard University
Cambridge, MA 02138
U.S.A.

Dear Gordy,

Greetings from Merry Old England. Hope
you had a pleasant Xmas vacation and, in the
best American tradition, were inundated with
gifts. I can tell you one thing: Peter Paul
Pilgrim had his best Christmas ever!

We arrived at Heathrow Airport and were
greeted by James and June. James was outfitted in his full chauffeur's livery, complete
with Wellington boots. The children were, as
was their father, duly impressed.

I was much more impressed, however, by
the Rolls-Royce. We all piled into the Rolls,
and the first words out of James' mouth
were, "Where to, Madam?" I swear to God,
Gordy; I'm not bullshitting you.

To which June replied, "Home, James." I
could not believe my ears. Had I actually
heard and correctly recorded this conversa-

tion? Or had I been daydreaming? Could I somehow have been transported smack-dab into the middle of a P.G. Wodehouse novel? I pinched myself to make sure I was wide awake, and, sure enough, we were heading north toward Ely.

We arrived at Harlequin House, and, after a long nap to counter the effects of jetlag, we were feted like kings and queens and feasted royally. June had ordained that a welcoming banquet be prepared, and I, as guest of honor, was seated at the head of the table. Opposite me, located at the other end of the table, a location which must have been at least two blocks removed, was June. Had I wanted to converse with her during dinner, I should have had to either place a long-distance call or rent a megaphone. You get some idea, Gordy, of the size of this castle?

Seated directly to my left, giddy about entering her second childhood, was none other than Hortense Crimpet herself. The poor thing babbled on throughout the complete length of the meal—she may very well have been speaking in tongues for all I know—and never, to my knowledge, made one coherent comment the entire evening long. She's as loony as I had imagined her to be.

And on my right sat His Grace, the Archbishop of Canterbury, as strange an old coot as I've ever come across. I'm convinced he's momentarily escaped death by hiding out in dotage. He barely introduced himself to me before he started out the conversation on a pleasant ecumenical note by voicing his earnest hope that I wasn't a Papist. I assured him I was apolitical, the result, I conjectured, of the fact that my mother was a conservative Republican and my father an ultramontane Democrat.

His response to this revelation was, "Please pass the salt, Mr. Leonard." I'm sure, had I said, "Your Grace, your royal fly is open," his response would have been, "Please pass the salt, Mr. Leonard."

Not dissuaded by my subterfuge, he continued to pursue the subject dearest to his heart, for he then asked me what my church preference was. I answered that I preferred red brick with ivy growing up the sides and a nice rose window. He greeted this bit of news with the same blank stare that my response to his previous question had generated. Raconteur that he was, he skillfully parried my sally, responding with, "Please pass the pepper, Mr. Leonard."

Sensing that I might have scored a point, I decided not to abandon my advantage, so I continued the discussion in the same vein before he had the chance to pose another question. I further elaborated that I was very fond of fan vaulting as executed in some of the Gothic cathedrals in Albion, but, of all the churches I had ever been in, my favorite had to be the *Wieskirche* in Bavaria with all of its rococo splendor, although placing a close second, third, and fourth were the Sainte Chapelle in Paris with its glorious stained glass windows, the churches in Ravina with their magnificent mosaics, and the monasteries of Moldavia with their colorfully painted façades.

As if I had just said "Long live the Pope," his aspect colored an angry red, and the veins on his forehead became turgid and empurpled. He was pissed! He gave me a most unchristian dirty look and turned away from me to talk with the children. He didn't address another word to me the entire evening, a snub which suited me just fine. Would that his decrepit ladylove would have also given me the silent treatment, I might have enjoyed the meal.

Gordy, I swear to God I haven't exaggerated a thing. The whole conversation took place exactly as I have just described. If there has ever been a couple who deserves to be enshrined in *The New Yorker's* "There'll-always-be-an-England" column, it's these two crazies. I ate, drank, and listened numbly to Nanny nattering on about nothing.

Trying to carry on a conversation with her is about as challenging as staying awake through a Barbara Pym novel. In fact, just listening to her nearly lulled me to sleep. There were moments during dinner when I actually felt as though Nanny might invite me to a jumble sale or rip from my hand the wine I was downing with so much gusto and supplant it with a cup of hot milk and Ovaltine. Welcome to England and the exciting world of Barbara Pym.

The entire week following our reception banquet was spent busily preparing for the wedding, an occasion which turned out to be the social highlight of the Christmas season. The kids found plenty to do and made themselves quite useful; they really pitched in and volunteered to help wherever, and whenever, needed. Nanny fell in love with them. She insisted that Erica be her junior bridesmaid and that Jason and Justin serve as acolytes. The three of them responded to the challenge with great aplomb and made me proud. I'm pissed she didn't ask me to be an usher; I knew I had lost all hope of ever being a groomsman when, at our welcoming banquet, I failed to correctly respond that the Church of England was my church preference.

The ceremony went off without incident. One might say they were hitched without a hitch (sorry about that). And everybody who was anybody—with the exception of the Queen, for obvious reasons—was there. They must have gone through *Debrett's Peerage* and sent an invitation to anyone listed therein. After the reception, the happy couple—with reliable old James at the wheel of the Rolls—took off, destination unknown, for a two-week honeymoon. (Lucky for the honeymooners that they had James along to guide them, for, forgetful as the two of them are, they probably would have failed to remember their destination five minutes after having decided where to honeymoon. Then their destination would truly have been unknown—to anyone.) Their departure left June, the kids, me, and a household staff of thousands alone in the manse.

I'm going to hold my tongue, Gordy, and not reveal too much about what passed between us when we two consenting adults were finally left to our own devices. My lips are sealed. I'm much too much of a gentlemen to go into a detailed account of how we passed the midnight hours. If, however, you must know, she's a real tigress in the sack, but you never heard it from these lips. Far be it from me to say anything crude about the morals or mating habits of the woman I love. Besides, I'm not the type to kiss and tell.

Suffice it to say, however, that, after the kids went to bed and the servants retired for the evening, June and I talked each night into the wee hours of the morning and discovered that we were intellectually, emotionally, and sexually compatible. We decided she was the woman for me, and I, the man for her. You have already guessed what I am about to tell you, have you not? My announcement, therefore, should come to you as no surprise.

Surprise, Gordy! I asked her to marry me, and she accepted my proposal.

We wanted to wait until the spring, but I was there, she was there, the kids were there, and, thus, the timing seemed perfect. So last Friday, in the presence of my children and her servants, the village curate joined us in Holy Wedlock. The kids fly back to the U.S. of A. tomorrow, and I'll miss them terribly. However, I've already phoned

Betty and made arrangements to have them come and spend the summers at Harlequin House. I also called my office, told my boss I quit, and advised him that he could take all of his rate books, mortality tables, insurance contracts, and related forms and trash them in the nearest dumpster.

And the icing on the (wedding) cake is that, just this very morning, we heard that *Love Among the Scones* has been nominated for five Emmys. Can you believe that?

Let me close my letter by reporting one bit of news that I bet you never anticipated hearing after everything I've written concerning the subject. Despite her aversion to it (By "it," I mean her general aversion to the genre not her specific aversion to *Tempestuous Summer*.), June has placed *Tempestuous Summer* with her publisher, and he loves it. He's simply crazy about it. I got a huge advance—five figures. Call me a liar, but I swear it's the truth. And they're already talking about a movie contract which would mean megabucks.

Jesus Keerist, Buddy, what can I say? "All's well that ends well," to quote the Bard. I'm a lucky guy. My book's about to be published; I've got a pocketful of change; I've got my kids every summer (quality time rather than quantity time); and I'm married to a woman whom I absolutely adore. Such a felicitous turn of events couldn't have happened to a nicer guy, wouldn't you agree, Gordon?

It's all just like a fairy tale. With a

little luck, with the grace of God (the bestowal of that blessing to be procured through the intercession of God's loyal servant, His Most Holy Senility, the Archbishop of Canterbury), and with a whole lot of effort on both our parts, I think this might just work out.

There's a damn good chance that we'll live happily ever after.

Yours, from that sceptered Isle,

Joseph E. Leonard I

Joseph Leonard, First Duke of Harlequin House, Lord of the Manor, and Master of the Hounds of Harlequin: Alcuin and Aethelred

P.S. Should you ever get disillusioned with academe, give it up, without a second thought, for a career as a romance novelist.

Printed in the United States
3952

9 781401 029494